# Spin the Bottle

## Wayne A. Barcomb

Writers Club Press
San Jose New York Lincoln Shanghai

Spin the Bottle

Published by Writers Club Press
an imprint of iUniverse.com, Inc.

For information address:
iUniverse.com, Inc.
620 North 48th Street
Suite 201
Lincoln, NE 68504-3467
www.iuniverse.com

ISBN: 0-595-09715-4

Printed in the United States of America

To Susan, my partner is this endeavor as in all else.

# Acknowledgements

I am indebted to a lot of people who taught me about crime and criminals and how to catch them. I particularly want to thank Boston FBI agent, Charlie Walsh, who not only read the manuscript, but offered critiques and suggestions to enhance the book's authenticity and credibility. Detective Ray Pierce, Criminal Assessment and Profiling Unit of the New York City Police Department, also read and critiqued the manuscript and made valuable suggestions. James Fox, the renowned criminologist at Boston's Northeastern University was the first person I talked with about my plans for this book, and he started me off on the right foot.

Three outstanding mystery writers, Stuart Kaminsky, Peter King, and John Lutz took time away from their own writing to read the manuscript and offer encouragement.

And finally, I'm indebted to my wife Susan, whose long publishing experience and editorial expertise saved the day more times than I would like to admit.

Wayne Barcomb
Sarasota, Florida

# Chapter One

She never truly hated her father until that night. It began as the others had. The voices awakened her around midnight. She buried her face under the pillow but the voices found her.

"You stupid cow. You're so dumb, you still don't know how to do it right, do ya. **Do** you?"

A loud slap. "Paul, please."

The light from the kitchen intruded into her room, and she wished her bedroom had a door. She would close it to shut out the sounds, the words, the slaps, the sobs, and the screams. The screams were the worst.

"Paul, please," her father's voice mocked her mother's plea. "I'm sick of your whining. Shut up!" More scuffling, another slap. "No? O.K., I got a better idea."

The little girl raised her head from under the pillow, sat up and looked out the open window, and wished she could climb out and go far away. Her eyes closed and she was walking with her mother in the warm night. A shiny car stopped, and a tall handsome man with a kind voice asked her if she and her mother would like to go away with him. He said her mother was the most beautiful woman he had ever seen. The three of them drove away in the handsome man's car. She did not know where they were going, but it would be far away and they would be forever happy.

"Oh Paul, it hurts so much, please. Please. Oh! God! God, help me. I can't stand it."

The child slipped out of bed, tiptoed to the doorway and peered into the kitchen. She saw her mother lying on her back on the floor. Her father was sitting on top of her, with his hand up her skirt. She knew where her father's hand was.

She stood staring at her mother and father. Her mother lay between the radiator and the refrigerator, one shoe on, one lying half way across the room. Her blouse was torn, and she could see one of her mother's nipples bruised and bleeding. Her left eye was swollen, and the rest of her face was red and wet from tears. Her father's hand was over her mother's mouth.

She smelled the sweat and whiskey from her father. Her father was probably already drunk when he got home. When he was like that she wished he would go away and never come back. But he was her father and she was ashamed of those thoughts.

"You bit me. You bitch!" her father screamed. He pulled his hand away from her mother's mouth, and blood trickled from the side of his index finger.

She stood in the doorway, watching, as her father pulled his other hand from her mother's skirt and slapped her hard. A wine bottle rolled from under her, and her mother's legs sent it clattering across the floor. It came to rest at her feet, and she stared down at it.

Her mother suddenly came to life, arched her back, and rolled her father off. Her knee shot into his groin, and she started to get up. Bellowing with pain and rage, her father grabbed her ankle.

She watched her father drag her mother until he could get his hands on her throat. He began choking her and banging her head against the floor. Her mother tried to slide away and got as far as the radiator. Again he grabbed her and pounded her head against the edge of the radiator. Blood gushed and began forming a small pool on the floor.

She rushed to her mother who lay still, the color draining slowly from her face. She hugged her mother. "Mamma, Mamma."

A blow sent her sprawling. When she focused her eyes, her father stood over her. "You get in your bed, now, Tookie! You hear me? Now! You say one thing—one thing and you'll get the same thing your mother just got. Now get in there!"

Never taking her eyes off her father, she slid across the kitchen floor to her bedroom. When she reached her room, she grabbed two of her dolls and dropped on the bed sobbing.

Through the doorway she could see her father leaning over her mother's body. She watched him feel her mother's wrist with his fingers and shake his head. He stood over her mother, sucking on the knuckle of his finger. His eyes seemed to be everywhere and then she saw him look toward her room. She was afraid and closed her eyes and made believe she was asleep.

"Tookie, wake up sweetheart. Daddy wants to talk to you."

She moaned and stirred.

"Wake up, Tookie. Talk to Daddy."

She opened her eyes and looked straight into her father's bloodshot eyes. They always bulged and they scared her. She squirmed but he held her fast. She smelled the whiskey and the sweat. The hard bristle of his unshaven face scratched her face. The mole behind his ear brushed against her neck. The mole was big and hairy, and she hated it. She wanted to be free, to go to her mother. But, he held her face next to his.

"Tookie?"

She hated that stupid name he called her. Her mother called her Lucky. Her lucky charm. She liked that.

"I want you to listen to me, sweetheart. Daddy's gonna call the police, and tell them about Mommy. They'll come over here in a little while and talk with me, and they'll talk with you, too. Now here's what happened, and here's what we're gonna tell the police. Mommy and Daddy were sitting at the table in the kitchen. We had a little argument, and Mommy got mad and hit Daddy in the face. Then Daddy hit Mommy back, first in the face and then here." He touched her breast.

"Then Daddy hit Mommy once in the eye. You were standing in your doorway and you saw it. Mommy saw you and jumped up to go to you to put you to bed. She slipped on the magazine on the floor and fell. When she fell, she hit her head on the radiator, and it got cut open. That's what happened, sweetheart, and that's what were goin' to tell the men when they come over to talk with us."

She wanted to get away from him, wanted to be out the window with her mother and the handsome man. But he held her arms hard, smiling and nodding. Her arms hurt and she hated looking at the ugly gold tooth.

"But, Daddy, that's not what happened."

Even before he hit her, she knew it was coming. She closed her eyes and felt the pain as his open hand smacked across her face. Tears filled her eyes, but she was afraid to open them.

"Now, you listen to me and you listen good. You're gonna tell me exactly what I just told you, or you'll get a lot worse than you just got. You hear me?"

She opened her eyes. He was still holding her by the arms, his eyes bigger than she had ever seen them. Traces of spit trickled down the sides of his mouth. She stared and nodded her head slowly.

"That's better. Now you tell me what happened."

She slowly, haltingly repeated the story.

His face softened, and the grip on her arms relaxed. "That's a good girl, sweetheart. Now let's do it a couple more times just to be sure." Three more times he had her run through the story. Each time she told it more convincingly.

"Oh, you're a good girl, sweetheart. Daddy's gonna take good care of you."

Her eyes closed again, but the smells of her father were making her sick. She struggled to hold back the vomit in her throat.

"Now, Tookie, I'm going to call the police and tell them about the accident, and they'll be comin' over soon. You stay in bed. They will probably want to talk with you, after they talk to me. You be sure and tell them just what you and me went over together, right?"

She nodded. Her father went back to the kitchen and she lay in bed, hugging her dolls, trying not to cry.

She listened to his movements and sounds and crept out of bed and peeked into the kitchen, watching him. He picked up the wine bottle, washed it off, and smashed it in the trash can. Then he pressed a magazine hard against her mother's bare foot and placed the magazine near the radiator. He picked up her mother's shoe from the far side of the room, put it under one of the kitchen chairs, removed the other shoe and set it next to the one under the chair. With a damp paper towel, he washed off traces of blood between her legs and inner thighs. Removing her stained panties, he tore them into shreds and flushed them along with the paper towel down the toilet.

Her father stood hunched in the middle of the kitchen. He poured some more whiskey, drank it, picked up the phone, and called the police.

Tookie heard him tell the policeman there'd been an accident. She wiped her nose and eyes with the sleeve of her nightie and watched her father as he hung up and sat at the kitchen table. She wanted to go to her mother again, but she was afraid.

She was almost asleep when the doorbell rang. Her clock said ten minutes after one.

"Mr. Gale? I'm Detective David McNally, and this is Officer Gamache."

"Yeah. Come in. Come in." Gale fumbled into his shirt pocket for a cigarette and clumsily worked the pack out.

Tookie could see the two policemen standing in the middle of the kitchen looking at her mother's body sprawled across the floor. The man in the suit knelt and felt her pulse, at the same time looking at her puffed eye. "I'm afraid she is dead, sir." He rose and faced her father.

When she heard the man say her mother was dead, she ran back to her bed and buried her head under the pillow. She didn't want to see or hear any more.

Gale flicked the sweat from his forehead, never taking his eyes off McNally. He'd dealt with cops before, and he knew he would have to be on his guard. McNally looked to be in his late thirties, good looking, even seemed kind of gentlemanly. Not like other cops he had known. Nice navy blue suit, white shirt, silk tie. But cops could fool you. The guy's handsome face showed an intelligence that unsettled him.

"Can I use your phone, sir?"

Gale nodded.

"Hello. McNally here. The lady's dead. Get the Medical Examiner over here and the State Police and the photographer." He hung up and looked over at the body again. "Mr. Gale, could we go sit down in the other room? I'd appreciate it if you could tell us what happened. I'm sorry. I know this is difficult for you."

"Sure, sure. That's O.K. I understand. I…I…." Gale sobbed and swallowed hard, closing his eyes.

McNally and Gamache glanced at each other and back to Gale. "Thank you, sir," McNally said.

McNally nodded to Gamache and Gale led them into the small living room, off the kitchen. He snapped on the overhead light. Still holding his crumpled pack of cigarettes, he pulled one out and held the pack out to the two cops. "Cigarette?"

They declined.

McNally made Gale uneasy, but there was something about Gamache that he just didn't like. He looked like all cops; cocky, big-shot attitude; Brass-buttoned, blue uniform stretched across his fat belly, big gun and nightstick hanging off him.

"Mr. Gale. Can you tell me what happened here tonight?" McNally asked. A gentle friendliness had slipped into his voice.

Gale was careful. He knew cops too well. They were just like those pricks in the Merchant Marine. You get in a little trouble and they suck you in by making you think they care about you, being nice to you. Then just when you start to trust them, they grab you by the balls.

He had told the investigating officer in the Merchants why he had beaten the woman in Seville. He trusted him and thought he would understand. Before he knew it, they had kicked him out, telling him he was lucky he wasn't going to jail. Now he had to deal with these two fucks.

"I came home from work about midnight Officer. I worked late, and then I stopped for a few beers. My wife likes to wait up for me if I'm late. She was sittin' at the kitchen table, sleepin'. When I come in she woke up in a bad mood. She was pissed at me for comin' home so late without callin', you know?" He nodded at the officers but got no response.

"Anyway, I tried to ignore her. I poured myself a little nightcap and suggested we go to bed. But she kept at me, gettin' herself all worked up. So, we had some words, and she throws a magazine at me. Then, all of a sudden she sucker punches me in the face. I'm caught by surprise, and I hit her back, first in the chest and then the face. I mean, hey, she really belted me.

"Then I look up and I see my kid standin' in the doorway. Sarah, my wife, saw her too and jumped up from the table to put her back to bed. She slipped on the magazine on the floor and she fell backwards and hit her head on the radiator. That was it. It all happened so fast. Her head just cracked open." He ground the cigarette out and looked back at the officers.

Both men stared at Gale. He squirmed, crossed, and uncrossed his legs. For Christ sakes, say something you assholes.

Finally McNally spoke. "Mr. Gale. How long had your daughter been standing in the doorway?"

"Quite a while, I guess. I noticed her right after I hit her mother the second time. She sort of whimpered, and when my wife saw her, she jumped up to go to her, to put her back to bed. That's when she slipped on the magazine."

McNally glanced at Gamache. "What happened then?" asked McNally.

"Well, I run over to her, and so did my daughter. Sarah was moaning and bleeding from her head where she hit the radiator. I could tell from the gash in her head and from the blood that she was hurt bad. A few seconds after I got to her, she stopped moaning and passed out."

"Passed out?"

"Yeah. Her eyes kinda rolled back and her head slipped to the side, and she was gone."

"What do you mean, gone?"

"I mean she was out cold."

"Did you think she was maybe just knocked out or what?"

"No, I seen dead people before, when I was in the Merchant Marine. I knew she was dead."

"What did your daughter do?"

"She ran to her mother. When she saw the blood she started screaming."

"And then?"

"Well, I didn't know what to deal with first. My wife is layin' dead on the floor, and my kid's hysterical. I picked my daughter up and carried her into bed, calmed her down, and told her I'd take care of Mommy. Then I went back to Sarah and felt her pulse. I couldn't feel none, and that's when I called you."

McNally nodded. His eyes never left Gale.

Gale wanted a drink.

"Mr. Gale, can we go back into the kitchen?"

Gale was tired. He wanted Sarah out of here. He wanted the cops out. He wanted to go to bed. "Sure."

The crime scene unit arrived and went to work. The photographer began taking pictures while the medical examiner worked with the body and a state police artist sketched the death scene. Two paramedics sat at the kitchen table.

Gamache sat next to the paramedics. McNally and Paul Gale stood in the middle of the room. Gale watched the crowd of people taking over his kitchen like they owned it and wanted them the fuck out of his house. He started to say something but McNally interrupted him. "Mr. Gale. Can you describe for me just how your wife stepped on the magazine and how she fell? Could you show me how it happened? Walk me through it?"

"Look, Officer. What do you want from me? I mean my wife is layin' dead in front of me. It's one-thirty in the morning. My kid's in there, maybe asleep, maybe not. I got seven strangers in my kitchen, and I'm dead tired. I been through a lot tonight. I just don't want to talk no more." His voice broke, and he closed his eyes.

McNally covered his face with his hands and rubbed his eyes.

"Uh, Dave."

When McNally looked up, Gamache was standing by the little girl's bedroom. She stood in the doorway, her eyes red, tears trickled down her cheeks.

McNally looked at Gale. "Your call, Mr. Gale. Do we talk to her now?"

Gale looked at his daughter. Their eyes locked. He nodded his head slowly, and she slowly nodded back.

McNally looked from Gale to the little girl.

Her eyes remained transfixed on her father.

"Sweetheart, Mr. McNally would like to talk with you for a minute. Can you come out and sit down?"

Tookie stared at her father. She knew what she had to say, and she knew she could do it. She walked into the kitchen and looked around for the first time.

She saw her mother lying on the floor. The policeman standing by her bedroom smiled at her. She could see the window in her bedroom, and she wished she could float through it again. Suddenly the handsome man was in her house, standing in the kitchen, smiling at her. She looked back at him, and she knew that everything was going to be all right.

He smiled again, and he spoke. "Honey, can you tell us what happened here tonight? Can you?" The handsome man's voice was soft like her mother's.

The little girl stared straight ahead. "My father did it. My father killed my mother."

# Chapter Two

The young woman lay in bed. She was tired but unable to sleep. Painful memories tormented her and the familiar scenario kicked in on schedule. As always, she was a detached observer, floating in the space and time of today, watching those events of long ago.

She saw the little girl standing in the doorway, watching the beautiful, gentle woman being choked and beaten to death. She heard the little girl scream and watched her run to her mother. And then she felt the father hurting the child. She heard her crying softly.

The handsome, kind man was in her house, and she hoped he would take her away with him. But the father's bulging eyes stared at her and she was afraid again.

The images picked up speed, fast forward. the police taking the father away; the trial; the little girl, sitting on the witness stand; the guilty verdict; the father being led away, and leaning over to kiss her good-bye. The child reaching out, tears running down her face. The father embracing her and hissing into her ear, "I'll kill you some day for this, you little bitch."

The tears came before she finally fell asleep.

\*　　　\*　　　\*

She opened her eyes and lay still for a moment, staring into space. But there was no space, only the beige walls.

Her headache arrived as expected. She squirmed in bed, flailing her legs until the bedcovers lay on the floor. Her temples throbbed, and she squeezed them until her fingers ached.

The sun streaming through the window raised her spirits, and she willed the bad thoughts away. But they would come back.

Ten-thirty a.m. She couldn't remember when she'd slept so late. She sat up and stretched. Her bedroom glowed in the bright sunlight of a beautiful Saturday.

She eased herself off the bed, padded into the bathroom and took a Percocet. The hot shower warmed her body and calmed her. She closed her eyes and turned her face upward into the cleansing waters, waiting as she did every morning, for the water to wash away the foulness.

The Monet exhibit was at the Metropolitan. She would take a long walk in the sunshine and spend a few hours with her favorite artist.

She tried to focus on the beauty of Monet, but the ugliness stayed with her. It never left. No matter how hard she tried, how busy she kept herself, how many years separated them, he was always there.

By one o'clock she was on her way. She walked briskly with long graceful strides, head high, her hair shining in the sunlight. By the time she reached the museum her mood had softened.

The paintings took her breath away. All the Monets she had studied and loved in college were there. The series of *Haystacks, Rouen Cathedral in Morning Sunlight,* and the *Cathedral in Full Sunlight.* The pure color harmonies of his *Waterliles,* the naturalism of *Gare St. Lazare,* and the dream-like colors of *Impression Sunrise.*

"That's the painting generally regarded as the one that gave Impressionism its name," she heard a man's voice just behind her. She turned, not sure if he was talking to her. A man of about thirty stood directly behind her, looking over her shoulder.

"A hostile art critic wrote a negative article about an exhibit that included this painting by Monet. He said they were all just a series of impressions: 'slap happy daubers', he called them. Coined the term

Impressionism from the title of Monet's *Impression: Sunrise*." He said all of this quietly, matter-of-factly and stood smiling, awaiting her response.

"You're quite an authority," she said.

"No, not really. It's just one of those isolated facts you sometimes remember from a college course. I love Monet though, do you?"

"Yes, I do." She looked at him curiously. He was a few inches shorter than she, slender, almost frail looking. Boyish came to mind. "Well, I just got here," she said moving away from him toward the *Haystack* series. "I've got a lot more to see. Thanks for the lecture."

"I guess it wasn't much of a lecture, but it was nice talking with you. Enjoy the exhibit." He turned and headed in the other direction.

She watched him, hands in pockets, bounce off on his toes. He was cute.

She was absorbed by the paintings and followed the taped Monet lecture on her rented ear-phones. Two hours of concentrated art history left her tired and hot and longing for the beautiful day outside. She yawned and half promised herself to come back tomorrow.

"How'd you like it?" a familiar voice asked from behind her.

She turned. Her quirky friend from the exhibit skipped down the stairs two at a time. "I liked it," she said and continued walking.

He caught up to her, smiling broadly, part of his sandy brown hair sticking up in back. His hands were stuck deep into the pockets of his chinos, and he rocked back and forth as he spoke. "I went over to the Egyptian exhibit, then came back here for some more Monet and was just finishing up when I saw you. Two hours in here on a day like today is enough for me. But I'm really glad I finally got to see Monet and I love the Egyptian exhibit. I'm going to come back and spend some more time when the weather isn't so beautiful." He nodded toward the front door, "Are you leaving now, too?"

For a moment, she was tempted to say she wasn't. He had already committed himself to saying he was leaving. It was a perfect chance to get rid of him. "Yes, I am," she heard herself say.

"Good, I'll walk out with you, if that's O.K.," he said.

She shrugged and headed for the door.

"Uh, my name is Jack Beatty," he said, holding out his hand.

She shook it. "Hi."

They reached the front door, and Jack tried to maneuver himself into position to open it for her. She beat him to it, opened it herself, and was out into the bright sunshine. She squinted and dug her sunglasses out of her purse without breaking stride. "Well, I'm heading down this way," she said, starting to walk downtown.

"I'm going that way, too. Do you mind if I walk with you?"

She looked at him. He was still smiling, but he looked uncertain, vulnerable. "Sure, why not," she said.

He scurried along to keep up with her long strides. "Uh, could we slow down a little? I'm a terrible jogger." He stuck his tongue out in mock panting.

"Sorry, I always walk fast." She slowed down.

"Oh, that's much better, thanks. I think I might make it now. By the way, what's your name?"

She hesitated. "Uh, my friends call me Lucky." The name tumbled out. It was so weird.

"Lucky? What a great name. Well, it sure is nice meeting you and having a chance to chat with you," he said, his head bobbing awkwardly.

The blocks ticked away as they made their way downtown. Jack was a talker. He was one of those people who were funny without trying to be. Comical was the word her aunt liked to use. The herky-jerky movements, his hands thrust deep into his pockets, and his wide-eyed enthusiasm amused her.

Within a few blocks he had laid out his life's history. "I'm from Iowa. Got my B.A. in art history from the University of Iowa. Been in New York for just a year. After graduation, I stayed in Iowa City and worked as a designer at the University of Iowa Press. Boy, was that a bore. I really think I've got some talent. New York is where the real opportunities are for people like me."

His head was bobbing and nodding again, and she had to suppress a chuckle at how intense and serious he was.

"You ever been to Iowa, Lucky?"

"No, I haven't. Someday maybe."

Jack laughed. "Iowa's not a place anyone goes to on purpose, like Hawaii or California. Iowa is a place where you live or visit because you have to, like business or something. Uh, you like living in New York?"

She walked with her head high, body erect. Jack kept turning, leaning toward her, looking up at her face to get her attention.

"It's O.K.," she replied without looking at him.

"Don't mind me. I'm just inquisitive about people. Probably too nosy. Sorry."

She glanced over at him. He had dropped his head in a sheepish way. He was cute, in a dumb, boring kind of way. No sex appeal. But harmless. That was it. That's why she let him walk with her. He was cute and harmless. Kind of just right for the mood she was in today. It was O.K. to let herself be distracted by him for a while. When he became too tiresome, she would get rid of him.

"I love New York," he said, starting up again. "I feel like I'm in heaven. I'm starting to do pretty well now too." His head went up and down again in that way she was beginning to find appealing and annoying at the same time.

"That's good."

"I'm a free-lance designer. I do mostly interior and cover designs for magazines. Hey, you know walking with you is stimulating in more ways than one. I've really worked up an appetite. It's five-thirty. Uh, you think you might like to get a bite to eat?"

She was about to say no until she turned to look at him again. He had this boyish grin on his face, eyes arched, head bobbing hopefully. He sure was different. She was beginning to get kind of a kick out of him. She was hungry and the idea of heading back home to fix herself something had no appeal. "Sure, why not?" she said and smiled.

"Oh!" He sounded surprised.

He took her to a nondescript restaurant that seemed to fit him. "I found this little spot one Saturday afternoon after the movies. They start serving at five. Pretty unusual for New York, and the food's not bad."

She was tired and hungry, and the pasta tasted good. Jack had a couple of martinis before dinner, which made him even more talkative. He ordered a glass of wine with dinner and halfway through the meal he ordered another.

"Who's your favorite author, Lucky?" he asked.

She noticed his face was flushed and he was talking louder. "I like a lot of authors."

"But who's your favorite? Everybody's got a favorite."

"John McPhee."

"You gotta be kidding. I don't believe it. He's one of my all time favorites," he proclaimed loudly.

She gave him a quizzical, 'oh come on now' look.

"No, it's true," he protested.

She put her finger to her lips. "Jack, keep your voice down."

"Oh, sorry, Lucky. I've got a little medical condition, I'm not really supposed to drink much…and I don't, let me hasten to add. Guess I'm overdoing it a little, I'm enjoying you so much."

"It's been fun, Jack, but I do have to go in a few minutes."

His eyes fell. "Oh, damn. Well, anyway, I still can't get over our taste in authors. I've got every book McPhee ever wrote. *A Sense of Where You Are, The Headmaster, The Pine Barons, Coming Into the Country…*"

"You have *Coming Into the Country*?"

"Course, why?"

"Nothing."

"Well, how come you asked about it?"

"It's just that I've been looking for that book, and haven't been able to find it. Probably out of print."

"Well, look no further. You can borrow mine."

"Thanks, but I'm sure I can get it at the library."

"Listen. Tomorrow's going to be a lousy day. Supposed to rain all day. Perfect day to read. I only live two blocks from here. Five minutes. Walk over with me and I'll get you the book." He was bobbing and nodding again.

God, he read my mind, she thought. Relax and do nothing but read all day. Nothing good at home and it was true that she'd been dying to get her hands on *Coming Into the Country*.

"Come on, Lucky. Give me five more minutes with you. I'll get you the book and put you in a cab home."

Actually, it was no big deal, and it was an interesting coincidence. It would be worth an extra five minutes. "O.K." she said, "let's go."

They were at his building in five minutes, a brownstone like hundreds of others in the city. "Are you up for a little climb? I'm on the third floor."

She hesitated. He'd been slurring his words on the walk over and he no longer struck her as cute. She thought about asking him to run up and bring down the book. It started to sprinkle.

"Come on, Lucky. We're going to get wet."

She shrugged and scurried in with him out of the rain. Jack led the way up the stairs. She could barely see in the dim light of the single bare bulb in the hall. The rickety railing swayed when she grabbed it. The building was quiet except for the clicking of her heels on the bare stairs and Jack's unsteady shuffling just above her. She wished she hadn't come.

By the time they reached his door, Jack was puffing and mumbling. The smell of alcohol coming from him in the closeness of the airless hallway made her nauseous. She stood, watching him fumble through the pockets of first his coat, then his pants looking for the key.

"Aha! Success."

The front door opened directly into a small living room, dominated by a large sofa and bookcases running the length of the far wall. She was impressed with his collection of art books.

"Here, why don't you sit for a minute, and I'll go hunt for the book." He disappeared down a small corridor that probably led to his bedroom.

Instead of sitting she wandered over to the bookcase. There were several by McPhee but no *Coming into the Country*. She wondered why he wouldn't keep them all together. "Maybe he's been reading it." She discovered two others she hadn't read and pulled them out and sat on the sofa.

Jack returned, carrying a bottle of wine and two glasses. "I can't put my hands right on that damn book, but I know it's around here some-where. Let's take a break in the action though and have some wine. Then I'll find it for you." He sat next to her, his shoulder and knees brushing hers.

She moved away. "What are you trying to pull, Jack? I came up here to get the book you offered, not to watch you drink. Forget the book. You're drunk. I'm going home." She started to get up.

Jack put his hand on her shoulder. "I'm sorry. Please don't go. I'll get the book for you now." As he stood, he leaned over her, putting his arms on the back of the couch, one arm on either side of her head. "But first, I just want to do something I've wanted to do ever since I first saw you. I want to kiss you, Lucky."

She started to get up again, but he moved his arms closer, each arm holding her head firmly against the couch. He leaned closer, his face now inches from hers.

"Goddamn you!" she yelled.

She tried to slide her head out and under his arms but he held her firmly. He straddled and sat on her. Before she could move again his lips were caressing her face. His breath stank of alcohol, and she could smell the musky odor of his perspiration. She managed to move her head away. His big eyes moved in on her face. One hand slid down between her legs.

"No, no! You bastard!" she screamed, arched her body, shoved and rolled him off her. In the same motion, her hand found the wine bottle and brought it smashing down on his head. He rolled onto the floor and she brought the bottle down again. The bones in his nose crumbled and blood poured out and into his mouth. He lay on the floor, his eyes rolling crazily. She pounced on him, grabbed his head, and smashed it over and over on the hard wood floor, now slimy with his blood and pieces of scalp. "You son of a bitch. You'll never hurt me again."

He was like a rag doll in her hands. She arched her back and sat bolt upright, charged with energy and release.

Slowly, she relaxed her hold on him and collapsed over his body. She closed her eyes and lay over him for long minutes, her quick heavy breathing the only sound in the room.She wasn't sure how long she had been lying on him, She raised herself and felt a stickiness in her hands. Dark stains covered her sweater and she realized for the first time that her hands and clothes were covered with his blood. She stared at the lifeless body and felt no remorse, no shame, only an odd sense of rectitude.

Her legs nearly buckled as she pulled herself off him and stood for a moment in the silence of the apartment, steadying herself. She went into the bathroom, washed herself, took the towel and carefully wiped it over everything she could remember touching. Returning to the living room, she cleaned up, then stood over the man she had killed. There was one more thing she needed to do before leaving.

# Chapter Three

She awoke in some confusion. It felt like morning but the bedroom was still dark. No matter. She was wide awake now. The events of her evening after the museum floated through her mind, a dream sequence, mingling with childhood memories and the long-forgotten words of the psychologist. "When denial no longer works, anger will emerge. It's all right. It's normal

Anger. She buried her head under the pillow and sobbed. His face was there with her. The ugly thyroid eyes; the stink of his breath pressing against her, his sweaty body dirtying her. But she had fought back and discovered the power of her anger. It was a good feeling. "It's normal."

\*　　\*　　\*

When Frank Corso awoke he knew it was nowhere near time to get up. He lay still with his eyes closed, hoping to drift off again. But the harder he tried, the more awake he became. He opened his eyes and looked at his watch face, glowing in the dark. Three-fifteen. He had slept only a few hours, and the prospects for more didn't look good. Images of Carla flashed across the darkened room.

He was wide awake. Sleep was out of the question. And there was no way he was going to keep lying there, playing mind-fucks on himself. He got up and turned on the computer. Six weeks behind his deadline. Two phone calls last week from his publisher, telling him he's holding up the book. All the other contributors' chapters are in except his.

That was bullshit and he knew it, but this was the first time he'd missed a deadline and he didn't like it. He was nearly done and he could finish it tonight.

He put on some lights, padded into the small kitchen, and made some coffee. His stomach growled. "I'm up now, might as well make something to eat," he said aloud. Since he'd been living alone again, he'd begun talking to himself. It was when he had some of his best conversations.

Actually, living alone wasn't all that bad. He could read all night if he wanted to, get up and cook at two in the morning, watch TV in bed any time of the night—something that really pissed off Carla. He missed her a lot, but he didn't miss the wild mood swings.

The marriage didn't leave him with much but he did get the kitchen stuff. Carla hated cooking and refused to go near the kitchen. She was better in the bedroom. "You're the culinary artist," she'd said. "You might as well keep all this crap."

It didn't take him long to whip up an omelet with cheese, ham, peppers, onions, tomatoes, and sliced mushrooms. He gently and carefully slid it onto his plate, admiring its symmetry. The omelet was good and so were memories connected with it; he and his father sitting in the kitchen at five-thirty, when his mother and sister were still in bed. They would talk and watch the sun come up. Silvio taught him how to fold the omelet in half before turning it so it wouldn't break up.

They liked sharing the early morning hours, getting a head start on the rest of the world. It was their time together before he went off to school, and his father strapped on his holster with the gun in it and left for work.

It was during one of their morning talks that he told his father he wanted to be a cop instead of a doctor.

"Frankie, you're smart enough to be the best doctor in New York," Silvio said.

He was afraid he had disappointed him and felt a twinge of guilt until his father grinned. "But you're going to be the best cop in the whole goddamn country. I have no doubt of that."

The strong coffee gave him the jolt he needed to forget about sleep and he went to work in the small study he'd created out of a dressing area off the bedroom. The two walls were lined with fiber board bookcases, overflowing with books on psychiatry, psychology, psychopathology and a section devoted to books and treatises on the mind of the serial killer. His magazines, many of which contained his own articles ran the gamut from semi-pop publications like *Psychology Today* to the academic *American Journal of Psychiatry*. It was where he spent what little time he had to himself in the apartment. What was left he spent in the kitchen with his other creative passion.

At five-thirty he put the finishing touches on the third chapter, printed and proofread the manuscript and shut off the computer. He sat back and closed his eyes, wondering why it is when you have all night to sleep, you lie there wide awake, and when you have to get up, you feel like you could sleep forever.

After a hot shower and a shave, he brushed his teeth and gulped down the Lipitor pill he took daily to keep his cholesterol down…another thing he shared with his father. Feeling better, he wandered around the apartment, dressing in stages. First his underwear and socks, then to the kitchen to make more coffee. He was more of a morning person than ever now, since becoming an insomniac. Three, four hours of sleep was about it for him. It had been like that for nearly a year, starting about ten minutes after the break-up with Carla.

He liked having the time to himself in the early morning hours, poking around the apartment, enjoying the solitude of his own time and space. Once he hit the precinct the world changed.

He slid a piece of bread into the toaster and pushed the lever down. It popped back up. Twice more, same result. He glanced at the note stuck on his refrigerator, "Buy toaster." It had been there for a week.

Back in the bedroom with his coffee, he slipped into a pair of tan slacks and brown loafers. Time to call his father. Hell, seven-thirty in the morning was the middle of the day for Silvio. He'll be wound up, ready to talk all day.

"Hello." His father's voice boomed through the small bedroom.

"Hi, Dad."

"Frankie. I had a feeling it was you. Where you been? Haven't heard from you in almost a week."

"That's why I'm calling. Starting to think about Florida?"

"Yep. We leave January second. Three months in the sun. Can't wait. How's the writing coming?"

"All right. Just finished the three chapters for the *Handbook of Criminal Investigations*."

"You got three chapters in this edition?"

"Yeah."

"Jesus. They must like your stuff, give you three chapters. That's the bible, Frankie."

Frank smiled. It was the bible, but it contained about half the knowledge his father had stashed away in his head. Thirty-five years in homicide, retired for five, Silvio Corso was a legend at the NYPD.

"And a tough cookie, your old man. Don't kid yourself." Jerry never pulled his punches about anything or anybody. "He was no angel. He did what he had to do when he had to do it. So don't get carried away about the legend bullshit." That was Jerry, the first day he and Frank became partners.

"Hey, when you coming over the house, Frankie?"

"Get some Jets tickets from your buddy and let's get to a game before you leave for Florida. I've gotta run. Got a nine o'clock meeting with Jerry."

"Say hello to the old windbag for me. I'll get the tickets. Call ya."

He finished dressing. Blue and white stripped button down, maroon tie, and a blue blazer. It had been years since anybody at the station gave him any guff for the way he dressed. He learned his dress code from Silvio.

"Just because everybody else in the precinct looks like a slob, don't mean you have to. You're a gentleman, Frankie, and you dress and act like one. Always remember that."

He did. And he tolerated his reputation as the clothes horse of the department. Being dressed up made him feel good. He wore off the rack suits and jackets like they were tailor made for his tall, slender frame.

Dark, curly hair swarmed over his neck and around his shirt collar. His face had a high cheekboned leanness, with a long elegant nose that gave a sharpness to his profile. Any suggestion of over sleekness was removed by the thick eyebrows that gave him a rugged feral look. Deep brown eyes flashed with an intensity that dominated a room. It was the eyes with their don't-fuck-with-me look that backed off the wise guys in the station house that first day, when he walked in wearing the kind of pin-striped suit a cop would wear only to a funeral.

He drained the rest of the coffee and tried to focus on his meeting with Jerry, but Carla came out of nowhere. Carla and that hideous afternoon.

Funny how relationships end. Two people are close. Shit happens. A distance gradually develops. And bingo! You make a 180 degree turn and it's over.

\*       \*       \*

Jerry Blodgett thumped around the squad room. A narrow, vintage sixties tie dangled loosely from the neck of his short sleeved shirt. The shirt curved around a massive belly, toward a waist hidden from view. Jerry's efforts to stuff the shirttail back under his belt met with only momentary success. He shrugged and gave up. "Hey, Fraser, you seen Corso?"

Francis Fraser looked up from the button he was sewing on his shirt. "No, try his office."

"The fuck you think, I'm gonna wander around here lookin' for him without first tryin' his office? He's not there."

Fraser returned to his sewing. "I don't know where he is. I ain't his keeper."

Blodgett watched Fraser for a moment. "Francis, I got a hole in my shorts. I'll drop 'em off later."

Frank came out of the men's room. Jerry spotted him and motioned him over. Frank moved gracefully across the room looking out of place among the sweat shirts, jeans, sneakers, and leather jackets in the Eighth Precinct.

Jerry led him into his office and shut the door. "Frank, you got anything more on the Beatty case?"

Frank shook his head. "Not much." He looked through the glass walls at Fraser, who was finishing up with his button and bit the thread off. "Francis is getting to be quite a seamstress." He turned back to Jerry. "Harry and I have interviewed everybody in Beatty's building. Nobody saw or heard a thing, except for the people you talked with who live just below him. They heard somebody going up the stairs at about eight-fifteen, eight-thirty. Couldn't say if it was more than one person, because they didn't pay any attention. They were watching TV. Anyway, about ten minutes later they hear this commotion and thumping on the floor. Lasted for just a minute or two but long enough to annoy the guy. Says he was about to pound on the ceiling with his broom when it stopped. They could still hear somebody moving around up there, but more softly, not as heavy or noisy."

"Yeah. The killer was being careful. Cleaning things up and all. Pretty cool customer."

"Uh, uh. Whoever did this wasn't a cool customer. He tried to be, but this was the work of an amateur. O.K., fingerprints wiped off, but two books were still there on the sofa with prints on them. The killer picked up pieces of a broken glass, but missed three pieces. He left everything in the victim's pockets, so no effort to make it look like a robbery. This was the work of somebody who tried to cover his tracks but was sloppy.

"The hairs found on the body come from long, brown, untreated natural hair. Can't determine the sex."

Jerry took a sip from the Styrofoam coffee cup he'd been holding, made a face and dumped in two more envelopes of sugar.

"Two books by the same author still on the sofa," Frank continued. "I figure Beatty brought someone back with him. They sat on the sofa and had a drink. Maybe they were discussing the books."

"Yeah, looks like things started out O.K."

"Had to be somebody he knew, Jerry. Beatty was a highly educated guy, working in an upscale field. Look at the books in his apartment. He's got more money in books than furnishings. Whoever it was up there with him most likely came from a similar background."

"How can you be sure?"

"I'm not sure, for Christsake. But those two books by McPhee were there for a reason. Beatty wasn't reading them both at once. We've got two sets of prints on both books. He and his guest were probably discussing them. Two wine glasses, a couple of books. These were two guys having a discussion and something went wrong. I think we're looking for an educated person, somebody not unlike Beatty."

"What do you think went wrong?"

"I don't know, but this guy was really worked over. It's one thing to get whacked with a wine bottle, but that's not what killed him. He was hit on the front of his head with the bottle. The back of it was bashed over and over on the floor. He died of a subdural hemorrhage. Christ, the floor's all splintered from his head. Look at the way the back of it was split open. Somebody was very angry."

"What do you make of the wine bottle up his ass?"

"It's a statement, Jerry. It's not just a random act."

"You think the killer was a homosexual?" Jerry asked. "Came on to Beatty and Beatty didn't like it? Called him a faggot or worse? Course maybe Beatty was a fag and they had a lovers' quarrel."

"Yeah. But all of the people who knew him said there's no way this guy was gay. Nobody ever saw any sign of it. We know of at least two women he dated. They said he was a good guy. Drank a little too much. The autopsy showed a high level of alcohol in his blood. Intoxication level. He was drunk at the time he was killed. Also still had pasta and red sauce in his stomach, so he'd only recently eaten. Probably no more than an hour before he was killed."

"Yeah," Jerry said. He pulled a half empty box of sugar doughnuts from his desk drawer, took a bite out of one, and dunked the remainder in his coffee. Little pieces of powdered sugar floated on top for a moment, then disappeared.

"There's no sign of anybody having cooked", Frank said. "No pasta packages around. No empty cans. No dirty pots or dishes. A few items from breakfast still in the sink. Coffee cup, plate with dried egg and toast crusts, but no sign that anybody ate dinner there." He shook his head as Jerry pointed toward the doughnut box.

"So he got the pasta in a restaurant," Jerry said.

"Yeah and on this guy's income, you can bet it wasn't an expensive one. Beatty was not what you'd call a mover. Look at his wardrobe. One sport coat, an old suit, and a few pairs of chinos. I doubt he strayed far from the neighborhood. We'll check out all the cheap Italian restaurants first and go from there."

"Maybe he ate at a friend's apartment?"

"Not likely. If he ate at a friend's place, why would they come back to his for drinks? They'd have just stayed there."

"Yeah, well don't give up on the gay angle. The M.O. has all the signs. Lotta guys hide in the closet pretty effectively. You never know."

"Yeah. Anyway, we're making our way through everybody he worked with. I've had a good first session with his family. Nothing concrete yet, though. He was very well liked by the way."

"Yeah, well somebody didn't like him. Frank, I'm already takin' shit from Nolan on this. He doesn't want any waves to screw up his promotion. That lawyer wife a his is pushing him all the time. She's a social climber, married to a cop! What do ya' call that, Frank? There's a word for it. Oxie somethin'."

"Oxymoron."

"Yeah, that's it. Anyway, Nolan's gonna be all over my ass 'til we find the guy who did this. I agree with you. Had to be somebody he knew. He let him in, they had a nice friendly drink and the guy kills him."

"Jerry, you ever hear of a case where the killer jams a bottle up the victim's rectum?"

"No."

"I'll run this through the state homicide and lead tracking program and put it through VICAP. Maybe we'll find a similar MO somewhere around the country. I'd say this one's a tad unique."

"Yeah, well, I got an appointment downtown. Talk to you later." As he walked past Frank, he patted him on the stomach. "Hey, gettin' a little pot? You better start workin' out."

Jerry left for his appointment, and Frank headed over to Fifty-first Street to talk with a publisher for whom Beatty had done some freelancing. Beatty didn't move in a very wide circle. Shouldn't be too hard to get a handle on the people he saw professionally and socially. The killer was somebody he knew, somebody he felt comfortable with. Somebody like him.

He thought about Jerry's parting shot. "Gettin' a little pot?" Too much booze. He would start working out, try that little health club he'd heard about.

He reached the corner of Madison and Fiftieth and froze in his tracks. Not fifteen yards in front of him, Carla was crossing the street.

Bile came up in his throat. "Oh, Jesus Christ," he blurted and closed his eyes. When he opened them, all that was left of her were two long legs sliding into the back seat of a cab. She closed the door and turned to look out the back window. He was sure she saw him.

# Chapter Four

Mike Peters pushed a button on his console. "Denise, would you bring in the Mendenhall file and reviews?" He gazed out his window at the New York skyline while he waited for the file. His office, although not large, was comfortable, and typical of most New York publishing editors' offices, simple and functional. Manuscripts were strewn everywhere. Both side chairs bulged under the load of millions of typed words. Papers crept out of manila folders, battened down by thick rubberbands. The small table by the window was stacked high with fat, messy-looking folders, boxes, and three-ring binders.

"Mendenhall giving you trouble again, Mike?"

Mike turned from the window and watched his editorial assistant come toward him. Although they had been working together for nearly a year, he was still in awe of Denise's body, nearly six feet tall, broad shoulders, a waist you could put your hands around, tits that won't quit, and legs that start somewhere up around her shoulders.

Denise stood over his desk. "He's a lot to put up with, isn't he, Mike?" She threw her head back, her dark brown chestnut hair flying away from her eyes for the moment.

He wished she wouldn't do that. She was the best editorial assistant he ever had, and he was not about to do anything to screw things up. Anyway, he was happily married. He still wished she wouldn't do that.

"Yeah, he's pissed about the reviews I sent him on his manuscript."

"What are you going to do?" Denise set the file and reviews on his desk. She stood over him, totally oblivious, he was sure, of the effect she had on him.

"I don't know yet. The profs who've reviewed it are all at great schools, and their suggestions make a lot of sense."

"Why don't you get them all together with him and set up a focus group?"

Mike put his hands to his forehead. "That's a great idea, Denise. Let's do it. I'm sure I can get Mendenhall to come and at least listen. What would I do without you?" He smiled warmly at her.

"You'd hire somebody else and forget all about me pretty fast." She had said it matter-of-factly, without humor, without irony. It simply reflected her view of things. Mike watched her walk toward the door, her hips swaying.

He called after her. "Denise, the Bookbuilder's Association is having its monthly cocktails and dinner get together on Thursday. I've got some tickets, and a bunch of us are going over. Do you want to come?"

"Oh, Mike, you know I work out every night at my health club. Thanks anyway."

"O.K., just thought I'd ask…again."

At five-thirty, Denise turned off her computer. Mike was so sweet, but he just didn't get it. She didn't want to go to those publishing dinners. Her co-workers were all nice people but she just wasn't into those monthly mob scenes of drinking and schmoozing. She really did wish he'd back off.

"Is that you Denise? Are you still here?" Gina Ponte's voice floated across the cubicles.

"Yes, it's me. I can't seem to get out of this place."

Denise looked up and Gina was standing in the doorway. She hadn't entered yet but she seemed to fill the small room. Long black hair curled undisciplined around her neck and over her shoulders. Hoop earrings fought their way through the mane of hair, struggling to be seen. A fresh coat of lipstick covered her lips, giving them a puckered, waiting-to-be kissed look. She was nearly as tall as Denise and rivaled her good looks. Her coat was draped over one arm, a briefcase in the other hand. She came in and slumped heavily onto Denise's chair.

"What a day! David's getting ready for his trip to the coast. He's been running my ass off all day, pulling me in sixteen different directions, snapping at me, growling. Fun day."

"Sounds like a day like any other to me," Denise said.

"I tell you Denise. One of these days, when David gets on me like he did today, I'm going to smile sweetly, give him the finger, and walk off into the sunset."

Denise laughed, the first time all day. "No, you won't Gina. You thrive on the pressure and the give and take between you and David. If you walked out, you'd be in the next day, asking for your job back."

Gina shrugged. "You're probably right. But don't ever tell David that. I like to keep him guessing. I want him to think that one of these days he's going to go too far and bingo! I'm gone. How was your day?"

Denise leaned back in her chair and stretched her long legs. Even though she was about to leave and wanted to get to her health club, she was glad that Gina stopped by. "It was O.K. Mike's having his usual problems with Mendenhall, but we'll deal with him. Somehow his books always wind up being worth the trouble."

"Yeah. He may be a pain in the ass, but he's a doll, that Mendenhall. I almost flipped when I saw him in the office a few months ago. I wish he was one of our authors. I'd figure out a way to soften him up. On second thought, maybe I'd just keep him hard." Gina's laugh, phlegmy and watery erupted.

"He's married, Gina."

"So what. I'd just give him a little R and R, while he was away from home. That's all. Well, see ya. I've got to go." She was up and gone, leaving Denise with a smile on her face.

It was time to go if she wanted to be working out by six. The brisk October air felt good, and she enjoyed the seven block walk to the club.

Club Fitness was nothing more than a second-floor room about the size of a large living room. The place was well equipped with free weights, Nautilus machines, cardiovascular bikes, and treadmills. A small reception desk stood to the right of the front door, and there were two small locker rooms and showers for men and women. That was it. No frills.

Tonight, she was working on her back and shoulders. First, the back. Three set of twelve hyperextensions. Four sets of ten rowing half seated, half at the T-bar. Four sets of ten pull downs to back, and four sets of ten pull downs to front.

Next she focused on her shoulders, working with the free weights. First, a behind the neck press, four sets of ten. Then the rest of her shoulders routine.

After she finished, she closed out her session with fifty push-ups and lay on her stomach, resting. The club had filled up, during her workout. She headed for the locker room, weaving her way through the sweating, grunting men and women.

She had showered and dressed, and looked forward to the walk home. That was another thing she liked about the club. It was almost exactly halfway between her apartment and her office. She pushed through the doors as a tall, dark-haired man entered.

"Hi! Bye," they said simultaneously, laughing.

The cool air felt good. It was dinnertime and the street was crowded with chattering couples. The thought of sitting in a comfortable restaurant and having dinner with a friend flashed through her mind. Gina was always fun and she made Denise laugh. She made a note to be friendlier with her.

She'd been busy all week, never seeming to relax and unwind, grabbing a take-out salad in a neighborhood store run by the Korean couple, standing at the sink, eating tuna fish out of the can. Tonight she decided to treat herself. She made some pasta and a salad and poured a glass of red wine. She set the table using one of her good place mats and lit both of the candles. She dimmed the lights and slipped in a tape, sipped her wine, and ate slowly and deliberately in the flickering candlelight. It was so nice, everything so pretty. And no one to share it.

# Chapter Five

Crystal Wilcox stood on the corner of Forty-fourth and Seventh Avenue. It had been a beautiful day, but with typical fall-weather treachery, the night had turned cool. She wasn't dressed for it and had about decided to go home when her friend Vickie Torrez came around the corner.

"Crystal, honey, what you doin' out here? It's cold."

"Same thing you are, Vickie," Crystal replied. "It is getting a little chilly, though. Come on. I'll buy you a drink."

They headed down Forty-fourth Street, Mutt and Jeff, Crystal at five feet eleven towering nearly a foot over Vickie's five-one. Inside the bar they sat warming themselves over a couple of glasses of wine.

"I swear, Crystal, I'll never understand you. You got some of the richest, big shot Johns in the city after your body any time you snap your fingers. You got that gorgeous apartment that you ain't never got to leave if you don't want to, and you come down here and mess with the scumbags looking for a little cheap pussy or a quick blow job. Why?"

Crystal snickered, drained her glass, and ordered another wine. "Sweetie, why do you waste your time wonderin' about me? You got enough to do keepin' your own little butt humpin', takin' care of that loser you live with."

Vickie bristled. Raoul was a loser and he treated her like dirt, but that didn't give Crystal any right to talk like that. Still, she didn't want any trouble with Crystal. She was mean and everybody knew it wasn't healthy to argue with her or piss her off.

"I didn't mean nothin' Crystal. It's just that I have to put up with this crap. I got no choice. But you, you're beautiful, you're smart, you're a college graduate, and everybody knows you make ten times as much as the rest of us with all your high class clientele. And then when I see you down here…well, it just don't make sense." Vickie quickly put her hands up, afraid she'd gone too far. "But, hey, that's cool with me. I like seein' you. We always seem to get along O. K., right?"

Crystal played with her hair and smiled. "Let's just say I get off on gettin' down and dirty once in a while. Reminds me of my roots, O.K.? Come on, let's get out of here. Walk me down the corner while I get a cab."

They started down Forty-fourth Street. A man came out of a small bar and headed toward them. He walked unsteadily, slowly, in no hurry to get anywhere.

"Well, lookie here," Crystal whispered looking around the otherwise empty street. She grabbed Vickie by the arm and they stepped into a doorway.

The man reached them, humming quietly to himself. He was clearly drunk.

"Hi, honey. You want to party?" Crystal whispered.

The man stopped and looked at the two women standing in the doorway. He stood weaving, looking them up and down, and moved into the doorway with them.

Vickie gave him a big smile and rubbed him a little. "You want some fun, honey?"

He studied her, trying to focus. A sneer crossed his face. "Sheeit. I don't go with spics." He turned toward Crystal. "Maybe I wouldn't mind a little white meat."

Crystal's hand found his crotch and began rubbing him. "Hmm. You feel like a real man, honey. I want some a that, eat you right up. How 'bout a nice little blow job? Send you home happy." Now, she was really working him over. His eyes closed and little gurgling sounds came from him.

"Oh, Jesus. Yes, yes, where?"

"Come on, honey, I got a good spot. You got fifty dollars? That's all it's going to cost you."

The man nodded and walked along with Crystal. Vickie followed behind. Halfway down the block Crystal turned the man into an alley. "Vickie, honey, would you kinda keep an eye out while we do our thing? Won't be long."

Vickie nodded and stepped into another doorway. She was used to being called names, especially spic. But she still didn't like it. She wished she had Crystal's looks and brains and style. She sure wouldn't be walking the streets blowing guys in alleyways. She shook her head. "That Crystal's a piece of work" she whispered to herself.

"You son of a bitch." Crystal's voice came out of the alley. "What're you trying to pull?"

More yelling from Crystal. A man and woman rounded the corner about a hundred yards away and slowly headed toward them.

Vickie decided it was time to retrieve Crystal and get the hell out of there. She headed down the alley.

# Chapter Six

"Frank, I got your chapters a coupla days ago and read them last night. They're brilliant." The metallic, all-business voice of Bill Greenberg, Frank's editor at Kent Publishing Company sounded almost friendly.

"You being nice to me, Bill? Careful, you'll blow your image."

"Hey, I know I've been giving you a bad time about being late, but I have to tell you, the stuff you delivered was almost worth the delay."

"Oh. You mean I was getting paranoid over nothing?"

"I said almost. We're still going to have to scramble to meet the production schedule."

"Ah, that's the Bill I know. You almost had me feeling good there for a minute."

"Seriously, Frank. Those chapters are dynamite. In fact, I've got a proposal for you."

"Uh-oh."

"I'd like to talk with you about a contract to write a book for us in the Fahey *Criminal Justice Series*."

"Uh-uh. I already have a job. I'm a cop, remember? A few chapters and some articles here and there, that's one thing, but a whole book? No way."

"Come on, Frank. You know this is the most important series of books in the field. With the following you're developing with your articles and your contribution to the Encyclopedia, you're a natural for this series. We'll get you a nice advance."

Frank thought of the load on his Visa, maxed out on the Mastercard, and the valve job he needed on his car. "I don't know, Bill. That's a lot of work."

"Couple hours a night, a little bit on weekends, you can do the book in a year, year and a half. Professor Fahey's right here at NYU. Didn't you take your Master's with him?"

"You know goddamned well I did. Don't hustle me, Bill. I gotta go. I'll think about it."

\*       \*       \*

"Hey, Frank, let's go over to Tommy's and get a beer." Jerry stood over Frank's desk and grabbed him by the shoulder. "Come on, pal. Enough's enough. It's six-thirty."

Frank looked up from his computer and waved him off. "Give me a couple of minutes."

"Hurry up. I'm going to the head. See you downstairs." Jerry shambled across the squad room and out the door.

Frank liked Tommy's. It was where he went to unwind, often by himself. He liked it a little too much. His monthly bar tab was killing him. He hoped the little health club would take up some of the slack. But everybody needed a safe haven, a haven from all the bullshit and Tommy's was his.

Jerry ordered them a couple of beers. The barmaid slid Jerry's to him and set Frank's carefully in front of him as if presenting a magic potion.

"How you doin', Frank?"

"I'm O.K., how about you, Cathy?"

"I'm better, now," she said, squeezed his hand and wiggled to the other side of the bar.

Jerry took it all in and shook his head in disgust. "What'sa matter with you, Corso? That broad's been throwin' herself at you for almost a year now. And all you do is give her that silly-ass wimpy grin and act like a faggot." He drained his beer and nodded his head toward Frank.

"I'll tell you one thing. She come on to me like that, she'd a been taken care of a long time ago."

"Sheeit," Frank laughed. "You'd have a heart attack with somethin' like that. Anyway, Betty'd find out and kick your ass."

"You're probably right on both counts. What's new on the Beatty case?"

"We don't have a whole lot. I requested a state check of the automated fingerprint identification system...our friends from SAFIS. Neither set of prints we found on the books belongs to anybody who's been arrested since 1985. So...we know the killer hasn't been arrested before, at least in New York state and at least since 1985."

"Yeah. Too bad the automated check isn't available nationwide yet," Jerry said as he motioned for two more beers.

"No luck on the restaurants yet," Frank said as Cathy poured his beer for him. "He had a Visa card in his wallet but no restaurant receipt in his pocket. We checked with Visa but no charges have come in yet. We'll follow later in the month. Course he could've paid cash."

"Or the other guy could've paid," Jerry said.

Frank nodded. "There's something else that bothers me about this one, Jerry."

"What?"

"This could be the beginning of more to come."

"Yeah, I know what you're gonna say."

"You've got a signature here with that bottle in the rectum. This kind of behavior goes beyond the actions needed to commit the crime."

"Yeah, go on." Jerry knew he wasn't going to like what was coming.

"Well, you get an offender with fantasies and he's going to brood and daydream until he finally expresses and acts out the violent fantasies. However, just committing the crime doesn't satisfy all of his needs. He needs to go beyond it and perform a ritual...a calling card."

"And the bottle is the calling card here."

Frank gave him a double take. "Uh, yeah." He grinned and tapped the side of his head with his finger. "Now, what we have to worry about is that the signature aspect stays with the killer as an ongoing part of his fantasies. He's got to keep acting it out now, right?"

"Yeah," Jerry said softly.

"These creeps all start out with their fantasies and begin to live them. Ed Kemper, John Wayne Gacy, Wayne Williams, our own Son of Sam, Ted Bundy, Jeffrey Dahmer…"

"All right! All right," Jerry growled.

Frank watched his friend, a year away from retirement and trying to coast home. He felt Jerry's angst and hoped he was wrong about Beatty being the beginning of more to come. "Hey, let's talk about something else for a change. How's Betty?"

"She's fine. Listen, kid, there is something else I want to talk to you about." He clamped his arm around Frank's neck. "Come on. Let's go sit down at a table. I'll get us a couple more beers."

They settled in at a table. Frank poured his beer and watched Jerry pull out a cigar. Uh-oh, he thought. He knew the routine. He watched Jerry take his time unwrapping the cigar, suck on it, bite off the end, light it, look up, close his eyes, and blow the smoke out, looking real thoughtful. "Frankie," Jerry began. "You know you're the best and smartest detective in the precinct next to me, that is. I don't mind tellin' you that, 'cause you already know it. You're one of the best in the whole NYPD. Lotta people have their eye on you. You been doin' Silvio proud. Shit, even I learn somethin' from you every once in a while."

"Gee, thanks, Jerry."

"Don't be a wise ass. I'm tellin' you this because I'm worried about you. You got a great future ahead of you, kid, but you got to get over this Carla stuff. It's affecting your work. You're not yourself. You ever see her?"

"No. When she moved out and got her own place, that was it. We lost touch. I never even knew where she lived. Still don't."

"It's been what…almost a year? You gotta' move on with your life."

He wasn't in the mood for this. Jerry was wound up, probably been saving up this speech and rehearsing it. "Don't worry about it," he snapped. His eyes were now adjusted to the darkness and he looked around the bar. A young hooker sat across from them, looking nervous, ill at ease and yet, hopeful. She didn't even look old enough to be in the bar. A few stools away, a fiftyish man in a three piece suit sat alone, staring into space, not having much luck fighting back tears.

The city was full of people like that, sad people trying to cope with life, playing as best they could the hands they'd been dealt. He turned back to Jerry and saw the anguish in his face. He slid his arm up and hugged his friend. "Thanks, Jerry. I appreciate what you're saying. I'm going to be fine." He let go of Jerry and flashed his grin. "Tell you what. I'll go out and get laid tonight."

The joke fell flat. "You know, Frank, now that it's been almost a year, I guess I can tell you I think in the long run you're going to be better off. So does Betty, by the way."

"What do you mean?"

"I mean I think you were so nuts about Carla you didn't see some of the things we did."

"Like what?"

"Like…well, she had a short fuse, even with a pussycat like Betty. And she could be moody as hell. Jesus, when she'd get into one of those moods of hers, you just felt like you were walking on eggs around her. It seemed like there was always something bugging her."

"Yeah. I know what you're saying, but a lot of that was my fault. Even with the career what she really wanted more than anything was a husband who was there for her, a guy she could count on for the emotional security she needed. I wasn't there."

"Yeah, you say that, but I just don't think you should be bashing yourself, Frank. Takes two, you know? And hell, I may be way off base for saying this, and if I am, tell me to shut up. But you didn't really seem to know a hell of a lot about Carla. Hell, you know me, I'm just nosy, but whenever I'd ask you things about her, you didn't know much. You know…like family and all that. Just simple basic stuff."

Frank pushed his beer away. "Christ, we were married less than a year. It took me that long to find out her middle name. I told you her mother and father are both dead, and she never wanted to talk about her family, so I never pushed it, O.K.? You are a nosy son of a bitch, aren't you?"

"Yeah, well I'm a cop. I'm supposed to be."

"Carla was always just…a very private person. She…ah, hell, Jerry. Let's drop it for tonight, O.K.?"

Jerry nodded. He knew his friend and it was time to drop it.

*    *    *

Carla Sanders stood on the balcony enjoying a rare moment of solitude, a solitude she knew would be short lived. But it was nice to reflect and recharge, no matter how briefly.

It was hard to believe this was her life. So much had happened in the past year. And it all started the day Frank caught her in the sack with Henry. That nightmarish afternoon had been humiliating for all of them, but now standing on the terrace of a penthouse apartment looking out across the city, her city, it had all worked out for the best, except for Frank.

But things had moved so quickly, there was little time to think or worry about Frank. She had changed and grown and moved on, swept into the fast lanes of Henry Manning's world.

"I'm going to make you the top model in New York, Carla," Henry had promised. And now, a year later, she was getting close. She'd been on some spreads of a couple of obscure fashion magazines that hardly anybody read, but the pace was picking up. In January she'd be in Marabella and her agent was working on a cover for a major magazine.

Henry had taken her a long way, but he had become too possessive, and he was terrible in bed. Frank had spoiled her in that department.

Henry was definitely worth staying on good terms with, but the romance was over.

Tonight's party was typical of the world she'd been living in during the past year. Kenneth Amory was one of the world's leading fashion designers. His wife, Claudia, was the winner of this year's Tony Award for best actress in a musical.

At first she had been thrilled and honored to be invited to such affairs. Now, she was considered a catch.

Her reverie was abruptly shattered. "Carla, for God's sake. I heard you were here. How are you?"

She turned and said hello to Linda Kellerman, a woman she hadn't seen in probably a year and a half. She greeted her as if she had just seen her yesterday. "Hello, Linda, nice to see you," she said. She remembered Linda as a pain in the ass, always trying to push her way into her and Frank's circle of friends.

"I've been out of the country for the past year, but I've been hearing about you. You're doing great." She lowered her voice. "Sorry to hear about you and Frank. How's he doing?"

Stupid, intrusive question, "I don't know. I haven't seen him in a year," she said, lighting a cigarette.

"Oh! Well, he was some gorgeous guy. Is he still a cop?"

"I really don't know that, either. Why don't you call him up and ask him? Excuse me, Linda. There's someone I need to see." She swirled past Linda and into the living room.

"Well! Excuse me," Linda called.

Carla spotted her agent, Randy Stern pushing his way though the crowd toward her. "Carla, I've been looking for you all evening. I need to talk to you for a minute." He led her into a quiet corner of the spacious room. "Listen, I've been talking with Bruno Mori from Milano. He's interested in you for a part in a movie he's putting together in Italy. If he likes you, and you test O.K., he might want you for another he's going to be starting right after this one. The thing is, you'd have to be in Italy for the better part of about six months but…"

Carla was shaking her head.

"Hey, Carla, the money'd be great, and you can always zip back here from time to time as needed. I mean it's not like…"

"Randy, I really don't want to be out of New York for a while. O.K.? I just need to be here. The thing in Italy sounds interesting, but the timing just isn't right."

Randy started to speak again, but she shut him off. "No."

"O.K., I hear you. I'll pass on this one, but you owe me."

Carla looked around the room. "Randy, who is that darling young man standing over there in the blue jacket?"

Randy scanned the area she directed him to. "Oh, that's Rob Sturgis. He's the big new stud on that soap The Young Lions."

"Hmm. Is he gay?"

"Shit, no. Not from what I hear."

"Would you ask him to come over? I'd like to meet him."

# Chapter Seven

Paul Gale sat outside the warden's office of the Massachusetts State Prison at Norfolk. Today was the day for which he'd waited eighteen years. He fidgeted nervously and his heart pounded. Through the room's two windows he could see the fading late autumn colors of the trees and the deep blue October sky. He glanced at the guard sitting next to him. I won't miss seeing you anymore, asshole, he thought, resisting the temptation to say it aloud.

The guard looked back malevolently at Gale, seeming to read his mind. "You'll be back, Gale. We'll keep your cell warm for you."

The phone on the secretary's desk buzzed. "Yes, sir, I'll send him in." She hung up the phone, and without looking at the guard indicated that the warden was ready to see Paul Gale.

"All right. On your feet, Gale." The man's voice had the tone of one accustomed to telling people what to do.

Gale struggled to his feet, the chains and handcuffs rattling as he did. The guard held one elbow as Paul shuffled across the room toward the warden's office.

When they entered the office, Warden John Bulger slid his desk chair back and stood. A slender, scholarly looking man, he appeared more like an academic. He spoke softly. "That's all right, Quigley. You can wait outside." Warden Bulger walked around to the front of his desk, and leaned against it, facing Gale. He did not offer him a chair.

Gale shifted from one foot to the other, his restraints the only sound in the room.

The warden continued to look at Gale. His face was hard and unfriendly and Paul's discomfort mounted. "Well, congratulations, Gale. You're finally going to be leaving the system. I can't say that we're going to miss you."

So that's it, thought Gale. The prick's gotta give me some shit before I leave.

"Gale, I know you're leaving tomorrow, and I should wish you good luck, and hope that you stay out of trouble. I also want to tell you that I don't like you. The guards don't like you, and very few of the inmates like you. The law says you've paid your debt and we have no choice but to set you free. I want you to know that I don't feel good about it. I think you're an evil person, who's not been rehabilitated. You've simply learned how to go along. Frankly, I believe you're the kind of person, who should never leave prison."

Gale's face twitched. "Sorry you feel that way, sir. I done my time, and stayed outta trouble, and the parole board says I'm ready to leave." He couldn't resist a slight smile.

Warden Bulger shook his head. "People don't change, Gale. Especially not scum like you. How many people did you assault in Walpole?"

Gale stood, silent, his eyes on the floor.

"Well, you got your parole. Now, get the hell out of here. My office is beginning to smell." He walked to the door, and opened it. "Quigley. Get this scumbag out of here."

The cab carrying Gale angled on to Route One and headed north toward Boston. Gale sat back, enjoying the fresh air blowing through the open windows. A million thoughts raced through his mind. But for the moment, he reflected on the session with the warden. It had taken him a long time to learn. Constant fights and other troubles kept him at Walpole way beyond the norm. Year after year he would come up for his automatic parole hearing, and each time he was denied.

How many times had he thought of his daughter and how she'd put him in Walpole? Only every day. He finally got smart and learned how to go with the flow and put up with all the shit. It paid off. First the transfer to Norfolk. Medium Security. Piece of cake after the tough maximum security at Walpole. And now, here he was after eighteen years, paroled and cruising along Route One to Boston, a free man. He leaned back and lit a cigarette.

The cab driver turned around. "Excuse me, sir. Did you notice the No Smoking sign in the back? I'm very allergic to cigarette smoke, and I ask my passengers if they could please not smoke."

Gale took a deep drag on the cigarette. Without inhaling, he exhaled a great cloud of smoke, most of which settled into the front of the car.

The driver coughed. "Sir, could you please put the cigarette out?"

"Hey! You don't tell me what to do. Just shut up and drive the cab."

The driver slowed down and turned to look at his passenger. The look in Gale's eyes told him to drive and say nothing more. They continued in silence.

The cabby dropped Gale at the Park Plaza Hotel. When he reached his room, he lay back on the queen-sized bed, the first real bed he had been on in eighteen years. He closed his eyes and fell into a deep sleep.

# Chapter Eight

As usual Frank was surrounded by students when he finished his lecture at NYU. Once a week he spoke for an hour on the Violent Offender to graduate students in Criminal Justice as part of the guest lecture program.

He had mixed feelings about it. He enjoyed teaching students and loved the intellectual give and take. Since this was his second year, it no longer required a lot of preparation time and the students loved it. That was part of the problem, he thought as he tried to make his way through the jam of students wanting to talk with him. Most were female, serious about wanting more discussion with their favorite teacher. It was the other ones who were getting to be a problem. They'd call him at the precinct, even at home. He knew better than to encourage anyone and he was not about to get involved, even though some of them were tempting.

"Mr. Corso, I'm intrigued by your comments about fantasy being more than an escape, but how it becomes the focal behavior." She was a good student, but she was also a toucher. He took a step back.

"No question, Shelly. What I'm saying is a sexual psychopath is able to maintain contact with reality. But his world of fantasy becomes as addictive as an escape into drugs." He looked over her shoulder and saw Susan Barsky beckoning. He managed to extricate himself with a smile. "Excuse me, I have an appointment. See you next week."

He took Susan's hand in both of his and squeezed it. "Thanks for rescuing me. What a surprise."

He was still holding her hand in his. She placed her other hand on top and they stood for a moment facing each other the way old friends do.

"Come on. You look tired," she said. "I'll buy you a drink."

They settled into their favorite spot at the edge of Washington Square. "So what's with you, Frank? Where've you been and how've you been?"

"I've been around and I'm O.K." The scotch tasted good. He looked across the room and back at Susan. She was his buddy but she knew him too well, knew too much about him and that made him just a little uncomfortable. "You teaching at night now, too?"

"No, I had some work to do in the library and then I figured you might be teaching tonight so I thought I'd stop over. That O.K.?"

Frank grinned and shrugged. He held up his empty glass. "My turn to buy you a drink."

Susan sat back and watched him. He knew she wasn't just looking at him. She was studying him. The psychologist in her. Always working. She wasn't exactly hard to look at herself.

"I've been seeing your articles in the journals. They're very good."

"Thanks."

"And Fahey tells me you might be doing a book in his Criminal Justice Series. Articles. Lecturing down here. And if I know you, you're putting in at least seventy hours a week for the good old NYPD. That sound about right?"

"Yeah, I guess so."

"Frank, you're pushing yourself too hard. Anything or anyone in your life besides work?"

"Ooh. That didn't take long. No small talk, no foreplay. Just get right to it, huh?"

She continued staring at him. He knew she would until he gave her a straight answer. "Anyway, the answer is no." He was about to say he didn't have any time but thought better of it.

"You know, Frank, my record as a therapist has been pretty damn good. I really do help people. You gave me a lousy eight months and then you call it quits…just when we were starting to make some progress, I might add."

He noticed the two little drops of perspiration form on her upper lip. Not unappealing. "Yeah, well I figured eight months of fun and games every week was enough."

"Dammit it, Frank, that's how it works. Of course it's painful. She hurt you badly, but we were working that through. And then what do you do, all of a sudden cut it off like that." She snapped her fingers and glared at him.

Now there were four beads on her lip.

"Sorry, Suze. I know we were making progress. And you're the best."

"Then why did you stop?"

"I told you. I'm not big on pain."

"Frank, you've got to move on with your life. Look at you. What a waste. You may be the best-looking man in New York City. If I weren't your therapist and friend…"

"Ex-therapist," he broke in.

"O.K., ex-therapist, but not ex-friend. I care about you, you jerk."

Five beads.

"Have you seen her at all?"

"Funny you should ask. I just saw her this afternoon. First time in a year. She was getting into a cab."

"Did she see you?"

"I think she did. But the cab took off, and that was it."

"The job going well?"

"Very well."

"Are you sleeping any better?"

"Not much."

"When's the last time you had a date?"

"Susan, are we having a therapy session?"

"Yes, and this one's on the house."

*     *     *

Back home in his apartment he made himself a hefty scotch on the rocks and slipped in a CD. He didn't know which one it was and he didn't care. Last Sunday's New York times sat undisturbed and unread on the sofa where he'd thrown it five days ago. The soft sounds of Yanni drifted across the small living room. Good choice, he thought as he sat down in his favorite and only easy chair, put his feet up on the ottoman and took a deep breath.

The scotch tasted good and helped him relax. It helped but it wasn't enough. He was tired and he felt depressed. Why the hell wouldn't he be?

Trying to do too much. His case load was ridiculous, the lecturing, articles, and now here he was about to take on a whole book. It's crazy.

It was good to see Susan. She was right, as always. They were making some progress and she knew him better than anybody. Didn't take her long either. Scary, actually. Maybe that's why he stopped seeing her.

Jerry was right if that was any consolation. Carla was starting to get weird, and in the long run he'd be better off without her. When would the long run begin?

He went to the kitchen and poured another scotch, this one bigger than the last, so he wouldn't have to get up again so soon. He glanced at the picture of his father and him with the mayor at his father's retirement. Shit, Silvio was a Borough Commander by the time he was forty. Hard to believe it had been eight years now since he'd made detective. So full of piss and vinegar. He was going to be Henry the Eighth and turn every case into another fucking Agincourt.

It didn't work that way, but he'd get there. Two tours at the F.B.I. Academy at Quantico, giving his own seminars, the writing, teaching. All adds up. He finished off the scotch.

Funny, when he was a holier than-thou graduate student he wrote a thesis on career police officers and their problems. Divorce rates off the charts, boozers living in drab little apartments. It was all so clinical, so easy to analyze with the condescending superiority of a college kid who didn't know shit about the real world.

Anyway, this was it, the real world, his real world. Maybe a graduate student'll call him for an interview.

Yes, life was complicated. He still had the bad vibes about the Beatty killing. It had been almost two weeks now. If he was right about the signature and the timing, something was going to happen again…soon.

Jerry. He'd learned so much from him, but now Jerry was just coasting, not wanting to rock the boat. Jerry would lean on him down the stretch. It was O.K.

He set the empty glass down and checked the refrigerator. He found a chicken breast, which he sliced on an angle, cut up the aging green pepper, and a few shallots, sprinkled in some herbs, a little fresh garlic, and put it all in a frying pan with some wine. He was in his element, feeling a little better. He turned the heat down and whipped up some pasta with tomatoes, olive oil, basil, and more fresh garlic.

He ate his supper while reading the page proofs of one of his articles. At eleven o'clock, feeling groggy, bone tired and generally screwed up, he flopped into bed, popped in a Beatles CD and slipped off to sleep to the strains of *Hey, Jude.*

# Chapter Nine

It was six a.m. before Gale stirred. There was much to do today, and he was eager to get started. He opened his small suitcase and removed an envelope. Inside was a cashier's check for $10,280. At Walpole, he had opted for the work program, averaging just over twenty hours a week for sixteen years in the plate shop, making automobile number plates. He earned twenty-five dollars per week, kept half the money for cigarettes and other incidentals, and the other half was deposited to his account. The check now would provide him with a nice little nest egg, until he could get back on his feet.

He stood in the center of the hotel lobby gazing at the lively, chattering people. Mostly, he watched the women. Two flight attendants bustled past him. He liked their little tight skirts and the scent of their perfume. It was the first time he'd smelled perfume in eighteen years. A young woman with her back to him leaned over to pick up a glove she had dropped, exposing part of both thighs.

"Goddamn!" he muttered and headed for the check-out counter.

In the bank across the street, he used his certified check to buy nine thousand dollars' worth of travelers checks and took the rest of his money in cash. He called the train station for schedules. A train was leaving for North Adams in an hour and a half, at eleven thirty.

By the time he settled himself into his seat on the train, Gale's longing for a woman had become overpowering. The walk to South Station was particularly tantalizing. They were everywhere; big-breasted, long-legged, hip-swinging, lusty-looking women of all ages and sizes. South Station offered no reprieve.

If I don't get a piece a ass soon, I'll go nuts, he thought, hunkering deeper into his seat.

He forced himself to think of locating his daughter. He did know that she was in New York City. Tom Foy, the one friend Gale had in North Adams, had heard from Gale's sister-in-law, his daughter's aunt, that she was in New York. He also heard she'd changed her name. But to find anybody in New York, he needed more to go on. Twice from prison he had phoned her aunt in North Adams, and both times she had hung up on him. "Damn it, Janet. I'm her father. I got a right to know where my daughter is and to see her," he had pleaded.

"You have no rights, you pig, and anyway, I don't know where she is." And she had hung up.

On the second call, she hung up as soon as she heard his voice. There'll be no hanging up this time, he thought and smiled.

"Excuse me, conductor. You got a bar?"

"It's in the club car, sir. Three cars down."

Gale stood at the entrance to the club car, staring at the gleaming chrome. He'd never seen a club car on a train before, never been on a train for that matter. He made his way across the room, settled into one of the small tables, ordered a beer, and lit a cigarette. A mirror directly across the way reflected his image. He was now balding, with only a few stringy wisps left on the top of his head. Years ago he had grown a goatee beard, now salt and pepper and neatly trimmed. He thought it gave him a distinguished look. The gold tooth still dominated his mouth. His thyroid condition had worsened in prison, and his eyes bulged wider than ever.

He had entered prison a slender wiry young man of thirty. In prison, he put on about thirty-five pounds, and if not fat, he was burly, heavy set. Unlike most inmates, he had spent no time developing his body. He was soft and flabby. The years of smoking had taken a further toll on a voice that had always been guttural and raspy.

All in all, he was not unhappy at the image, staring back at him. Not bad for a guy of forty-eight, he mused as the waiter set his beer down.

"Bring me another one now, before you get busy," he called at the waiter, heading back toward the bar.

The door to the club car opened, and a woman made her way across the room. Gale's eyes shifted toward her.

She looked to be in her early forties, short, a little on the heavy side. Her longish black hair was too dark to be natural, and her makeup was a bit much for the time of day and the setting. But Gale was looking only at her chest. He took a long drink of his beer and smiled at her as she came toward him. She smiled back.

The small room had only two empty tables. She sat at the one next to his and ordered a beer.

Gale watched her, trying to think of something to say to start a conversation. Nothing would come. She made it easier by pulling out a cigarette and fumbling around in her pocketbook. He leaned over and flicked his lighter. "Can I give you a light?"

She looked at him for a moment "Thank you. I can never find anything in this thing." She nodded toward her pocketbook.

She took a deep drag on her cigarette. As she did, her breasts expanded, moving suggestively under her tight sweater.

Gale swallowed hard. "Uh, where you headed?" he asked.

"Oh, I'm going to Greenfield. That's where I live. I was in Boston for a couple days visiting my daughter. She's a nurse at City Hospital."

"A nurse, huh? Must be a smart girl."

"Well, she's hard working, that's for sure. She put herself through the Fitchburg State College Nursing Program. I couldn't afford to send her there on what I make, so she did it pretty much on her own. Got both her B.S. and R.N."

"What about her father? Didn't he help?"

"No. Him and I were divorced when she was only ten years old. He took off out West somewhere, and we've never heard from him since." She finished her beer and glanced over her shoulder.

"Uh, could I buy you another beer?" Gale asked, moving his chair closer to her table.

"Well, I guess we got a couple hours more to Greenfield, so sure, why not?" she lit another cigarette.

He braced himself for the first big puff. "What kinda work you do?"

"I'm a waitress at Bill's in Greenfield."

"Hey, I bet you serve a mean meal." his thick bronchial laugh filled the room. The laughter started him coughing.

She reached across the table and hit him several times on the back. "Ooh! That's a bad cough you have there. It's the cigarettes, you know."

Her touch made him rock hard. She was the first woman to touch him in eighteen years. "Yeah," he wheezed. "Someday I'm gonna cut these things out. But hey! Today we're havin' a good time. So maybe I'll cut 'em out tomorrow, right?" He erupted again. His hacking laughter infected his companion and she joined in, laughing, wheezing, and coughing along with him.

"We're a great pair." Gale barely managed to get the words out, tears of laughter streaming down his face. "Hey, what's your name, anyway," he asked, finally settling down.

"Lois. Lois Fachetti." She drained her glass.

"How 'bout a couple more beers, Lois?" Gale was now sitting at her table. "Waiter," he yelled loudly across the car.

The waiter held his finger to his lips, held his hand up, palm out, and nodded.

"You haven't told me your name, yet," Lois said, leaning forward.

"Uh, oh yeah. My name is Paul. Paul Gillis," he said.

"Paul Gillis. That's a nice name. How far are you going, Paul?" Lois asked, taking another chug of her beer.

Gale made a quick decision. "Well, actually, I'm going to Greenfield, too."

Lois Fachetti's eyes lit up. "You're going to Greenfield? What a nice surprise."

"Yeah," he said. "I'm going up to visit an old buddy of mine to discuss a business deal."

By the time the train reached Greenfield, Paul and Lois had bonded. They were also drunk.

They made their way unsteadily off the train, Paul carrying their suitcases. On the platform, Lois staggered against him. He slid his arm around her to hold her steady. Her heavy breasts pressed against his chest. He started to kiss her, but she giggled and pulled away.

"Take it easy, honey. Not right here, in front of everybody. Tell you what. I'm going to take you home and make you the best lunch you ever had. How's that sound?"

"Lois, baby. You just made yourself a deal. Let's go. You got a car here?"

"Course I do. It's right over here in the lot. It ain't much, but it gets me where I want to go And right now, where I want to go is home with you, honey." She giggled again, and pinched him in the stomach.

Once inside the car, Gale leaned over, and kissed her hard. His hands groped her body.

"Hey, easy honey, easy. We got all day," she said huskily. She squirmed away, hitched her skirt down, and started the motor. "Now honey, you gotta let me drive, and not be fuckin' around. Oops, excuse me, Paul. That just kinda slipped out. I don't usually talk like that, you know."

Gale's wheezy laugh erupted. "Oh, baby, I love it when you talk dirty to me. You can say fuck all you want."

"Well anyway, Paul, we have to be careful driving. They're tough on drunk drivers in this town, so let's just cool it 'til I can get us home."

On the way to Lois' house, he noticed a Greyhound bus station at end of the main street. Lois turned right at the bus station, and after less than a mile, she turned into a dirt road, and stopped in front of a small cottage, one of only two houses on the road.

"Well, this is my little haven from the world. It's close to town, but nice and private."

Gale set his bag down in the little entry hall and looked around. The house was a dump but he wasn't there for the ambiance. The kitchen and combination living-dining room were all cramped together. Looking down the narrow hallway, he could see the bedroom. That was the only room he was interested in. The house smelled of perspiration and cheap perfume. There were so many cigarette butts in the ashtray, he had to throw his in the sink.

"Sit down, Paul. I'll get some lunch started. How 'bout a nice big Western omelet, some toast and coffee? But first we're gonna have a couple Bloody Mary's, O.K.?"

She turned, and Gale was leaning against her. He kissed her. Her arms went around him squeezing, her pelvis undulating against his. Her tongue filled his mouth.

"Oh, Jesus, Paul. It's been so long."

"Me, too, baby," he whispered. He grabbed her by the hair, and pulled her head back. She moaned and clawed at him and found his crotch.

"Ooh, baby." He moved her toward the bedroom.

They fell heavily onto the bed and he had her clothes off in seconds. He buried his head between the tits he had longed for all day.

"Oh Jesus Christ," he muttered. "Baby, baby."

Lois sobbed, then took one of her breasts into her hands, and guided it into his mouth. He took it hungrily sucking and nibbling. Lois moaned and grabbed at him.

"Oh, fuck me, honey. Fuck me."

He rolled over on top and entered her. Like two savage animals, they clawed, and bit, and humped and sucked until they lay still, panting, satiated.

They both drifted off to sleep. After about thirty minutes, Gale awoke, ready for more. He reached out for Lois, and began fondling her. She moaned and stirred and turned her back. Gale grabbed her and tried to turn her around. She resisted.

"Honey, not now. I'm tired. Let me sleep for a while." She moved away.

"Goddamn it. C'mere," he snarled, turning her around.

"No," she said thickly, and without opening her eyes, put her hand up to push him away. Her finger accidentally stuck in his eye. He screamed and recoiled.

"You bitch!" he screamed and slammed his open hand across her face. Her eyes opened wide in surprise and fear. She reached out instinctively, her nails raking his face. He roared and hit her again. Grunting and panting, he pulled her off the bed and threw her on the floor. She screamed, and he was on her, his hand clamped over her mouth. With his hand still covering her mouth, he mounted and entered her again. She managed to get his hand off her mouth.

"You're crazy, you bastard," she screamed.

He climaxed and began pounding her again. She stopped squirming and lay still. Twice more, his fists came down, then he slowly disengaged himself from her. He staggered into the kitchen, rummaged through the cabinets, and found a bottle of vodka. Three shots of the vodka calmed him and he walked back into the bedroom. Lois lay on her back on the floor, between the bed and the wall. Blood covered her face, and part of her cheekbone was exposed. He couldn't tell if she was breathing or not.

He snickered. "She ain't going nowhere for a while, one way or the other."

He finished his drink, washed himself, wiped his prints off the things he'd touched, dressed, and left. It was a few minutes to five when he reached the bus station. He was in luck. There was a bus leaving for North Adams at five thirty-five.

# Chapter Ten

Frank sat alone at a small table in a corner of Tommy's, eating a corn beef sandwich and enjoying a cold Heinekins. A man with jowls that rippled like a water bed whenever he moved sat at the bar surrounded by plates of food. The man sipped a highball and took intermittent drags on his cigarette along with shoveling in the food. Real gourmet. Another guy with a death wish.

The wine bottle thing rattled around in his head. It wasn't your run-of the-mill thug. Somebody really got off on this.

He'd talked with at least a dozen of his contacts in the gay community, checked every gay bar within twenty blocks. Nothing.

"Frankie, if this boy was gay and looking for action, believe me I'd have known about him," Bruce Dion, Frank's most reliable connection had assured him. "If he was as adorable as these pictures, he would have had all he could handle. He was cute, wasn't he?"

Beatty seemed to have all the profile of being straight. He dated a few women at work, asked at least four others out, and was turned down. Nothing in his apartment or personal effects to indicate any gay activity. Switch hitter? Not likely.

He thought about how much time he'd spent over the past nine years checking out people's sex history. He'd become a voyeur, digging into people's perversions, jealousies, infidelities, and lust. People die for bad reasons all the time, and if you dig deep enough, chances are there's a sex angle somewhere. What is it on this one?

\*      \*      \*

Paul Gale stood on the front porch of the house and rang the doorbell. The door opened, and a small, gray-looking woman in her early fifties stood behind the screen door. Gale recognized his sister-in-law.

"Yes?" The woman looked tentative, nervous.

"Hello, Janet," Gale said quietly.

She stared at him. Something in the voice tried to jog her memory. "Do I know you?"

Gale smiled. "Yes. It's Paul."

Janet continued staring for a moment. Recognition lit her eyes. Her mouth fell open, and she whispered, "Paul? Paul Gale?"

"Yes. Can I come in?"

Her mouth was still open, but she said nothing, shaking her head slowly.

Gale remained smiling, trying to appear friendly.

Janet regained her composure. "What do you want with me"?

"Janet, except for my girl, you're the only living relative I got. I was released from prison yesterday. I don't know a single soul in the outside world. I wanted at least to start out by thankin' you for bringing her up, and maybe just talk a little, that's all."

"I have nothing to say to you. I told you that on the phone."

"Janet, please. It's been eighteen years. I've changed. I'm sorry for what I did and I've paid for it. Please, can I just talk to you, maybe a cup of coffee? I'm tired. I come a long way."

She softened. "How did you get here?"

"I took a bus from Boston."

"Are you planning on staying in North Adams?"

"I don't think so. I come up here to see you, talk with you a little."

The two of them stood facing each other for a long moment. Finally, Janet broke the silence. "All right. You can come in for a few minutes. It's against my better judgment, but I don't guess it'll do any harm to talk for a few minutes."

She opened the screen door. Gale smiled and stepped inside.

She led him into the kitchen. "Coffee?" she asked without looking at him.

"I'd love some. Thanks."

Gale looked around the house as if expecting someone.

Janet noticed. "No, I never got married, if that's what you're wondering. I've lived here alone for twenty-four years, and that's the way I like it."

Who the hell would want to marry you?, he thought.

"Well, what's on your mind? I don't have a lot of time."

Over coffee they made some small talk about North Adams, her job, and some mutual acquaintances, before Gale finally got around to his reason for being there.

"Janet, tell me about my little daughter, huh? What was she like as a girl, teenager? What's she look like? Did she go to high school? College? Is she married? Kids? My God! Everything."

"There's not much I can tell you. She was a good kid, but very shy. Kept to herself pretty much. Her and I never really talked much. She went through high school with good grades, mostly all A's, a few B's. Smart girl."

"She go to college?"

"She got a scholarship to go to U Mass. After that, I never really saw all that much of her. She hardly ever came home, except for the big holidays. In the summers she had different jobs, working day and night, mostly waitressing. Ate most all her meals wherever she worked. Pretty much only slept here. Like I said, her and I had trouble communicating, so we never really talked much. To tell you the truth, I never felt like I really knew her."

"I understand she changed her name."

Janet looked at him for a moment, lowered her eyes, and said nothing.

"Come on, Janet. What'd she change to?"

Janet hesitated. "I don't know, Paul. I didn't like the idea and tried to talk her out of it, but she was eighteen, so there was nothing I could do about it. Said she didn't want any part of any North Adams family names. She wanted a new one."

"Don't worry about it. Tell me some more about her."

"Well, after she graduated, she got a job and lived in Boston. Then we gradually lost touch. She called a couple times when she first went to Boston. I tried to ask her about her personal life. She got huffy, we had a few words, and that was it. She never called again. I tried calling her about five or six weeks later, but the number was disconnected and there was no other listing for her in the Boston area."

Gale stared at her. She looked away, and he wondered if she were telling the truth. "What's she look like?"

"Well, like I said, I haven't seen her in about five years. But she's very attractive, tall, nice figure. Pretty girl."

"You mean to tell me, Janet, that after you brought that girl up, you just lost touch with her, and you and her ain't had no contact in five years? I find that hard to believe." His voice had taken on a less friendly tone.

"Look, Paul, that's just what I'm telling you."

"Do you have any idea where she is today?"

"No, I don't."

He was getting agitated. His voice rose. "Boston, New York, Chicago, Denver, California? I mean no idea at all? Come on, Janet. I don't buy that."

Her eyes darted toward the door. She stood up warily. After eighteen years, she still mistrusted Paul Gale, and he still frightened her.

"I don't have anything more to say to you, Paul. I think you'd better leave." She headed toward the front door.

Gale grabbed her wrist. "Look, Janet. I want to see my girl. I'm her father, and if you know where she is, you tell me. Now sit down. I'm not through talking to you."

"You're hurting my arm. I've told you everything I know. Please go."

Gale twisted her arm roughly. She screamed. He increased the pressure. "One more scream, and I'll break it, I swear. Now I'm gonna ask you one more time, and I better like the answers this time, or you're gonna have a broken arm. Where is she?"

Janet grimaced in pain, and began crying. But she said nothing.

He grabbed her wrist again, and pulled her close to him. "Listen to me, you little bitch. You know what I'm capable of doing, don't you?"

She whimpered and nodded.

"Then I'm gonna ask you one more time and you say a word to anybody about our little visit and I'll come back to see you again. And you won't like what happens. Now, are you gonna tell me where I can find her and what she changed her name to?"

"Yes! Yes!" she screamed.

# Chapter Eleven

Janet Kately had always been afraid of Paul Gale. She remembered the first time she visited her sister and Gale at their Hathaway Street house, Gale flew into a rage because his dinner was cold and wound up throwing it at Sarah. Janet never forgot the hatred in his eyes. Over nothing.

She knew of the fury Gale felt toward his daughter back then. She'd been standing next to her in the courtroom when Gale whispered his horrifying threat. His visit convinced her that the man hadn't changed. If anything, he'd gotten worse.

Calling the police would be futile. Gale had done nothing. And, if she did and word somehow got back to him, she feared for her life. Even now, she worried what he might do to her if he found out she had lied. It hadn't been five years since she talked to her niece. It had been only a year.

But she couldn't lie about the phone number and address. she tried but he wouldn't let up. He would have broken her arm, maybe even killed her. Now she wished she hadn't known Lucky's phone number and address.

She had tried so hard to keep in touch with her, but it got more difficult over the years. Janet smiled as she thought of the birthday and Christmas cards that her niece never forgot. Every once in a while she would even get a little money with a nice note. She thought of their last phone conversation and even now, it broke her heart.

"Aunt Janet, it's getting so hard even talking with you lately. It just brings back so many bad memories that I thought I had pushed away. Try and understand. It's not you. I'm trying to work some things through here and I'm just not doing very well at it right now. I'm having trouble sleeping, and when I do sleep I have these awful nightmares…and…it's just not going to be good for me to talk with you for a while. Please try and respect that." And she hung up.

Janet reluctantly did respect Lucky's request. In spite of her sadness she smiled as she thought of the nickname Lucky, the name only she and Sarah used. She felt so helpless. She remembered the years of counseling, her niece leaving the doctor's office in tears, hurrying home and burying herself in Janet's arms, sobbing.

"She's in a spiral of anxiety, depression, and rage," her psychologist, Dr. Coleman, had told Janet. "And I'm not having much luck yet penetrating it. I'm afraid the anger inside her is accelerating. Each time I talk with her, I can feel it stronger. She's trying to suppress it, but it's taking a toll on her. I'm worried about her."

For the first few years while under the state psychologist's care, she would talk about her mother's death. "Oh, Aunt Janet. If only I had done something. If I had called the police when I heard what was happening to Mommy." By the time she was twelve, she no longer talked about it. The withdrawal, depression, and mostly the anger the psychologist had warned Janet about were obvious. Her niece would spend hours in her room looking out the window, doing nothing, saying nothing.

And the rage. The rage was frightening. Janet ran her hand over the long crack in the glass top coffee table, thinking back years ago to the night Lucky had flared up over something…Janet could no longer remember what…and had grabbed her aunt by the shoulders and flung her across the room onto the table. She then rushed to her aunt cradled her in her arms and cried uncontrollably. Even now, Janet could feel the intensity of her anger, so out of proportion with the incident.

Janet nervously dialed the number, and within seconds a vaguely familiar voice answered.

"Hello."

Janet took a deep breath. "Hello, sweetheart. This is Aunt Janet."

Nothing.

"Hello, honey. Are you there?"

Finally, "Yes, I'm here. How are you, Aunt Janet?"

"I'm fine. How have you been? Are things O.K.? Are you doing all right?" Suddenly, Janet wanted to know all about her. Everything.

"I'm fine. I hope things are well with you."

"Oh, yes, I'm fine. The roof still leaks. I still hate my job, and I'm getting fat. But other than that, I'm doing fine. Uh, you sound like you're busy?"

"I am."

"Uh, sweetie, the main reason I called is to tell you that your father is out of prison."

Janet waited. Silence.

"Are you there?"

Silence.

"Hello! Hello! Hello!"

"Yes," the voice, a deep whisper.

"Lucky, did you hear what I said?"

Her mother's nickname for her. It had been so long. "Yes."

"Well, please listen carefully. He came to my house yesterday. At first I didn't know who he was, and then when I did, I refused to let him in. He gave me a long sob story and I felt a little sorry for him. So like a fool, I said he could come in for a minute. You know me. I couldn't turn away a rabid dog if I felt sorry for him. I did feel a little pity for your father, in spite of what he did. Well, once he got in he started pressing me for information about you. I wouldn't tell him anything but he got mean and abusive. He twisted my arm, and hurt it so bad, I had to give him your address and phone number.. Oh, God! I'm so sorry I never

ever should have let him in. The man has not changed. He's as mean and vicious as ever.

"He took the only two photographs I had of you. He knows what you look like. Please be careful, Lucky, please."

Lucky drifted away to another time, a little girl sitting in a car with her mother and a handsome man; a little girl standing in a doorway staring at a handsome man in a blue suit. "My father did it."

"Honey, what did you say?" Her aunt's voice jolted her. The headache pounded in her head.

"Nothing, Aunt Janet."

"I'm sure he's heading for New York. Please be careful. Maybe you should call the police."

She grabbed a kitchen knife and began slashing a magazine. Her hand shook so badly the knife slipped from her hand and fell to the floor. She tried to focus on what her aunt was saying. "Did he say he was coming to New York?"

"No, but he was very eager to know where you are. He's going to go to New York. I know he is."

Her throat was dry and she wanted a glass of water. "Aunt Janet, what does he look like?"

"Well, he has a beard, sort of a goatee, and he's put on quite a bit of weight. He's lost most of his hair. He looks very different, but he still has those bug eyes and that gold tooth."

"Well, thank you for calling, Aunt Janet. I appreciate it, but please don't worry, and don't say anything to anyone else. If he threatened you, you know he's capable of following through, so just keep it to yourself and say nothing, O.K.?"

"All right, if you think that's best."

"I do and again, thanks for calling and telling me."

"Oh, honey, please be careful. I still do think about you a lot. Maybe we could talk once in a while? Just keep in touch a little? I remember those nice cards you used to send me."

"I have to go now, Aunt Janet. Good-bye."

She sat by the phone in the kitchen for several minutes, staring, her breath coming in short, loud gasps. She tried to swallow, but her tongue was too dry. Sweat gathered under her arms and began trickling down her ribs. The hateful words uttered in the courtroom pierced her eardrums as they had so many years ago.

\*         \*         \*

"Hey, Denise."

Denise looked up and saw Gina Ponte's head hanging over the cubicle. "Stop working so hard. You're making the rest of us look bad."

"I work for a slave driver, remember?"

Gina came around and sat down. "Well, slow down. I want to pick your brains about setting up a focus group. Dave heard about Mike's, and he wants me to set one up for him."

"Oh, gee, Gina. I can't. Not now. I'm really busy."

"Oh, come on, Denise. Tell you what. I'll take you out to lunch, and we'll do it then. I'll take you to that new hot spot, the Blue Wave. Twelve-fifteen O.K.?"

Denise held out her palms in surrender. "O.K."

The Blue Wave had only been open for a month, and it was already a big hit. California trendy, bright, sunny and loaded with green plants and brass.

The waiter took their orders. Gina also ordered a glass of Chianti, Denise a diet coke.

"You can bring my wine now," Gina told the waiter.

"You bet." His smile lit up the table. He turned to Denise, and graced her with another smile. "How about you, miss. Would you like your coke now?"

Denise looked away and nodded. "Yes, thank you."

"Jesus. How'd you like to take him home with you?" Gina watched the waiter walk away. "Look at the tight little buns on him."

"Gina, you've got a one-track mind, I swear. Anyway, what do you want to know about focus groups?"

Gina finished her wine, ordered another, and helped herself to more bread. "Well, just tell me how to set the damn thing up. How do I get started?"

Denise went over the focus group procedure, while Gina finished off her wine and the basket of bread.

"Jesus, Denise. I think I am really ready to roll now. I'll knock 'em dead. I think I might just buy you another coke, and I'll have a tad more of this Chianti." She beckoned the waiter over and ordered the drinks.

Denise looked at her watch. "I've got a lot to do today before Mike's trip," she said. She tugged nervously at her hair, nearly as long as Gina's. Denise rarely wore makeup and wondered if she looked out of place sitting in such a sophisticated restaurant with Gina and her exotic makeup.

The waiter arrived with their lunch and Gina's third glass of wine. "All right!" Gina said, hoisting her glass.

He set Denise's salad in front of her, along with another of his dazzling smiles.

"Uh, how do you like working here?" Gina asked. "It must be fun."

He turned away from Denise, and flashed the smile in Gina's direction. "Yes. It's O.K." A customer at another table motioned to him and he moved away.

"Dennie, this is great, isn't it?" Gina said. "We should do this more often, maybe have dinner some night. You're not so wrapped up with some guy, are you, that you couldn't spare a night on the town with me?

"No, but what about you? From what I hear, you've got a different guy every night."

Gina took a long sip of her wine and leaned forward. She beckoned Denise toward her. "Let me tell you a little secret. That is strictly bull. But it's good P.R." She leaned back and reached for more bread. "Now, that's not to say that I don't get my share."

Denise nodded, not sure what to say.

"What about you, Dennie? I know you don't like to talk much about yourself, but hey, I'm nosy. Is there anybody special in your life?"

Denise tugged at her hair again. "Anybody special? The answer to your question is no! There's nobody special in my life."

"Well, that's pretty emphatic. But anyway, I bet you get a lot of attention. They're out there. And if they are for me, then they sure must be there in droves for a lady like you." Gina lit a cigarette and looked out the window. "Yes, men are wonderful, aren't they? They're just…they're…men are assholes!"

"Gina!"

"Oops! Sorry, honey. Guess I got a little carried away there. Must be the wine."

Denise studied her friend, puzzled by the abrupt change in her, even the expression in her face. "Well, I must say, that was a quick turn-around. Maybe there's some objectivity in you after all." Denise checked her watch again. "Hey. I really do have to get back. But this has been fun. Let's do it again."

"We're going to. Let me get the check from handsome, and we're outta' here."

He appeared with another of his killer smiles. "Was everything all right, ladies?" He looked at Denise as he set the check in front of Gina.

Gina set her credit card on the table. "Just perfect," she said. "Especially the service."

He ignored Gina's comment and continued smiling at Denise. "I hope you enjoyed the meal and the service as much as I enjoyed waiting on you," he said directly to Denise.

She lowered her eyes. "Yes, thank you."

Gina broke in. "Just take the goddamn credit card, O.K.?"

Again, Denise was startled by the suddenness of the change in Gina. The waiter froze for a moment, then smiled politely. "Sure," and he left.

" Think you just blew that one, Gina"

"I told you men are assholes. Come on. Let's get out of here." The now distant waiter returned with the credit card receipt. Gina signed it and they left.

# Chapter Twelve

Gina Ponte trudged up the stairs to her apartment. She was still fuming over her episode with the waiter. Here she's just trying to be friendly with the little twerp and he's practically raping Denise with his eyes.

She poured herself a glass of wine and flicked on the TV. *Hard Copy*, something about a young girl who killed her mother for having an affair with the girl's fifteen year old boyfriend.

She thought of Denise and Denise's discomfort at the waiter's heavy breathing all over her. She and Denise were having such a good time, and this jerk had to spoil it. She never should have gotten so friendly with him. All part of the stupid charade. Hot pants Gina—a different guy in the sack every night. Party girl. It really was tiresome.

She channel surfed. Couldn't even concentrate on the pap on TV. It was still early. She dialed the phone.

"Hi, Cathy. Whatcha doin'? Yeah, me, too. Come on, I'll meet you over at Patrick's for a drink and a bite to eat. Sure, that's O.K.. You take your hot bath and watch your video. That's probably what I should do, too. O.K. Talk to ya' soon."

She hung up the phone and dialed again. "Hi, Andrea." Same question. Same result. One more call. No answer.

She finished her drink, went into the bathroom, and combed her hair. It was getting so wonderfully long. She loved the look it gave her, especially with the big hoop earrings and dramatic eye shadow and matte lipstick. She looked at the scale and decided against it. Anyway, it was the end of the day. Not a time to weigh herself. Why bother? She knew the pounds were going on at an alarming rate. She was a big girl, but this was getting ridiculous.

She decided to go for a jog…a little one. Maybe just enough to work up a sweat and make her feel as if she was doing something constructive.

Even with her turtleneck under the sweat-shirt and the sweats hugging her legs, she was chilly. But after a couple of blocks, she warmed up, and the run was feeling good. Nothing heavy, no point in overdoing it. Just a nice easy cruise along the avenue. After fifteen blocks, she headed over one block east and turned back toward home. Within a few blocks of her apartment she'd had it and slowed to a walk. The candle-light flickering across the picture window of Jenny's Place brought her to a halt. She peered in and entered.

Several young women sat at the bar, talking quietly. A couple of them greeted her as she entered. "Hey, Gina, out for your monthly two-block run?"

"No, six miles, and I need a drink." She slid onto a stool at the end of the bar and ordered a diet coke. She was halfway through it when a voice in back of her inquired softly, "Mind if I join you?"

She turned and saw a small blond woman of about thirty smiling at her. Gina looked her over for a moment before smiling back. "Sure, have a seat."

*     *     *

For much of the afternoon Denise puzzled over Gina's behavior at lunch. The incident made her realize how little she really knew Gina. There was a chip on her shoulder that she'd never seen before.

Her health club was a little more crowded than usual, and by the time she had changed, there were already several men working out. Her eyes were drawn immediately to one.

Puffing along on the treadmill was a tall, very handsome man with longish dark hair. She dismissed him, and headed for the nautilus. On the way he noticed her and nodded, flashing a friendly smile. She recognized him as the man who was coming in as she was going out a week or two ago, and she nodded back.

Her workout was long and satisfying. She concluded with a hundred push-ups, and when she finished, she felt as if she could do another hundred. Her body vibrated with energy. She headed for the showers and saw the stranger walking toward the men's locker room.

She showered and dressed quickly. Feeling pleasantly tired and hungry, she looked forward to dinner and turning in early for a good night's sleep.

As she headed through the club and toward the door, she noticed the new guy wearing a leather jacket and jeans walking toward Charlie, the club manager. He moved with a graceful elegance, but there was also a macho vitality about him, a study in contrasts that she found kind of intriguing. Was he a construction worker or a college professor? She figured he could be either.

He stood talking with Charlie as she hurried by them and down the stairs. The street was quiet, uncrowded. It was also very cold.

She pulled up the collar of her coat and tugged her gloves on, bracing herself for the long walk. She had walked for about a block and was just approaching the intersection, when a car shot out of Fifty-first Street, jumped the side walk, and bore down on her. She stood transfixed, unable to move. The large black machine was all she could see. It was so close she could see the wide eyes of the terrified man behind the wheel. She closed her eyes and waited for the impact.

She was hit about waist high and felt herself moved off the ground and through the air. The impact was hard and sudden, but it was not what she expected. She felt the hot breath of a human being across her face, as she lay somewhere, uncertain where. Her eyes were still closed, but she knew she was alive. She opened her eyes and rolled over, disentangling herself from another set of arms and legs.

"Are you all right?"

She looked up, and saw a man staggering to his feet, holding his hands out to her. Just to the left and behind her, she saw the black car, imbedded in the window of a convenience store.

"Are you O.K.?" the man asked as he helped Denise to her feet.

Her legs felt like rubber, and she was shaking badly. "I…I don't know. I think so," she said, her voice quivering. She staggered and leaned against him. His arm slid around her waist, holding her steady. Her head began to clear, and she saw that he was the stranger from the club. "What happened?" she asked, moving slightly away, and standing on her own.

"Well, I came out, and headed up Second Avenue, all of a sudden this car shot out of nowhere and jumped the light and I saw you about to get zonked. I just hit you with an old fashioned body block." He rubbed his shoulder, and smiled. "By the way, your workouts are paying off."

At the mention of the car, they both turned toward the convenience store. A crowd had gathered, and the driver, an elderly man, was being helped out of the car. He looked bewildered and frightened, but appeared to be unhurt.

The man was mumbling to a man and woman, ministering to him. "The brake. Meant to put my foot on the brake. Hit the damn gas pedal."

A police car pulled up, and two officers jumped out and took charge. An ambulance arrived and the old man was gently moved into it.

A man stepped out of the crowd. "Officer, I saw the whole thing. I can tell you what happened."

Frank was satisfied that the young man would give the officers a report and saw no need to get involved. He was more interested in the woman and her well being at the moment. They walked slowly along Second Avenue.

"You sure you're O.K.? You look a little green."

"Oh, God. I think so, but I've got to sit down somewhere."

"Here, let's go in here." He opened the door to a coffee shop and led her to a booth and slipped her coat off. "I'll get you some black coffee and some water." He went over to the nearest waitress and returned with her in tow.

"Here, honey, you drink this good strong coffee and let me get you some water," the waitress said. She poured them both coffee, and returned with a large glass of water for Denise.

Denise held the mug with both trembling hands and sipped the coffee, pausing for a deep breath after each sip.

He handed her the glass of water. "Here, try to drink all of this."

She took the glass, again with both hands, and took long deep gulps of the water. The water seemed to restore her, at least enough to manage a brittle smile.

"Well, I think I'm going to live," she said slowly guiding the glass to rest on the table. She looked quizzically at him.

"You're going to be fine. My name is Frank, by the way." He held out his hand, and she feebly shook it.

"I'm Denise Johnson. Thank you, Frank. I think you just saved my life." Her eyes flicked to face him for an instant and quickly returned to the table.

He moved his head downward trying to find her eyes. "You're looking better already."

"Oh, well thank you." Her hand darted up and brushed her hair back. It fell again and again the hand went up. She glanced at him but again quickly looked away.

Up close she was even more beautiful than when he'd noticed her at the club. His first reaction was that she reminded him of Carla. Not a good thought and he dismissed it. He wondered if she had noticed him.

He got his answer. "I've seen you at the health club," she said.

"Yeah, I've seen you, too." He grinned. "I'm afraid I'm not in your league up there."

"You just have to be patient and stay with it." She finished her coffee.

They sat for a moment, neither saying anything. Frank broke the silence. "I noticed that you go through a pretty strenuous routine. Been doing this for a while?"

She peered into the coffee cup, studying its contents. "Yes. I…I'm kind of a jock, I guess."

He smiled at that. "Whatever you're doing, it's working."

She looked up and smiled back. "Thank you." She closed her eyes and a little shiver went through her.

"You O.K.?"

"Yes, I was just thinking about what happened out there. I'd be mashed between the car and the store right now if it hadn't been for you. Thank you again."

"You're welcome. I'm glad for the chance to meet you, even under these circumstances. Actually, I staged the whole thing." Her smile came more easily this time. He liked the way she smiled. He liked the nervous little shyness about her.

Denise rubbed her shoulder and made a face. "You sure you weren't a linebacker in college?"

I guess I did hit you pretty hard. You'll probably be sore tomorrow."

"At least I'll be here tomorrow," she said. Her stomach suddenly rolled, an audible gurgle. She put her hand to her mouth and giggled.

"Uh, what's that? I didn't quite get it all."

"Oh, God. Excuse me, I'm so embarrassed. That's my stomach telling me it's time to go home."

"No, that's your stomach telling you you're hungry. How about some dinner?"

"No, I don't think so. I really do have to get home. But, thank you again. It's been a pleasure meeting you." She reached for her coat.

He moved quickly around to her, helping her with her coat. "I wish I could've picked a better way, but I've enjoyed meeting you."

He left the money for the coffee on the table, and they walked out and stood on the sidewalk for a moment. People rushed by in both directions, everyone in a hurry. A car horn tooted and Denise instinctively jumped and staggered. Frank held her. She smelled good, and he liked standing there holding her in his arms.

She moved away and gave him the shy little smile that he liked so much in the restaurant. She staggered again, but recovered quickly. "Oh God, I'm sorry. I guess I'm still jumpy and a little dizzy. Must be from sitting all that time and suddenly getting up."

"You sure you're going to be all right?"

"Yes, I'll be fine, really."

"Well, let me put you in a cab."

"No, I'd rather walk. I need the fresh air. It's not far."

"I'll walk along with you just in case."

She started to protest, but was hit with another wave of nausea and dizziness. He braced her again. "Thank you," she said and they began walking.

They walked slowly at first, but Denise gradually began to pick up the pace, and they were soon at her building.

"Well, I think you're going to survive," Frank said. The wind had picked up and it was getting cold. But he didn't want her to go in.

"Yes, I'm going to be fine. The walk helped. Good night, Frank." The wonderful little smile flashed. "And thanks again."

"Good night, Denise. Hope to see you soon at the club."

"Me too," she said and went inside.

*      *      *

Relaxing in her apartment, the full impact of her brush with death hit her, and she felt exhausted. It had not been a good day. No longer hungry, she decided to go to bed.

She sat on the bed, slowly taking off her clothes. Her stomach gurgled again and Frank Corso's remark came back to her. "What's that? I didn't quite get it all." He's a nice man, she thought.

Frank had been walking for four blocks when he realized he'd been thinking about nothing but Denise the whole time. None of the usual crap that rattled around in his head. Just a good feeling from the hour or so that he had spent with her. He decided that if an hour with her could make him feel this good, he'd have to give it another shot.

# Chapter Thirteen

After leaving Janet Kateley's house, Paul Gale spent a few days in Boston at a small hotel. The first morning there he awoke at seven and picked up the phone. He stared at it for a moment, took a deep breath, and began punching out the numbers.

Perspiration rolled off his face onto the phone. The phone continued ringing. Finally a woman's voice answered.

"Hello."

Gale's temples pounded. His stomach began to cramp.

"Hello." The voice sounded irritated. "Hello."

He hung up the phone and smiled.

He thought of his upcoming move to New York and reflected on the events that made it possible, beginning with his conversation with his ex cell-mate, Larry Cardillo, several months before.

"Paul, how you gonna go live in New York? You know you can't even leave Massachusetts to visit New York, let alone live there. You'll violate your parole!"

"I know. I know, Larry. That's where you come in. I need your help. You said your cousin, the guy that owns the restaurant in New York, owes you some favors, right?"

"Come on, Gale" said Cardillo. "I can't ask him to give you a job."

"Why not? I can go to New York if I have a job, a place to live, and most of all, somebody to sponsor me. You know that, Larry. Now, can you get your cousin to do this for you?"

"I dunno, Paul." Cardillo sat on his cot and lit a cigarette. After a long silence, Cardillo got up and faced Gale. "Paul, I ain't the kinda guy who forgets. I know I'd be a dead man today if you hadn't pulled those goons off me in the laundry. I'll talk to Tony and see what I can do. He does owe me. I'll see what I can work out for you."

It did work out. Tony Breda not only hired Gale but also got him a room in a friend's rooming house. The room wasn't much but it was better than his accommodations of the past eighteen years. He settled in, took a shower in the bath down the hall, and dressed for a night on the town.

He had always wanted to see Times Square. Plenty of action there, he'd heard, and a guy could find just about anything he wanted. Might just go find himself a little pussy.

He enjoyed the walk, taking his time, stopping to look in store windows along the way. He continued to be shocked at the prices of things. Wonder how much a piece a ass costs today, he pondered.

It was a little after ten, when he reached the Times Square area. He turned on Forty-second Street and stopped. Instead of the sex shops, dirty movies and massage parlors he'd heard about, it looked more like DisneyWorld. "The hell's this?" he muttered.

The glistening new buildings and yuppie crowd were not exactly what he'd expected. He felt out of place among the well dressed men and women, hurrying by, and the gawking tourists looked like a bunch of yokels. Where the hell were all the hookers?

He started walking west until he hit Eighth Avenue and turned uptown. This looks a little more like it, he thought, passing several small bars that looked like his kinds of joints.

After a few blocks, he was about to enter a bar, when he stopped. "Uh, oh. Look at this."

A tall black woman headed his way. He watched her approach, spike heels, short, tight skirt rolling around her hips as she swayed toward him. "Come on, baby," he whispered.

He could see her face now, mouth open, smiling. He liked the way she licked her upper lip with her tongue. A sweater a size too small highlighted a pair of tits aimed straight at him. She slowed down, as she approached him.

"Want to go out, honey?" she whispered.

He was already hard. "Sure," he barely got the word out.

She continued past him. "Follow me," she said without breaking stride.

She led him along Eighth Avenue for a block before stepping into a narrow doorway. Gale quickly caught up to her in the doorway. She faced him, leaned against him, and slid her hand down to his crotch.

"Ooh, honey. You are ready, ain't you?" She gave him a little squeeze. "You ready to go out, honey?" she smiled, still holding him.

"Yeah."

"O.K. What you wanna do? We can go to my place. You gotta use a rubber, and it'll cost you a hundred bucks. But I'll show you a real good time, honey." She was rubbing him now, working him over.

"Yeah. Let's go to your place. Where is it?" he whispered, reaching for her.

She stepped away and out of the doorway. "It just down Eighth Avenue a few blocks. Follow me, but make sure you stay behind me. We don't want no shit from the cops, you know?"

"Yeah, yeah. O.K., let's go."

He fell in behind her, and watched her walk. He liked the way the curved outline of her ass strained against the tight skirt. That ass would be his in a few minutes.

She turned into the hallway of an old building and held the door open for him. "I keep a place right here on the first floor," she said.

He stepped into the small room. It wasn't much, an unmade double bed, a wooden chair and a small sink.

She set her sweater on the chair and stood facing him. "O.K., honey. Let's get our business out of the way first." She held out her hand.

"Oh yeah, sure," he said, and pulled out two fifty dollar bills.

"Thanks, honey."

He watched her stuff the bills into her purse. "O.K., honey. Take your clothes off, and let's get to it."

Her tone was different from the one on the street. She was all business.

She unzipped her skirt and let it drop to the floor. Gale watched her sit on the bed in her panties. He dropped the last of his clothes on the floor and moved toward her. She threw him a condom.

"Here. Put that on."

She knew many ways to please a man and expertly employed them all. Gale grunted, moaned, and bellowed, as she worked him to a frenzied peak. It didn't take long for him to climax, after which she immediately rolled him off her and began dressing. He lay for a moment with his eyes closed, panting, slowly catching his breath. When he opened his eyes she was nearly dressed.

"What do you think you're doin'?" he demanded.

"I'm gettin' dressed, honey. We done our thing. You had fun, didn't you?" She finished dressing and picked up her purse.

Gale bounded off the bed and grabbed her arm. "Yeah, I had fun, but we ain't finished. For a hundred bucks, I want more'n a few minutes. Now take your clothes back off." He threw her hard on the bed.

She glared at him, her eyes blazing. "I don't know who you think you're fuckin' with, but I don't want none a your shit. We finished. I gave you a good time. That's what you paid for, and that's what you got."

She got off the bed, and Gale moved toward her. In a second, she had a knife out of her purse, opened, and pointed at him. She moved it back and forth in front of her, clearly no stranger to handling it.

"Now, you better get out of my way, mister, or you gonna get yourself cut up bad," she hissed.

Gale stepped back and went into a little crouch. He would have to be careful but he was enjoying this. She moved around the bed and backed toward the door. He stood, naked, watching her.

She reached her free hand in back of her, groping for the doorknob. As she did, her head turned slightly to the left. Gale lunged first to her right, toward the knife, then quickly moved left. She slashed in the direction of his first move. His open left hand chopped hard at her extended arm, and the knife fell to the floor. He was on her, throwing her across the room, and picking up the knife in one movement.

She sat cowering on the floor, fear, and fury in her eyes. Gale held the knife and looked down on her. "Now, who do you think you're fuckin' with, honey?" he asked, taunting her. "Get up and take your clothes off. I told you we ain't finished."

She got up slowly, never taking her eyes from him.

"I said get undressed. You gonna show me a good time, honey."

She balanced herself against the chair, as she took off first one shoe and then the other. She continued to glare at him, hatred in her eyes.

"Now, let's just get this knife outta the way, so nobody gets any ideas, and we can really have a good time."

He turned and threw the knife on the other side of the room. The moment he turned, she raised a high heeled shoe and brought it down on his head. His knees buckled, and again she hit him in the same spot. Blood gushed from his head, and the room spun. He staggered against the wall. She hit him again, and he went down. Through the blood dripping into his eyes, he saw her move toward the knife lying on the floor near them. His hand went out and grabbed her leg. She fell. He saw her arm go up and start to bring the stiletto heel down on him again. Now struggling for survival, he rolled hard into her. The shoe came down on his shoulder.

He shook off the pain and was on her, striking her face with his fist. She cursed, and tried to break away from him. He held her fast, but she was strong, and he knew he couldn't hold her long. His eyes searched and saw the knife, inches away. He grabbed it and buried it into soft flesh. She gasped and squirmed away from him.

He pulled it out and again thrust it harder into her. She shuddered and fell back, blood poured from her stomach and side. She lay motionless. He disentangled himself from her, and sat for a moment against the wall. He reached for his pants, retrieved his handkerchief, and wiped the blood from his eyes and head. The rest of his naked body was covered with blood, mostly hers. He finished wiping his eyes, and the room gradually came back into focus. The woman lay quiet, blood surrounding the knife imbedded in her stomach.

He staggered to his feet and felt his head. His stringy hair was matted with blood, and he felt two large bumps. The skin was broken, but the cuts didn't feel serious. They were now bleeding only slightly.

He leaned against the sink for balance and washed the blood from his hands, face, and head. He sponged the blood off the rest of his body, tore a piece of the sheet, placed it over the cut areas on his head, and put on his cap. Wincing from the pain, he dressed slowly, went over to the hooker, pulled the knife out of her, washed it off, and put it in his pocket.

Before leaving he opened her purse and retrieved his hundred dollars plus the rest of her money, another two hundred. He looked at her lying on the floor. "Tough shit, honey," he sneered and left.

# Chapter Fourteen

Crystal Wilcox sat on the couch in her living room reading Hemingway's *The Sun Also Rises*. Of all his books, this was her favorite. She'd read it several times but never tired of reading about Lady Bret Ashley, with whom she liked to identify—intelligent, beautiful, over-sexed, and self-destructive. There's no past or future, only the present. She liked that. It suited her. "We do what we do," she said aloud as she got up to pour herself a glass of wine.

The phone rang. "Hello, Crystal. How are you?" There was no need to identify himself. She recognized the measured, cultured voice.

She went into her act. "I'm just fine, honey. Nice to hear from you. Must be you're in the mood to party."

Even his laugh had breeding. "I'm in the mood for you, Crystal. Can you come over?"

She gave him the dirty laugh he liked. "Well, I was just reading a good book and relaxing with some wine. The wine's getting me a little mellow, if you know what I mean."

"I know what you mean, Crystal. Now, how about grabbing a cab, and I'll see you in twenty minutes."

"See you soon, honey." She hung up the phone and stared at it for a moment, smiled and went into the bedroom to change.

\*　　\*　　\*

His apartment, like those of all her uptown Johns as Vickie called them, was elegant and tasteful. She liked it and she liked him. He was dependent upon her for satisfying his desires. He placed himself completely under her domination when they were together. She liked the feeling of control she had over him. And he paid her large sums of money to punish him and to be made submissive to her.

She fulfilled his needs. But he filled a need in her far more than he could know.

"I have some Chateau Margaux for you, Crystal. Let's have some and relax a little before we get into things, shall we?"

She sat down on the sofa with him and crossed her long legs. "Yes, I would like that. Foreplay comes in many forms, doesn't it?"

"Yes, indeed. You know I find our conversations almost as enjoyable as the other aspects of our relationship."

She snickered. "Sure you do. Hmm. The wine's delicious. Subtle but still a little mischievous."

He laughed, genuine and spontaneous this time. "Crystal, you are a wonderful piece of work. You know that, don't you?"

"Yes, as a matter of fact, I was recently told that by a friend, a colleague so to speak."

They sat together on the sofa, enjoying the wine, discussing a range of subjects, Crystal easily holding her own with him. She did like him, as much as she was capable of liking any man. He was a gentleman.

Yes. Most importantly, he was a gentleman. And he did what he was told. She pointed to the cigarettes on the mantle. "Get me a cigarette," she commanded. She watched his slender body move across the room. He was small and brittle looking, another thing she liked about him.

She got up from the sofa and stood waiting for him. As he handed her the cigarette, she knocked it from his hand and without warning, slapped him hard across the face. He staggered backward and she slapped him harder. He fell to the floor and she was on him, straddling him with her legs. "Are you ready for your obedience training, you scum?

"Yes, yes," he whispered.

\*    \*    \*

The photo shoot was finally over, and Carla couldn't wait to get outside into the fresh air. The studio was hot and oppressive and everyone had become cranky.

"Come on, Carla. Let's get out of here. I'll buy you a drink." Jenny Slade was as beautiful as Carla. Tall, pencil thin, honey blonde hair, teal-colored eyes. Carla liked Jenny and enjoyed working with her. She was a real pro and a class lady.

"Sounds good to me. Let's go." They loped along the avenue, two thoroughbreds gliding gracefully through the crowds.

It was still early when they slipped into the cocktail lounge of the Pierre Hotel. The Pierre was Carla's favorite. Whenever she felt like winding down alone or with friends, it was where she went. The bartenders knew her and made sure nobody hassled her. She could relax and not be bothered by jerks trying to hit on her.

"Carla, this is the first chance in ages I've had to sit down and talk with you."

"Yes," Carla sighed. Life is hectic, isn't it?"

"Must be," Jenny said. "If you have to turn down an opportunity to do a movie in Italy."

Carla smiled. "You've been talking to Randy."

"Yes, I was flabbergasted. I think Randy still is. Sounded like a fabulous break. I mean, that's what we pay people like Randy for, isn't it? Movie offers don't grow on trees, sweetie."

"I know. And I know that Randy's still pissed too. I don't blame him, but I've just got too much going on here right now. I...I can't afford to be away from New York. Maybe I'm stupid and overconfident, but I feel sure there'll be other and better chances, particularly when I get the exposure I expect to be getting this year."

"I understand what you're saying but this is a bird in the hand. And as Randy said, you could always buzz back here for a day or so when necessary. It's not that big a deal."

"I know me and I just couldn't stand that kind of crazy commuting. Anyway, I told you I don't want to be away from

New York for a while." Her voice took on an edge that told Jenny it was time to change the subject.

"How's your social life? Had time for any?"

"A little. I've been to some parties, met some interesting men. Some dates here and there. Nothing serious."

Jenny looked pensive for a moment. "Carla, do you ever see or hear from, or talk to Frank?"

Carla smiled. "Someone else asked me that the other night."

"Must have been a woman. He's a beautiful man."

"Anyway, the answer is yes, and no and no. I did happen to see him on the street just the other day as I was getting into a cab. First time I'd seen him in a year and I haven't heard anything from him. Actually, I have been thinking about him these past few days since I saw him on the street."

"Well, I was just curious. The few times I met him I envied you."

"Yes," Carla sighed. "Frank is, as you put it, a beautiful man. I wish it could have worked, but it didn't and life goes on, right?" She lit a cigarette, took several quick, deep drags, and looked away.

Jenny studied her for a minute, watching her puff nervously on the cigarette. "Carla, you know how much I like you. I enjoy the few times we get together. I think we could become very good friends. So take this as said from the heart…from your friend."

Carla turned and looked curiously at her.

"I've been with you twice now in the past week. You've been nervous and edgy as hell. I know the signs. I've been at this business longer than you, and I know what it can do to you. Take a few days off. Get some sun and relax. Nothing's going to go away. It'll all be here when you get back."

Carla put her cigarette out. "Thanks, Jenny. I appreciate your concern. I have to run now. Thanks for the drink."

The streets were even more crowded now that the nine to five crowd was out. Twice she nearly collided with people in too much of a hurry. She hated the crowds and with the holidays approaching it would get worse. Jenny was right. She was edgy and cranky. Getting away for a while really would be the best thing in the world for her. But not now.

*     *     *

Paul Gale had settled into a routine in New York, alternately working one week days and one week nights. Whether lunch or dinner, he was constantly buried under mountains of dirty dishes, glasses and pans, scraping and rinsing before loading them into the dishwashers, all under the watchful eye of Peter the chef and master of the kitchen.

Peter was a large, surly Slav to whom Gale took an instant dislike. The feeling was mutual, and Peter took great pleasure in riding herd on him. "Gale, vot you pudding da glasses in der for? Dey go in da odder cupboard. How many times I gotta tell you? You stupid or vot?"

Gale quickly learned to keep his mouth shut and endure Peter, painful though it was. Vince, the manager, and the waiters and bus boys had all warned him about Peter.

"I know you got some connection with Tony, Gale but you better understand that Peter can fire you on the spot, and Tony won't protect you," Vince said. "He needs Peter much more than he needs you or me. Breda owes his success to Peter's cooking, and believe me they both know it. So, if you need this job, then don't mess with Peter."

Gale did need the job. Living in New York was expensive beyond anything he had expected. He'd never developed any discipline or savvy when it came to spending money, and he knew that without the job, his money would be quickly gone.

He found coping with Peter increasingly difficult and feared that it was only a matter of time before he told Peter off or attacked him. "This is worse than fuckin' Walpole," he would mutter to himself as he rinsed spaghetti sauce off the endless stacks of plates.

His day ended at four p.m., when, smelling of garlic, perspiration and a variety of kitchen odors that clung to him and his greasy clothes, he trudged wearily back to his room "I gotta do what I came here to do and get the hell out of here."

The encounter with the hooker had excited him, and he wanted more. He had made some dumb mistakes with her and almost paid for them with his life. He hadn't really planned to kill her, but once it happened, he liked the high it gave him, even more than the sex. Taking her money was a plus.

More than anything, however, he wanted his daughter. Since leaving prison, he thought of little else, and after hearing her voice on the phone the first time, the fantasies about her numbed his mind. Sex with her and killing her blended together. It was impossible for him to draw a distinction between the two acts. He tried to envision how he would kill her to make it slow and painful, but always the act was blurred, then replaced by his sexual fantasies.

He knew where she lived and what she looked like. She couldn't have changed much from the pictures he got from Janet. They were only a few years old. He had been to her apartment building but getting her alone was going to be harder than he thought. He would figure out something but it had to be his way, in the same room with her, touching her, feeling her body. He would be in command, watching the fear in her eyes, building slowly up to the point where she would realize what he was going to do to her. Sweet Jesus, how he wanted her. But he was a patient man. Patience was something he learned in Walpole. And he was smart.

# Chapter Fifteen

The early November evening was damp and chilly. She pulled up the collar of her coat and began walking. Not a good night to be outside. But she'd been restless and uneasy all evening. She'd tried taking a hot bath, but tonight all it did was enhance the strange feeling of pleasure she had derived at the moment of killing Jack Beatty. It was as if she were two people, one watching the act in horror, the other reveling in joy and satisfaction. Lying in the warm water, thoughts of Beatty only increased the agitation building within her.

The wind picked up and rain began to fall, but she continued, oblivious to it. No feeling. Only the vague sense of her life, whirling apart. Some of the confusion and hatred that had burned inside her for so many years had been released. She needed to release more. Memories of long ago began appearing in magnified close-ups. She was aware of things happening to her, a new sense of purpose, a way to bring about a thawing of her hurts until the day when all the memories could be erased and the hurts would disappear forever.

She was somewhere on the West Side and stood in the rain waiting for the light. The light changed but she didn't move. She was in her other world, an actor in the close-ups of distant memories.

"Hey, you better come in outta' the rain."

She felt something touch her arm and saw a man holding her, beckoning her toward the door of a small bar. She stared at him.

"Hey, you all right? Jesus, you're soaked. Come on. We gotta' dry you out." The man led her inside where the acrid smell of cigarette smoke hit her.

"You're catchin' cold sweetie. Come over here and sit down and lemme get somethin' warm in you." He led her to a table in a corner of the bar and took off her coat. "You sit right here. I'm gonna' get you a drink. Getcha a little whiskey. Warm ya right up. That sound good?" He took off his own coat.

Her eyes focused on him, seeing him for the first time. He was a small man, wearing a New York Mets "T" shirt and jeans. He rolled his pack of cigarettes into the left arm of his "T" shirt and headed for the bar.

"Hey, Billy, gimme a coupla rye and sodas and try to hurry it up, will ya?" He motioned toward the woman at the table.

He brought the drinks over to his table and sat down. He slid her drink closer to her. "Come on, sweetie, drink up. Make you feel better." He lit a cigarette.

The woman hesitated. He picked up the drink, handed it to her, and guided it up toward her mouth.

"That's it." The glass touched her lips. "Atta' girl, drink up."

She took a sip, letting it warm her. Then another.

He laughed and a hacking cough erupted. "Goddamned cigarettes," he rasped.

Her expression changed.

"Hey, what're you lookin' at me so mean for? You O.K.? I mean, can you talk? You ain't said a word since I first seen ya."

She continued studying him and when she finally spoke, the voice was deep, purring. "Where am I? What's the name of this place? Who are you?"

"Hey! She can talk. Ooh, what a voice. You're in Barney's and my name is Joey. I found you standing outside in the rain and brought ya in here to dry off. Seemed like you were lost or somethin'. What's yer name, sweetie?"

"Lucky," she said, still examining him.

The door to the bar opened again and two men walked in, looked around, and headed straight for Joey.

Joey was looking at his woman and didn't see the men approach him. She turned, just as the larger of the two grabbed him by the hair, and spun him around.

She started to get up from her chair, but the smaller of the two men stood so close he blocked her.

"Hello, Joey. You little creep. Did you forget your debt today?" He pulled Joey's head down flat onto the table and stood over him.

Only half of Joey's face showed. The other half was flattened against the table. "Tomorrow, Tony, tomorrow," Joey's half face whispered. "I'll have it for ya' tomorrow at noon."

Tony held him fast. "You better have it tomorrow, or you're history, Joey."

The woman grabbed her coat and managed to squeeze her chair away from the other man. "Excuse me." She looked at Billy, and edged her way past the two men.

Billy bounded over to the group. "O.K., Tony, give it a break. That's enough."

The woman headed for the door and stood on Seventh Avenue. The rain had stopped. She started to cross but stopped and returned, stood for a moment and began walking slowly along Seventh Avenue.

"Hey, I thought I lost you, Lucky."

She turned and saw the ugly little man standing on the sidewalk, grinning at her. Disgusting vermin. But she was strangely pleased to have him back.

"Whad joo say, Lucky? Come over here, where I can hear ya." He went over to her, and put his arm around her waist. "Ooh, you're a lotta' woman, ain't cha?"

He steered her back onto the sidewalk and started walking her downtown. "Come on, sweetie. Let's go back to my place and have a little drink. Come on, I'll show ya the way. It ain't too far."

He led her along Seventh Avenue. She heard his stupid prattling, but she neither cared nor heard what he was saying. She liked the feeling building inside her. The dullness left her eyes and she gradually heard his words.

"What do you like to drink, Lucky?"

"Whatever. Maybe some wine, if you have any."

His eyes brightened, "How about I get us a couple bottles. There's a store in the next block."

The rain had stopped and she stood outside the liquor store, waiting. She hugged her body to ward off the damp chill of the night and watched the little fool inside buying his wine.

She wanted him badly now. No need to resist the feeling taking hold of her. The anger was building, but she also liked the other part, the excitement, the erotic tingle. She liked that.

They reached Joey's place and entered through a small doorway between a coin operated laundry and a pawn shop.

"Here we are sweetie. See, that didn't take long, did it?"

Joey pulled out a key chain ladened with keys and unlocked the door. He led the way up the stairs. "I got a nice deal here. I'm the Super of the joint. Get my place for nothin' plus a few bucks, besides. I have to take care of the five apartments and kinda keep an eye on things, but it ain't hard. It's a good deal."

They reached his apartment on the second floor over the Laundromat. She noticed that Joey's was the only apartment on the second floor.

He opened the door and snapped on the light switch. She coughed and turned away as a cockroach skittered across the floor.

The apartment turned her stomach as much as Joey did. It wasn't really an apartment, just one room with a bed, a small table, and two straight back chairs. The sink had a hot plate on it, surrounded by dirty dishes. A refrigerator stood to the left of the sink, and to the right was a bureau. A clothes bar, jammed between the refrigerator and the wall, held two pairs of pants and a few shirts. She looked around for the bathroom.

Joey read her mind. "Uh, if you have to go to the toilet, it's out in the hall."

She nodded.

"Christ, you're a quiet one, sweetie. But that's O.K. I like 'em quiet. Sexy and quiet, my kinda woman"

He pulled a bottle of whiskey from the cupboard under the sink. "Hey, what's your name anyway?" He stuck his head back in the cabinet.

"I told you. It's Lucky," she said watching his every move. "Lucky, you little scumbag," she whispered to herself.

"You say somethin', Lucky?" he asked, pulling out two glasses and wiping them off with a dirty towel that had been sitting on the sink.

"No, just humming," she was still smiling, not taking her eyes off him. She tried to figure out his age, but it was impossible. He could have been anywhere from thirty to fifty. No matter. She moved in closer to him.

"Oh, you must be havin' a good time, huh? Well, I'm goin' to show ya an even better time, honey." He poured himself a large drink of whiskey and poured her wine into a water glass.

Joey handed her the glass of wine. At the same time, he slid his arm around her waist, and squeezed her buttocks. "Oh, baby, what a beautiful ass. You gonna' give Joey some a that ass, ain't ya, honey?" He nibbled on her neck.

She shuddered and stepped away, wondering how many women this vermin had defiled, what kinds of filthy thoughts he lived with. "Easy does it. We don't want to rush this." The deep voice. Different.

Joey looked surprised, pleased. "Hey, I like your style, Lucky. O.K. O.K." He drained his glass and poured some more. "Yeah, you're right. We got all night and we're goin' to enjoy this, ain't we?"

"Yes," she smiled. "We're going to enjoy this."

Joey finished his drink and walked over to her. His hands slid over her shoulders and onto her breasts. "Nice and easy does it, honey. Just take it slow."

He was touching her there. And she knew where he would touch her next. "No," she said and threw him hard on the bed. She picked up the unopened wine bottle from the table and walked over to him.

"Ooh. You like to play rough, do ya? I like that." He bounded off the bed and grabbed her by the neck. Surprised by his strength she found herself being pulled onto the bed, still clutching the wine bottle.

She lay for a moment on the bed, smelling the foulness of his body and the alcohol. Her body stiffened and she screamed. She gushed with a surge of exultation and joy as she flung him off and rolled over on top of him.

"Oh, I love it honey." Joey panted, pulling roughly down ward on her hair expecting her to roll off him. She hit him hard in the face with her fist.

Joey's eyes opened wide in surprise. A trickle of blood dripped from his mouth. "You whacko! You're crazy," he screamed, his bulging eyes fixed on her, back arched, lips slightly parted, her face a mask of ecstasy. It was the last thing Joey saw before the bottle crashed over his head.

# Chapter Sixteen

Frank slept late the day after his encounter with Denise. It was the first decent night's sleep he'd had in months.

He rolled over and felt a sharp pain in his shoulder. The pain puzzled him for a minute until he remembered the body block he'd thrown at Denise. He'd been thinking about her a lot since the brief time they'd spent together. Maybe that's why he slept well.

She was still on his mind as he dressed. He thought of her on two levels. Her wholesome good looks were unique. No question about that. There was also a shyness about her, a gentleness.

He liked thinking about her, especially since having spotted Carla for the first time in over a year. He walked through the living room on the way to the kitchen. That's all his living room was, a passageway between the bedroom and kitchen. He never used it. The sofa and chair he'd bought at Pier I on the way back from lunch one day still had the plastic covers on them. Should have saved his money and got his car fixed instead. But then he never used that either. It'd been sitting in his parents' garage in Jersey for nearly a year.

He made some coffee and eyed the brandy bottle that stood next to the cups. Not a good idea to start sucking up booze in the morning. What the hell. He splashed a little in. The brandy warmed him more than the coffee. He didn't guess there was any harm giving himself a little extra jolt before going out to deal with the dickheads of the world.

"Corso. Jerry's been callin' all morning for you," Ben Thiel, the duty sergeant greeted him. "Guy was knocked off in his apartment on Eighth Avenue a couple nights ago. Jerry and Harry Leonard are in the stiff's apartment. Better get over there."

"Relax, Ben. How about if I first get myself a little cup of coffee. That O.K. with you? You can go back to playing with yourself soon as I leave." He liked to tweak Thiel who was an officious little prick with peers and obsequious around authority. An ass kisser.

"Anyway, here's the address. They're waiting for you." Thiel handed Frank a piece of paper, and went back to his magazine.

The small room was crowded when Frank arrived. The body was on the floor and the medical examiner was still with him. A photographer took pictures, while an officer dusted the place for fingerprints. Jerry talked with a man at the kitchen table.

"Where the hell have you been?" Jerry growled at Frank.

"I had some things to do this morning, like catch up on some sleep. Where are we?"

"O.K., thanks for your help on this Mr. Quinn. I may want to talk with you later, but that's all for now. You can go." Jerry dismissed the man and turned to Frank.

"Poor little shit was really roughed up, Frank. Same M.O. as Beatty."

"Wine bottle?"

Jerry nodded. "Head bashed in with a wine bottle still full a wine when it hit him. Then it looks like who ever did it, just grabbed his head and pounded it over and over on the floor. Looks like he was then dragged over by the radiator where they really did a number on his head. Medical examiner says he died somewhere between ten and midnight night before last." He nodded again, anticipating Frank's next question. "Yep, same deal with the wine bottle."

"Who found him?"

"The victim was the Super of the building. The neighbors tell us that he was around every day, kind of on call. Nobody could reach him yesterday or last night, so this guy that just left called the owner of the building this morning. The owner sent somebody over with a key a little later about nine-thirty. The guy found him and called us. Harry's been talking with the man who found him and a couple of other people in the building. I think we got a pretty good fix on where he hung out. From what they tell us, we shouldn't have too much trouble tracking down where he was two nights ago."

"Hi, Frank." Harry Leonard came over and joined them. Harry was about Frank's age, two inches taller, and twenty-five pounds lighter. He looked like an adolescent, still trying to grow into his body, all gangly arms, and legs. His slightly hunched shoulders and droopy eyes gave him a hang dog appearance. In the rumpled sport coat that he wore every day, he reminded Frank of a crane in tweeds.

"What've you got, Harry?"

"We got some hairs on the body and on the bed, but they look like wig fibers. They also picked up some fiber material off the victim and off the bed. We got prints on the kitchen sink and the table."

Jerry broke in. "Joey Brewer, that's the victim's name, by the way, didn't stray very far from home base. Didn't have a real versatile social life. He was pretty predictable. Hung out in three joints, all within a few blocks from here. You won't see 'em mentioned in the society columns. The Mohawk Bar at Thirty-fourth and Eighth, Barney's Pub on Seventh near Thirty-fifth, and Sully's on Seventh between Thirty-sixth and Thirty-seventh. Chances are he was in one or all of them the night he got whacked. Frank you and Harry check out these joints this afternoon. See what you come up with. I gotta get back to the station. Talk to you guys later."

Frank went over to the body lying next to a radiator about eight feet from the bed. His pants and underwear were pulled down around his ankles and a wine bottle protruded from his rectum.

Vincent Craven, the medical examiner looked up at Frank. "I'm about to remove this little appendage, Frank. Anything you want to check before I do?"

"How far up is it," Frank asked.

"Pretty deep, maybe three or four inches."

"That took some doing."

"Absolutely," Craven said, standing and flexing his knees until they cracked.

Frank knelt and examined the bottle. "Like somebody was real angry."

Craven shrugged. "Yes, I'd say somebody was very determined to get it up there and stay. As you said, it took some doing."

Frank walked back over to the bed. The sheet and blanket were sprawled across the bed, half on, and half off, partly on the floor. He didn't figure Joey as a great housekeeper, but this bed was messed up big-time. Somebody had been flailing around on it. No question that's where the fight began. Was Joey on the bed with someone to begin with? A man? A woman?

He checked the rest of the room. Same scene as Beatty. Bottle of whiskey on the table a glass with some whiskey still in it. Glass of wine with the bottle standing next to it. Joey and his guest were having a friendly drink or so Joey thought when bingo! He gets zapped. He didn't figure he was in any danger. Same as Beatty. Whoever it was came into these guys' apartments only to kill them.

On the way to the Mohawk Bar Frank and Harry stopped in a coffee shop for lunch. Harry ordered a cheeseburger, double order of French fries, a piece of apple pie, and two glasses of milk.

"How long you been eating like this?" Frank asked.

"About a week," Harry replied, a hint of pride in his voice.

Frank shrugged. "Well, maybe you'll put some weight on. You are a skinny bastard."

"That's what I'm trying to do. I've got a new girlfriend, tells me she wants more meat on my bones. Says it'll improve my stamina. You know what I mean?"

"Yeah, you'd put on a hundred pounds if it would help you get laid."

Harry started to reply when Frank cut him off. "Harry you think it's a woman doing these guys?"

Their lunch arrived, Harry's taking up most of the table. He took a couple of bites of his cheeseburger before responding, nodding and chewing the way people do when they're trying to say something but need to get rid of some food first. "Could be," he mumbled through the cheeseburger. "The wine bottle's a sexual thing, but I'm still betting on a fag. Even though Beatty wasn't the type, the guy he was with might have come on to him and Beatty told him to back off Joey…who knows?"

"Yeah," Frank said watching Harry tear into his second cheeseburger, ketchup dripping down his chin. He made a note to avoid dining with Harry while he was on his weight gaining kick.

The bartender in the Mohawk Bar was shocked to hear of Joey's murder. "Geez, I'm really sorry to hear that," he said. "I'm not surprised though, in a way. I mean, he was an obnoxious little shit when he drank a lot, which was most of the time."

"Were you working the night before last?" Frank asked.

"Yeah. I work twelve, thirteen hours a day in this joint."

"Was Joey in that night?" Harry asked.

"No, I ain't seen Joey in over a week. Believe me, I'd remember if Joey was in here. He wasn't."

"You're sure?"

"Yeah, course I'm sure. You're talkin' only two nights ago, and I ain't seen Joey in over a week."

"Can you think of anyone who might have wanted to kill him?" Frank asked.

The bartender shook his head. "No, nobody that I ever saw. I mean he was just a little zero. Nobody got worked up about him one way or the other."

"Did he seem like the type to take up with a homosexual?" Harry asked.

"I don't know," the bartender said. "I never really paid that much attention to him to tell the truth. I never saw him with any fags. But then I don't know everybody who comes in here, you know?"

Like the Mohawk Bar, Barney's was dark and dreary and nearly empty. The bartender was washing glasses and placing them upside down on a dirty cloth, stretched out on the sink. One patron sat at the bar, a half-empty shot of whiskey, and a glass of beer in front of him. The smell of disinfectant permeated the bar. The customer belched.

"Come on. Let's get to it, and get out of here," Frank said.

They sat at the bar in front of the bartender. He continued washing the glasses, without looking up. Frank cleared his throat. "Be with ya in a minute," he said still not looking at them.

"How about being with us now," Frank said, as he reached over, and held his badge under the bartender's nose.

The man gave a little twitch. "What the hell do you guys want?"

"We're looking for some information about a guy who comes in here a lot", Harry said. "Might've been in here a couple nights ago. What's your name, by the way?" Harry took out a pad and set it on the bar.

"Uh, Billy," he said.

"You got a last name, Billy?"

"Oh yeah, sorry. Burnash. Billy Burnash."

Harry wrote in his notebook. "Billy, do you know a little guy named Joey? Joey Brewer. About forty. Got a couple tattoos on his arms, about here." Harry pointed to his arms, just above the elbows. "One arm says 'Born to' and the other has the word 'Lose' on it. We're told he was a regular in here."

Billy was nodding, before Harry finished talking. "Joey. Sure, I know Joey. He's in here all the time. I ain't seen him in a couple days or so, but I'd say you could call him a regular. What's he done? He in trouble?"

Corso leaned in. "Do you work nights too or just days?"

"Yeah. I work nights and days. I work two nights six to closing and then two days eleven to six. I alternate, ya know. Two days, then two nights, then two days, then… "

"I get the picture," Frank interrupted. "Were you on two nights ago?"

"Yeah. I worked last night and the night before."

"Was Joey in two nights ago?" Frank asked.

Billy frowned and put his fingers to his chin. "Hmm. Lemme see. He wasn't in last night," he said slowly, thinking his way along. "Now, when was he last in? Oh yeah. Sure. He was in two nights ago. How could I forget? We had a little problem that night. I thought for a minute Joey was gonna get roughed up real bad."

"What do you mean?" Harry asked.

"Well, Joey's sittin' at that table, over there with this broad. The door opens, and in come these two guys. They head straight for Joey, and they start workin' him over a little bit. Nothin' real heavy, you know, but I can tell, they mean business"

"Do you know who the guys were," Frank asked.

"Well, they…hey wait a minute you wanna tell me what this is all about?"

Frank leaned forward and spoke softly. "Joey Brewer was murdered two nights ago, the night he was here in your bar, the night we are now discussing. We are investigating a homicide, and we expect full cooperation from you. We expect you to answer all of our questions and to help us in every way that you can. That's what this is all about."

Billy turned white. His hand slipped off the bar, hitting one of the glasses, drying on the sink, and knocking it to the floor. "Holy shit!" He barely got the words out. "Jesus. Joey was such a nothin' little guy. Who the hell would want to kill him?" Billy asked, shaking his head.

"I mean he could be a pain in the ass sometime, but he was harmless. I mean, when you think of it, who'd want to take the trouble to kill the little nitwit?"

"Well, now that you're through grieving over Joey, do you think you'd like to answer some questions, Billy?" Frank asked.

"What about these two guys? Tell us what happened," Harry broke in.

Billy poured himself a shot of whiskey and downed it. "Well, like I said, Joey is sittin' at that table over there, with this broad he walked in with a few minutes before. These two guys come in and start workin' Joey over. They were givin' him some shit about some money they said he owed 'em. I was at the end of the bar, when they first came in, but when they grabbed him and slammed his head on the table, I shot over there. They weren't talkin' very loud, but I was close enough to hear what they were sayin'. They said Joey didn't pay 'em that day, like he was supposed to. Joey said he'd pay 'em the next day, and they let him up and said he'd better, or he's history. Jesus, I guess they meant it."

"Do you know these men, Billy?" Harry was off his stool and leaning over the bar, his face close to Billy's.

"Well, yeah, in a way. I mean I know their first names, and I know they're loan sharks, but that's about it." Billy looked around the bar, and his face twitched.

Corso asked Billy for a drink of water and when he brought it, Frank touched his arm. "Look, Billy. Don't worry about those two. Just tell us everything you saw and everything you know about them. We'll take it from there, and you're out of it. So, you've got nothing to fear, O.K.?" Frank smiled, probably the first time a cop ever smiled at Billy.

"One's name is Tony. The other is Ron. They're loan sharks, and they operate in this neighborhood. They come here once in a while for a couple drinks, but they never stay long. They hang around a joint called the Alcazar mostly. It's a few blocks from here over on Eighth Avenue. Everybody knows 'em over there."

"How long did they stay here, after they roughed up Joey?" Frank asked.

"Well, Joey took off pretty quick, after they let him up off the bar. They stayed and had a couple drinks each, and I heard 'em say they were going over to the Alcazar. Then they left. That's it."

"Do you remember what time it was, when all this was happening?" Frank asked, holding up his empty glass and nodding for more water.

"Yeah. I remember it was still early. Maybe nine, nine-thirty," Billy replied, as he handed Frank his water.

"Tell us about the woman," Frank said.

"Well, she seemed like spacey, you know. I mean, Joey was kinda leading her in like she didn't know where she was. I noticed for a coupla reasons. First, I'm surprised to see Joey with such a good lookin' broad. I mean even the usual pigs who come in this joint won't give him the time of day. And then second, she's pretty tall. Shit, she towered over Joey."

"She have heels on?" Frank asked.

"You mean like high heels, spike heels?"

"Yeah."

"I dunno. I couldn't tell."

"Joey wasn't very big," Frank said. "Most women would look big next to him. How tall would you say she was?"

"Ah, shit. I don't know. I didn't really get that good a look at her. I just know she was a lot taller than Joey. I'd say, maybe five-nine, five-ten, up to maybe six feet."

Harry was writing while Frank continued. "What'd you mean when you said she seemed spacey?"

"Well, she just sorta stared straight ahead. I mean she wasn't lookin' at Joey. Course, I can't blame her for that. He was an ugly little shit. She wasn't lookin' at nothin'. I dunno. She just seemed out of it."

"Drunk?"

"No. I can tell a drunk. She wasn't drunk. Just actin' funny."

"Did she seem like she was on drugs?"

Billy shrugged and shook his head. "I dunno. I'm no expert on that. Anyway, you gotta remember I was over at the bar and I never really got close to her." Billy looked around the bar hoping he might be needed elsewhere. He was running out of gas with the two cops.

Frank sensed it. "Billy, you're doing great. You've got a hell of a memory. Keep it up. Just a few more questions. Did Joey and the woman come in together or did they meet here?"

"They came in together," Billy said. "I remember doing kind of a double take when I saw them."

"Tell us some more what she looked like." Frank continued. "What color hair? Long? Short? How old? Was she pretty?"

Billy exhaled with a frown. "Yeah, she was a great lookin' chick. That's why I noticed her. Especially bein' with Joey. I'd say maybe late twenties, early thirties. Hair? Hard to say. Her coat collar was up when she came in and her hair was kinda tucked into it. I think she took her coat off later at the table but tell you the truth, I didn't even notice her hair.

"You couldn't tell if it was long or short?"

"Nooo." He dragged the word out, thinking along with it. "Yeah, I remember it was wet and it seemed like it was pinned up, you know?" He held out his hands, exasperated. "I just couldn't tell if it was long or short. I couldn't tell the color either, except it wasn't blond. I guess it was brown or black."

Frank noticed that Billy would be a great witness in a trial. He had remembered and answered all of his questions in reverse order. "Was she with Joey when Tony and Ron came in?"

"Yeah. But then when things got rough, she got up and left."

Corso frowned. "How long after she left did Joey leave?"

"Shit, I don't know." Billy looked around the bar again. "I mean I had other customers, you know? Once things quieted down over in Joey's corner, I didn't pay much attention."

Frank persisted. "Was it a long time? Did he leave right after her? Think, Billy!"

"Naw. It wasn't a long time. Maybe just a coupla minutes. Not long."

"Was that the last time you saw him or did he come back?" Frank asked.

"No. That's the last I seen of him."

"Did you ever see Joey leave with a woman before?" Frank asked.

"Nope. Not even the hookers who come in here would go out with him. Like I said that's why I was surprised to see him with just a good looking woman."

"Ever see him with a fag?" asked Harry.

"Naw. I think Joey was pretty straight. Course you never know I mean that was just my impression of him." He nodded toward a new customer sitting at the bar. "Excuse me. I gotta go wait on that guy."

"It doesn't sound like we're going to have a lot of trouble finding Tony and Ron," Frank said. "We'll go over to the Alcazar and talk to some people. If Billy knows what he's talking about, and we get lucky, they might even show up while we're there."

"I guess you could say they had a motive, huh?"

"You could say that," Frank said. He glanced at the pay phone on the wall. "I've got to call Jerry."

Harry was about to order another cheeseburger when Frank returned.

"Jerry's worked up. He filled in the captain on Joey, and Nolan's paranoid. He's bent out of shape about similarities between this one and the Beatty killing, and he wants a report this afternoon, before he leaves. You go in and write the report on what we've got so far. I'll check the Alcazar and Sully's. I'll be in later. Nolan wants to see Jerry and me at 4:30 in his office."

"O.K., Frank."

Frank headed for the Alcazar, encouraged by what they had learned from Billy. But the thing with the two loan sharks was just too pat, too easy. Guys like that just don't go around advertising that they're going to kill someone, and then turn around and do it a few hours later. On the other hand, fear and intimidation were the stock and trade of loan sharks, and maybe they wanted to send a message to the rest of the neighborhood. Maybe they really are that tough and that stupid.

He couldn't get the woman out of his mind. What would a woman like that be doing with a creep like Joey Brewer? Spaced out but not drunk. She came in with him. An unlikely pair for a date. So she's spaced, high on drugs. Maybe came from a party and little Joey spots her and sees she's out of it. Decides to take advantage and hauls her in here to work on her.

He remembered it was raining that night. And Billy said her hair was wet. Joey probably ran into her on the street outside and hustled her in here out of the rain. Could she have done him? Billy said Joey left very shortly after she did. Did he catch up to her outside?

Could there be a connection between Joey and Beatty and the loan sharks? Were they into Beatty too?

He reached the Alcazar and walked in.

# Chapter Seventeen

The Alcazar had the rancid smell and feel that bars have in the daytime. The place was dark, and it took a minute for Frank's eyes to adjust. A circular bar stood in the center of the room, with small tables clustered around one side of the bar. On the other side were a dance floor and a small bandstand. Against another wall to the left of the entrance, were several booths covered in green vinyl. He made a mental note to tell Harry about the sign at the entrance advertising Tuesdays and Thursdays as "Ladies nights. All drinks half price to unescorted ladies."

The bar was a mess of dirty glasses and empty beer bottles. He approached the bartender who was sitting on a stool behind the bar picking his teeth and asked him about the two loan sharks.

The man responded without looking at Frank. "Who wants to know?"

Frank showed him his credentials, which did nothing to change his attitude.

"Big fucking deal. What do you want from me?"

He really was tired of having to deal with creeps like this. Phony tough guys who liked to flaunt their dislike of cops. He leaned on the bar and swept his arm across it, sending the dirty bottles and glasses clattering on to the floor in back of the bar. Shards of broken glass exploded around the bartender's stool. "Sorry about that," he said. "I'm such a Klutz."

The bartender leaped off the stool, broken glass crunching under his feet. His eyes burned with hatred, a look Frank had seen many times.

"Anyway, the big fucking deal is I'd like you to answer a few questions about Ron and Tony."

The man hesitated, like he was debating what to do next. And then he looked toward the door. "Well, I guess today's your lucky day, because your two guys just walked in."

Frank turned and saw two men heading toward the bar.

"How's it goin', Russ?" the smaller of the two greeted the bartender.

Russ looked toward Frank, who introduced himself and showed them his badge. "I wonder if I could speak with you guys over in a booth," Frank asked.

They stood next to Frank and looked him up and down. The bigger of the two towered over Frank, standing six four or five. He studied Frank's credentials and badge, then dropped them on the bar. "Yeah, sure. Russ, give us a couple of beers first. You want one?" he asked Frank.

"No thanks."

Russ delivered the beers, and they settled into a booth.

"Well, what can we do for you?" Tony, the big one asked.

"I want to talk with you about a little guy named Joey Brewer. Name ring a bell?"

Tony and Ron looked at each other for a moment before Tony replied. "Yeah, we know Joey. What's the problem?"

"What makes you think there's a problem?"

"What, are you just coming in here for the atmosphere and shoot the shit with us about Joey Brewer?" Tony asked, lighting a cigarette.

"When's the last time you saw Joey?"

Tony shrugged and turned to Ron. "Ronnie, when's the last time we saw Joey?"

Ron was short and stocky and had a stubble of beard, which about matched the amount of hair he had on his head. He wore a blue shiny vinyl jacket over a gray sweatshirt. "Geez, I don't know. We see a lotta people. It's hard to keep track of who we see when." He gave a little smile showing teeth the color of lemons. Frank was glad he'd had the jolt of brandy before leaving the apartment.

"You remember where you were the night before last?"

"Night before last. Night before last. Tuesday. Yeah, we had a few beers in a couple a joints, then had a bite to eat, and went home. I was feelin' kinda sick, so we went home early. Right, Ron?"

Ron nodded. "Yeah, I remember now."

"You two live together?" Frank asked.

"Yeah," Tony replied. "What's this all about, anyway?" he asked.

"Did you guys go to Barney's Tuesday night?" Frank asked, ignoring the question.

"Barney's", Tony thought out loud. He turned to Ron, who nodded.

Tony hesitated for a moment. "Yeah, we were in Barney's for a while. In fact, now I remember. That's when we saw Joey."

"Oh yeah?" Frank replied. "You talk to him?"

"Yeah, we talked to him."

"What about?"

Tony flared. "Hey look, you wanna tell us what the hell this is all about? You come in here and start givin' us the third degree. For what? What's goin' on?"

Frank spoke quietly. "You want me to get a warrant and take you two punks down to the station for questioning? Want me do that? Or we can finish our little chat right here. It's up to you."

They each lit another cigarette. The booth was blue with smoke. Frank's eyes began to burn.

Tony exhaled in Frank's direction. He gave a final last minute poof toward Frank to make sure all the smoke reached him. That was bad enough, but it was the smirk that really did it. Frank slapped the cigarette out of his mouth and sent it skittering across the floor. Tony leaped to his feet and pulled his cocked fist back, ready to swing.

Frank was on his feet before Tony. "Go ahead, asshole, and we'll have you in a cell before you can light another cigarette."

Tony's eyes narrowed. He held his fist in position for another thirty seconds before he dropped it and sat down. The smirk returned, and he was Mr. Cool again. "O.K. Joey owed us a little money, and we talked to him about that. Sounds like you already been to Barney's, so yeah, we roughed him up a little. You know, just enough to let him know we want our money. That's all. Then we left. We came here and had a few beers, then stopped in the pizza joint on the corner, had some pizza, and went home, O.K.?"

Frank sat, staring at him, then turned to Ron. Ron smiled again showing his little yellow teeth. They squirmed and looked around the room, avoiding eye contact with Frank.

"What time was all this?" he asked. "How long did you stay here? What time did you get home?"

"Goddamn it!" Tony yelled. "What do you want from us? What's this all about?"

"Joey Brewer was killed on Tuesday night. You two were seen working him over and threatening him in Barney's. A few people noticed." Frank's eyes never left them.

"Holy shit," Ron muttered.

"Oh, I get it," Tony said. "You guys are gonna try to pin this on me and Ron, because we had a little tiff with Joey. Is that it?"

"Maybe. And maybe your telling him he's history if he doesn't pay up might get some attention."

"Well, screw you, pal. We had nothin', nothin' whatsoever to do with Joey Brewer getting killed. We walked out of that bar, and never saw him again."

"Nobody's accusing you guys of anything. Lot of things could have happened, and anybody could have done this. I'm just trying to get some help, that's all. I understand Joey was sitting with a woman. Did you get a good look at her?"

"No, we didn't pay any attention to her. Anyway, she cut out pretty quick. All I remember is she was pretty good lookin' and tall."

Ron spoke up. "Yeah, she stood up next to me, and I was eye level with her boobs."

"She have heels on or flats?"

"Heels? Shit, I don't know. It's hard to say, you know? With those tits, I wasn't looking at her feet. Tall broad though, maybe close to six feet."

"How about her hair?" Frank asked. "What color?"

"Yeah, her hair." Ron looked puzzled and glanced at Tony for help.

Tony spoke up. "Hard to tell. She had it covered with some kinda scarf. The little bit I could see seemed like it was dark. You know, maybe dark brown, black."

Frank's eyes still burned. He half wished that Tony had swung on him. "How long after the woman left did Joey leave?"

"He left right after she did," Tony said. "Couldn't wait to get the hell out."

After another twenty minutes or so Frank had pretty much the same information he got from Billy, and he took their addresses and phone numbers and left. He reached the precinct and brought Harry up to date. It was nearly 4:30 when he entered Jerry's office with the report.

"Jesus, I'm glad you're here," Jerry greeted Frank, as he walked in the door of the precinct. Nolan is ranting about his goddamn intuition. Says it's telling him that Beatty and this one are connected. He's scared shitless that we've got a serial killer on our hands. Give me a quick run-down before we go in to see him."

Frank went over everything. "We've finally got something to go on. It's not much but it's something."

Jerry stood up and tucked his shirt into his pants. He straightened his tie and put on his coat.

"Jerry, how long you and Nolan been working together, twenty years? You think he doesn't know the real you by now? Why do you have to fix yourself up to look like Tom Cruise every time you go in his office?"

"I'm insecure. Let's go."

Captain Joseph Nolan was about forty-five. He had been with the New York Police Department for twenty-one years and had worked his way up from rookie patrolman to the powerful position he now held. One of only a few black captains in the department, his ambition was no secret. He was bucking hard for Borough Commander and Chief and some day even Commissioner. Smart and savvy, he had a special set of antennae that went up, whenever he sensed a situation developing that could slow down his personal goals. More than anything else, he feared media attention or pressure. Whenever he sensed a problem, he was quick to take action to defuse it.

"Hello, Frank. Come in. Come in." Nolan did not get up, nor did he offer Frank and Jerry a seat. There was no chit-chit.

"Now, Frank, you may think I'm overreacting to the murder of this little nobody over on Eighth Avenue. And I know that you and Jerry and Harry have just gotten on it. So I'm not expecting you're going to turn over the killer to me today. However, let me tell you I have very bad vibes about this. It's a carbon copy of the Beatty case, and you don't seem to have much on that one yet. Now, what I don't want is to find ourselves in the middle of a series of killings that's going to get the wrong people's attention. Do you know what I mean, Frank?"

Frank knew what he meant. The last thing he wanted was to get on Nolan's shit list. He looked at Jerry.

"Jerry already heard my speech earlier today," Nolan said sharply "Now tell me exactly where we are on this one, Frank. What do you have, anything?" The captain leaned forward expectantly.

Frank handed Nolan a copy of the report and filled him in on what he and Harry had learned from Billy, and the two loan sharks. "We've got some leads now, Captain. We should have more later in the week."

"Well, I hope you do, Frank. But whatever, I expect action and results on both these cases…pronto. Keep in very close touch." Nolan wheeled his chair sideways and picked up the phone. They were dismissed.

"Get the picture, Frank?" Jerry asked as they headed toward the water cooler. Jerry's shirt had managed to come out of his pants again and his tie had unloosened. They each drank two paper cups of water and sat down.

Frank nodded. "Yeah, I get the picture."

Jerry got up and headed toward his office. He turned. "This is gonna get worse, Frank. I can feel it."

Frank went over to his own desk and slumped, tired and tense. He knew Jerry was right. It is going to get worse. His gut feeling told him the loan sharks didn't do these guys. They're scumbags and he'd like nothing better than to nail them for something, but it won't be this. No, somebody's out there getting their kicks, satisfying some sick need. And they're not finished. The time frame in between is going to get shorter. And Nolan is going to get nastier.

He took the three nerf balls from his drawer and shot a few hoops in the basket he'd rigged up. Three in a row. Not bad, he thought, for a guy with a bum shoulder. He felt the shoulder, smiled, and decided to go to the health club.

# Chapter Eighteen

Paul Gale was increasingly stressed out. His work at the restaurant had become unbearable. Since his first meeting with Tony Breda, Gale had hardly laid eyes on him. When he did, Tony ignored him, treating him like he wasn't there. He would breeze in and out of the kitchen from time to time, and on two occasions, Gale had greeted him with a friendly, "Hi! Tony." Both times Breda kept going, without reply.

Peter's dislike for Gale had reached the point where he picked on him constantly and made his life miserable. Gale loathed Peter and he knew he couldn't last much longer at Breda's.

But he had a plan. It was his plan that kept him going. The restaurant accepted no credit cards. Breda broke from all the credit card companies, because he tired of paying their percentages. The place was so popular that he never skipped a beat. Everything was cash, and it poured in.

The restaurant had thirty-three tables. Gale knew the traffic patterns and that the lunch crowd turned over twice on a good day like Friday. The average lunch tab per table ran close to a hundred dollars. The tables at dinner turned over three times, and the average bill per table at dinner, ran about a hundred and seventy-five dollars. The bar, which was always busy, was good for another five thousand. All in all, Gale figured that on a typical busy Friday, with lunch, dinner and the bar, the restaurant took in between twenty-five and thirty thousand dollars.

"Not a bad night's pay," he mused.

Gale also knew that Vince cashed out at night, after closing. More importantly, he knew that Breda demanded there be two people involved always, and that the second person, along with Vince was Peter. Vince and Peter were the two people that Breda trusted completely.

Gale knew the routine. On several occasions, since he started working there, he had been asked to stay on until closing and help clean up and get things in order for the next day.

Vince and Peter and a few of the older waiters liked to sit back, have a couple of pops, and unwind. Sometimes Breda joined them. After a while, everyone would drift on out and head home. Breda was always the first to leave, after one scotch and soda.

After everyone left, Vince and Peter locked up, and began the job of checking out the register validating the tapes, counting the money and putting it away in the safe for the morning deposit pick-up.

Gale's plan was simple. He had it all worked out. The key to it was the revolver, a Glock automatic he got through an ex con he had known at Walpole.

He'd go to work like always on the day after he finished with Tookie. Hadn't worked that one out completely yet. But he would, soon.

At his normal quitting time, four p.m., he'd slip down into the cellar from the door in the back corner of the kitchen. Nobody ever paid attention to him as he left for the day. Peter watched him like a hawk until four, but when he began to leave, Peter forgot about him. The door to the alley, through which he always left was next to the cellar door. Both doors were in the corner, out of anyone's sight. Be simple enough to open the cellar door, open and slam shut the door to the alley, slip down into the cellar and wait there until closing.

He smiled thinking of Peter and Vince alone, counting all that money, him coming up from the cellar, through the kitchen and surprising them. Then he would march them down into the cellar and have some fun. First, shoot Vince and then would come the sweet moments he had dreamed about since his first day of work. And for every humiliating day thereafter, he would make Peter pay with a slow, painful death.

"Vot's da matter, cocksucker? You stupid or something? You think you could shit on me day after day after fucking day, and expect to get away with it? Huh? Is dat vot you tink, you son of a bitch?" he would mock the terrified Peter.

Then do it nice and slow; shoot off both his kneecaps, and when he falls, lean over him, and slice his tongue off, cut down on him making too much noise. Then play with him some more, before finishing him off. "Take my time and enjoy it," he thought. "I'm gonna have all night."

After finishing with Peter, he would clean himself off in the kitchen change into clean clothes, scoop up the money into his overnight bag, head out the door, walk a few blocks, catch a cab to the airport, and take the eight a.m. flight to Los Angeles. No one came to the restaurant until ten in the morning. By that time, he'd be well on his way to L.A. There he'd catch a flight to San Diego, take a bus to Tijuana, and either bury himself there, or maybe later head further south into Mexico.

It would all be easy. But there was much to do first, and much to endure from his tormentor, before pay back time.

Two pay backs coming up soon.

*    *    *

After her adventure with Joey, she had gone home and slid into a hot bath. The soothing waters felt so good, they almost sucked her breath away. She washed herself slowly, gently massaging, and scrubbing her body until she was satisfied that the filth and foul smell of the scum she had punished was gone.

She drifted back to her incident with Jack Beatty. Her recollection was blurred and vague for many days until gradually it came into focus. She remembered clearly now how it had started with fear and anger, but when it was over, she was flooded with satisfaction.

It would probably be a while before she could fully comprehend her evening with Joey. But it would come. For now, some things she could remember clearly, some as shadows, some not at all. Mostly there were vague afterimages like the phantom traces of nightmares against the morning. The important thing was what she remembered clearly. He would never touch her again. She slid deeper into the soft water and thought of her mother.

The rest of her week passed without incident. Her life went on, but there was new meaning, a different dimension. She had her secret now, a hidden territory she could isolate and surround with silence.

Her doctors did know her. She wished she could tell them what was happening but of course she couldn't.

The words of Dr.Stein, spoken years ago, came back to her. "When you're with me, you rarely express anger. You cry a lot. When denial no longer works, anger often emerges. When you face up to how cruelly you were cheated out of your childhood, you will feel anger. And when it comes, it will come in a flood."

And her own words of only a few months ago to her current doctor, "When life is calm, I get the anger back or I feel depressed. I need to do something just to stir up that rush of adrenaline."

"That's all right. Nothing wrong with that," the doctor said. "Just be careful to channel that something in a positive direction."

She'd found her direction.

The newspapers had picked up on the possible serial killer angle of the murder of Jack Beatty and Joey and were playing it up. Each day she hungrily scanned every paper in the city and was disappointed if there was nothing. She made it a point to watch at least one newscast every day or evening. The police didn't seem to be making much progress.

She'd been more careful this last time, wiping off everything she had touched. She was learning. But there were other things on her mind, all boiled down to one, one person.

When she was alone she felt safe and secure in her own space. But though she took comfort from the solitude, she still clung to the need to live within society, to hope and dream about the possibilities of the future and the sense of self that she still sought.

It had been a cold walk home. She was chilled and tired by the time she reached her building. A crowd of revelers had just emerged from the building and stood chattering noisily on the sidewalk.

She wearily unlocked the door and entered the building, having failed to notice the short stocky man standing in the shadows across the street.

# Chapter Nineteen

Gina Ponte popped her head over Denise's cubicle. Her perfume preceded her and Denise turned and spotted her friend.

"My. Don't we look sexy tonight," Denise said.

"Come on, Dennie. Give me a break. It's Friday night. Everybody's going over to the Splendido. Get your coat and let's go." She was in the cubicle, playfully tugging at Denise. "Come on. Kiss your computer goodnight and let's go."

Denise looked her up and down and couldn't help smiling. The black slacks and sweater Gina wore fit as if they'd been painted on her. "You look like you're ready to howl," Denise said with a smile.

"Bet your sweet life, honey. Let's go."

"No, I can't. I'm going to the health club for a while and then I'm going to work on the curtains and comforter I've been making. I want to finish the curtains tonight and I'm coming down the home stretch on the comforter."

Gina shook her head. "I swear Dennie. You are so talented. You're the only person I know who can make a whole comforter."

"Guess you don't know many people," Denise said. "Anyway, thanks for the invite. But have a good time. I'm sure you will, knowing you."

Gina shrugged and left. Denise sat for a moment, half wishing she had gone with her. Gina was so much fun, one of the few people able to make her laugh. But all those phonies posturing and preening, all trying to impress each other. Who needs it?

Anyway, she'd been thinking a lot about Frank Corso. Surprising. Most of the men she'd met in New York weren't worth thinking about much. But he was so nice and God! Was he good looking! He had mentioned that Fridays were probably going to be the best nights for him to get to the health club on a regular basis. It might be kind of nice to bump into him again. She smiled at her choice of words.

And then, she really was looking forward to working on her home decorating projects. The material had set her back almost a week's pay but it was gorgeous and worth it. Now she couldn't wait to finish everything and get her bedroom looking just the way she'd seen the one in Elle Decor.

The club was crowded as usually on Fridays, but she was disappointed not to see Frank. He's probably got a date, she thought heading for the locker room.

When she came out she spotted him pumping away on the stationary bike. A good feeling came over her.

Frank spotted her and motioned for her to come over. His wave was so friendly that walking over to him seemed O.K

"Hi, Denise. How are you?" He wore a pair of gym shorts and no shirt. Sweat glistened on his body. Standing there, looking down on his nearly naked body, she felt an odd intimacy in spite of all the people around them.

"Hi. Looks like you're really been attacking that thing."

"Yeah, well I'm not sure who's winning. Right now I'd say the bike is."

She laughed and started to move away toward a nautilus machine.

"How long do you usually work out?" he asked.

She stopped and drifted back a couple of steps. "'Bout forty-five minutes or so tonight."

"That sounds good for me, too." He beckoned toward the juice machine. "Can I buy you a drink when we finish?"

"Sure."

Frank went back to his bike. She looked even better than he remembered. It had been a tough week. Nolan was pressing Jerry hard. They never liked each other and Nolan seemed to get off on riding Jerry if he was bothered. He had good reason to be bothered now, and he was turning the screws. Everybody on the Beatty-Joey Brewer cases was snapping at everybody else.

He watched Denise lying on her back, pumping the nautilus contraption up and down, her beautiful muscular body moving in an easy rhythm. She sat up and glanced over and caught him looking at her. He jerked his head down and fumbled with the tension control on the bike.

After about forty-five minutes they rendezvoused at the juice machine and sat together on a mat in the corner of the room. He liked sitting next to her and the slightly musky female smell she gave off. He'd noticed her sneaking looks at him, too while they were working out.

They sat with their backs against the wall, making small talk or at least he was trying to. She definitely was shy and he didn't feel like he was having much luck drawing her out. Over the past year, he was the one with the monosyllabic responses and indifference. Now, here he was acting like a school kid, playing twenty questions. She finished her juice and set the cup down. "I've got to go. I've really enjoyed seeing you again, Frank." She sounded like she meant it.

"O.K.," he said and started to get up. He groaned and held his back. "I think I'm too old for this stuff."

"No you're not," she laughed. "And don't you dare give up on it. I expect to see you here at least every Friday."

That was encouraging. "Tell you what," he said. "It only takes me a few minutes to grab a quick shower and change. I'll probably be out before you. I'll wait and walk you out, if you don't mind."

"Sure," she said without hesitating.

He waited for about ten minutes before she appeared. Her long dark hair gleamed, and the brown eyes had a luminous quality he must have missed before. The big bag she carried looked like the kind Carla used to tote around. He felt a twinge. She spotted him and broke out in a smile that made him weak in the knees. The Carla twinge disappeared.

She reached him in three long strides. "Hope I didn't keep you waiting too long."

"No," he said, his eyes playing across her. "But if you did, it would've been worth it." Her face flushed. She was actually blushing. He couldn't remember the last time he'd seen a woman blush.

The night was almost balmy, clear sky and a nearly full moon. He hated November. It was always gray, damp, and cold. Tonight was a rare treat. "Beautiful night," he said, as they stood somewhat awkwardly on the sidewalk. "Denise, you haven't had dinner yet, have you?"

She hesitated. "Well, no, but, I'm just going to make something light when I get home. I'm working on a project tonight."

"Oh. Well all that exercise has me hungry all of a sudden, and I don't have any strength left to cook anything myself. Too dehydrated and weak. If I don't eat soon, I'll probably get sick."

She started to giggle. "I think you'd better get yourself to a restaurant, fast."

"Can't," he said. "I get indigestion if I eat in a restaurant alone. Always have. I've got a solution, though."

She was already shaking her head. "I can't Frank. I really have some work to do tonight."

He looked at his watch. "Come on. It's not even seven o'clock yet. I know a great little spot just a couple of blocks from here. I also know the owner. We'll be in and out in an hour, you'll have performed a humanitarian act, and you'll be working on your project by eight-thirty. You like Thai food?"

"Oh, God! It's my favorite."

"See? I knew it. Come on…O.K.?" He reached out for her.

She stood her ground, watching him. He had made her laugh, the way only Gina could and there was a quality about him that made her feel safe, comfortable. Why not? She had the whole weekend to work on the sewing project.

The Thai restaurant was small and filled with delicious smells. The owner, a Thai woman of indeterminate age, greeted Frank with a hug and a kiss. "I miss you handsome. Where you been?"

"Awful busy, Mai Lee. Say hello to Denise."

She greeted Denise and seated them in a corner table. "We take good care of you, Frankie," she hugged him again and scurried toward the kitchen.

Denise watched her go and smiled. "Something tells me you have that effect on most women."

Frank's eyes twinkled. "You, too?"

She blushed again. "Guess I walked into that one."

They both ordered Pad Thai with shrimp and some Thai beer.

"This is wonderful," Denise said. "I'm glad you suggested it."

He smiled. "Me, too." She was easy to be with. None of the edge that most women in New York have. No B.S. Just…nice. "How about another beer?"

She looked at her watch. "It's ten of eight. Remember your promise?"

"Oh, yeah. What's your project?"

"Just some sewing I'm doing."

"Sewing? Like darning holes in your socks?"

"No," she laughed. "I'm making curtains and a comforter."

"You're making a comforter?"

"Yes, it's sort of my thing. I love to design and decorate things, mostly for my apartment. It's relaxing and I think I'm pretty good at it."

He nodded like he knew she'd be pretty good at it. "You mentioned you work for a publisher. What do you do there?"

"I'm an editorial assistant. I work for one of the hot shot editors. Sometimes he's a pain, but I've learned a lot from him. What do you do, by the way?"

He took a deep hit on his beer and gave a little laugh. "You don't want to know."

"Yes, I do. Now you've got me curious."

"I'm a cop."

"A…cop," she stammered.

"Did I say a dirty word?" Come on, it could be worse. I could be a lawyer."

She touched his arm. "Oh, Frank, I didn't mean to hurt your feelings. I'm sorry. I guess I just never thought of you as a policeman, that's all."

"Why not?"

"I don't know. I guess I thought all policemen wore white socks."

"What did you think of me as?"

She shrugged. "I guess I never really thought about it." She studied him. He sure was easy to look at. "A business executive, advertising, TV, a lawyer…Oops, sorry. What kind of a policeman are you?"

"I'm a detective, a homicide detective."

"Homicide?"

He watched the expression on her face and was sorry the whole thing had to come up. It really got tiresome, watching people react to his job. It's like everybody knows there are cops who investigate and solve murders, but nobody ever knows such a creature personally. It's O.K. in the abstract.

"Yeah," he said flatly. "Homicide. You know, like in murder?" Something about her attitude now was different and he didn't like it.

She picked up on the change in him, too. "Sorry, Frank. I just never met a real live homicide detective."

No kidding, he thought. What a surprise. Usually, if people reacted in a funny way to his job, he liked to tweak them. With Denise, he felt a need to justify himself. "It's something I always wanted to do." He resisted the urge to add O.K.? "My father and two uncles were police officers. I've been a cop for twelve years and it may sound corny, but I happen to believe in what I do."

Denise stared at him, impressed by his sincerity. "I'm sure you're a very good detective," she said softly.

He grinned. "Sorry for getting carried away. Didn't mean to jump on a soapbox."

"That's O.K. Your job must be interesting and exciting. What are you working on now?"

He looked surprised. "Well, that's a turnaround. I thought for a minute I had a contagious disease."

"I'm just fascinated by your being a homicide detective. Tell me more."

He looked at his watch. "I will another time. I promise. But right now, I'm going to keep tonight's promise, much as I hate to."

"Oh," she said, looking at her own watch. "That's right. I do have to go."

Frank paid the check and they left, after another hug from Mai Lee, this time for both of them.

"I'm going to catch a cab," Denise said. "But let's just walk along for a minute. It's such a nice night."

"Perfect," he said, glad for the chance to enjoy her a little longer. He lived his life like he was always ten minutes late for an appointment, but she had a way of slowing him down, even relaxing.

They walked for a few blocks, neither saying much. It was a comfortable silence, the kind that people have when neither feels any pressure to keep conversation going, but somehow there is communication.

A cab cruised down the street and she hailed it. "I'm going to catch this cab, but I hope I'll see you again...soon?"

He grinned and touched her face. "Count on it," he said, opening the door for her. He slipped the driver a ten dollar bill and turned back to Denise, who had the window down, her head partially out of it.

"Thanks again, Frank. I really enjoyed it."

"Me, too." He leaned in and gently kissed her on the lips.

The cab pulled away. Denise was still waving out the back window when it rounded the corner out of sight.

# Chapter Twenty

Crystal Wilcox drained her third cup of coffee of the morning at about the same time she finished reading the *New York Times*. Her day didn't really begin until she had digested it. She liked the *Daily News* for different reasons. It fed her need to keep up with the seamy other side of New York, her other world. The articles on violence, weirdos, druggies, and crime and punishment titillated her. It was a nasty, mean, sick world out there and the only way to survive was to be nastier and meaner than the rest of them.

This morning she was feeling pretty good. She stretched her arms and straightened her long legs along the length of the bed. The newspaper crinkled under her and some of it drifted off to the floor.

She slept well. No bad dreams that she could remember and her head felt clear for a change. Today might be a good day to visit the new super bookstore.

She got up and moved slowly to the bathroom medicine cabinet for the next stage of her daily ritual, her medication. She studied the two-tone blue and white capsule, hefting and assaying it as if the capsule were a little gold nugget.

The doctor prescribed it to keep her stabilized on an even keel, control her volatility. But it was difficult and he had twice in recent months increased the dosage. The spacey feeling it gave her was not unpleasant, and when she combined the medication with a few snorts of coke, she was off into a delicious never-never land. She gulped the pill down with some water, showered and dressed.

The bookstore was great. She took her time wandering through the aisles, browsing, losing herself in the world of fantasy. She picked out a couple of books on the Civil War, a P.D. James mystery, and a Phillip Roth novel, *Patrimony*, which she'd read before but wanted to re-read.

Upstairs in a quiet corner she found the section on violence in the United States, a subject in which she had some interest. There were books on family violence, street crime, mass murder, sex crimes—a potpourri of psychological analysis of violence. She selected a couple of them and turned her attention to a collection of books on Sadomasochism, another subject of interest.

She was reading through one when she sensed that she was no longer alone. She turned and a man stood directly behind her. "Jesus Christ," she blurted.

"Oh, I'm sorry if I scared you," he said, breaking out in a friendly smile.

"Well, you did," she said.

"Sorry," he said again. "I was just browsing around same as you." He glanced at the book she was holding. "I see we have similar tastes in books."

She eyed him, her head slowly nodding. He looked to be about forty, not bad looking, well dressed.

"You think so, huh?"

"Well, I don't know. That's an over generalization, I guess." He smiled again. "I'm a writer and I'm doing a book on violence in the U.S. I've been immersed in all of this stuff lately just thought I'd check out this store since it's new and might have something I haven't seen yet. Kind of a bonus to run into a beautiful woman like you."

She continued nodding. "No, shit. You think I'm beautiful, do you?"

He got the message. "Hey, I'm sorry if I offended you. I didn't mean anything by it."

"No, that all right. No problem," she said, reaching into her purse. "In fact, here, I've got something for you." She withdrew a can of pepper gas and sprayed it into his eyes.

She went down the stairs, paid for her books and left.

\*     \*     \*

It was Sunday and Frank was up early. Beautiful day for a football game. Jets and Patriots tied for the division lead. He smiled as the phone rang. "Hi, Dad."

"Frankie!" his father's unmistakable New York accent. "You wanna come by the house first or just meet at the Park?"

Another smile. Football and baseball games were still played at the park to Silvio Corso. He called Madison Square Garden the gym. "Meet you at the Park, Dad. It's another hour for me to get to the house and back to the Park. Meet you at Gate Eighteen at eleven-thirty and we'll have a bite to eat at Conlins. O.K.?"

"O.K., kid. See ya then."

Over coffee Frank read some FBI memoranda on profiling serial killers. He reflected on his most recent three weeks at the academy in Quantico. Great stuff and he'd learned a lot about serial killers—all male. There was actually very little on female serial killers. It just isn't something that's received much attention. But they're out there. Hell, in one study alone thirty-four female serial killers were identified and believed to be responsible for up to four hundred and seventy-one deaths. He'd also learned some other things. Ninety-seven percent of female serial killers were white and since 1975 there was a big increase in killing strangers, rather than family members. They were catching up to the men in this regard.

The violence of Beatty and Joey's murders didn't jell, though. Women still don't like to get their hands dirty. Poison is their weapon of choice followed by gunshots. Nice and impersonal. These two don't fit the pattern.

His stomach growled. Nothing in the refrigerator and no bread for toast. It was still only eight-thirty and there was no way he could wait until eleven-thirty, so he went down to the corner store for some bagels and orange juice.

On the way back to his apartment, someone called his name as he was about to enter the building. He turned and saw a tall man with thinning salt and pepper hair and a thick dark mustache smiling broadly and shaking his head.

"I don't believe it, Frank Corso. For Christ sake. How are you?" The man approached him, grabbed his hand, and pumped it warmly.

Frank stared for a minute, jogging his memory. No luck.

"It's David. David Weltman," the man's outstretched arms, palms up, telling Frank he should have recognized him.

"David!" Frank grabbed him and hugged him.

"That's better," David said. "Thought you forgot your old buddy there for a minute. I haven't changed that much have I?"

"Well, uh, let me see. Last time I saw you, was at that graduation party at Northeastern. You had hair then and no mustache and you were hanging all over Ginny Freeling. Ever get in her pants?"

David's hands went up to his head. "I still have hair." He looked at his reflection in the glass door and brushed back the strands he had left. "Yeah, I got into Ginny's pants. I married her. We got divorced a few years later. Haven't seen her since. How about you?"

"I was married for a while, but it ended in divorce, too."

They compared notes the way old friends do who haven't seen each other in almost fifteen years.

"You're a homicide detective. I'm impressed, I think."

"You're a television producer. I'm impressed...I think," Frank responded.

"Hey, Frank. I'm having a little shindig tonight at my place. How about coming? Be lots of good looking unattached women there. I'm over on East Seventy-second. What do you say?"

"Hmmn. I'm going to the Jets game. I…"

"So?" David interrupted," The game's over by four. Party won't get going 'til eight-thirty or nine." He gave Frank a card with his address and made him promise to come.

*    *    *

"Frankie. You're right on time." Silvio Corso stood in front of their appointed meeting spot. In his brown leather jacket, thick mane of silver gray hair and aviator sunglasses, he looked like an older, heavier version of Frank.

They hugged each other, and Silvio stepped back to look at his son. "Frankie, I don't see you enough anymore. Goddamn, I miss ya, kid."

"Hey, come on. You're seeing me now, so what's to miss?" Frank pulled a ten dollar bill out of his wallet. "Give me two points and I'll take the Patriots for ten."

"Shit," Silvio said. "Make it twenty and you're on."

They found a small table in the bar at Conlins, ordered two beers each and a couple of hamburgers. "I'm telling you Dad, Bledsoe is the best quarterback since Marino He'll pick these guys apart."

"Yeah, dream on, kid. I just hope you can afford the twenty. So, what're you doing? How's the writing coming?"

"Good. I just went over the proofs for the Crime Scene article and I've got a contract sitting on my desk for a book of my own. I sent you the article in *Crimes and Punishment* a couple of months ago. So…I'm keeping busy."

His father nodded and pursed his lips. "You gonna do the book?"

"I don't know. Haven't made up my mind yet."

"They offer you a big advance?" Silvio was eating this up.

"An advance? Yeah. Big? No."

"How much?"

"Five grand."

"Hey, that's not bad, Frankie. You do this one and they'll give you twenty for the next one."

"Oh. That's how it works, uh? What're you, a book agent now?"

"No. I just know what a great writer you are. Look at all the letters you get from your articles and all. You think your old man doesn't puff up his chest when I read those letters about you in the magazines? By the way, I had dinner with the chief the other night. He was down here for a meeting and called. We talked about the old days. I told him if I hadn't retired I'd a been chief today instead of him."

"What'd he say?"

"Told me I was full of it but that he wouldn't be surprised if the real cop in the Corso family became chief one day."

"Swell. You still milking him for compliments about me?"

Silvio chuckled and motioned for two more beers. "No. I didn't have to milk him. They poured out of him. You're a fair-haired boy, Frankie." He grabbed his son around the neck and pulled him roughly to him. "You're going places and you know it. I'm proud of you, kid. You're a chip off the old block." Silvio lowered his voice and leaned forward. "Chief's worried about these wine bottle killings. Sounds like you got a serial killer starting up. You got anything?"

Frank frowned and shook his head. "Not much. Same M.O. in both. Same fury, same no forced entry. Robbery doesn't seem to be involved. More like a killing of anger, rage. The victims most likely knew the killer."

"Gays?"

"I don't think so. The victims don't fit the profile. We're not ruling it out, but not likely. Chief tell you about the wine bottles?"

"Yeah. That's why I asked about gays. Killing a guy is one thing. Sticking a wine bottle up his ass tells me there's something else on the killer's mind besides murder."

"Dad, it could be a woman."

"Oh?"

"The second victim was seen with a woman the night he was killed. Tall, good looking woman, not the type this guy would've been with. No forced entry in either case. No indications in either victim's background of any contact with homosexuals. Course, you never know but people who knew them rule it out."

"What else?"

"The description of the woman with this Joey Brewer fits the type you might expect the first guy, Beatty, would've had in his apartment."

"Go on."

"There's no connection between these two guys. Their murders are random acts. Dad, we both know that homicide usually involves a killer and a victim who know each other or are related. The data doesn't hold up when it comes to serial killers."

"Yeah, but not with women. They don't usually kill strangers," Silvio said.

Frank shook his head. "Not so any more. Over half the female serial killers reported having killed strangers only."

Silvio arched his eyebrows and nodded just once slowly, his way of saying, "O.K., I didn't know that."

Frank continued. "Female serial killers usually kill because of abuse they've suffered in the past. So, we could be looking for a woman who's been abused."

"Pay back, huh?"

"Could be."

"What else?"

"The wine bottle thing. It's a sexual act. Perverted but definitely sexual. Not likely the act of a heterosexual man. And I'm not buying homosexual—at least not at this point."

"Prints?"

"Looks like our killer's learning from experience. We've got two sets of prints on a couple of books in Beatty's place."

"Nothing from the last one?"

"Yeah, we got some prints off the floor near the bed. Everything else was wiped clean."

"You check the prints from Beatty through SATIS?"

"Yeah. Nobody arrested in the state since '85 with these prints. It only goes back that far."

"You got a serial killer on your hands, Frankie. You're sitting on a time bomb. It's going to go off again. Could be any time now. Hey, we gotta go. Game starts in fifteen minutes."

The Patriots won and Frank collected his twenty dollars. "You know Silvio, I commit a felony every time I bet on a game with you. It's stealing. What'd I tell you about Bledsoe? Four touchdown passes convince you?"

He walked his father to his car, before heading for his own. Take care, Dad. I'll call you this week."

"O.K., kid. Frankie?"

"What?"

"Sign the book contract."

Frank was back in his apartment by six o'clock. He made himself an Absolut Martini on the rocks with a twist and sat down with Eric Hickey's *Serial Murders and Their Victims*. "The prime marks of the serial murderer are a sense of rage and nagging revenge carried over from early childhood." He smiled. Read a hundred of these books. Learned more from the old man than from all of them together.

*  *  *

David Weltman's apartment building was one of those glass facades, opulent, marble covered lobby, pretentious Upper East Side structures designed to intimidate the hoi paloi. Frank rode up in the elevator with a man and woman who had to be heading for David's party. Her hair, down to her waist, was the color of a ripe banana and looked like it had just been pressed at the dry cleaners. His was only slightly shorter and he wore a diamond earring in each ear. They were both in expensive black leather. The elevator smelled like a tannery.

David greeted Frank with the same enthusiasm as when they met earlier. "Frankie, you made it."

Frank looked around at the beautiful people being served drinks and hors d'oeuvres by a battery of tuxedoed waiters. "Was I supposed to bring something? A six pack? Chips?"

David, pumping Frank's hand, greeting other guests, and warding off the caresses of a theatrical looking blonde, didn't hear a word he said. "Come in. Come in. Make yourself at home. Relax. Have a drink. Circulate." Frank knew he'd never remember to do all those things, but no matter. David had quickly disappeared into the crowd. He grabbed some champagne off one of the trays and turned into the outstretched hand of a woman who was a dead ringer for Barbra Streisand and about the same age.

"Hi, I'm Leslie Gordon."

Frank was startled by her voice. It was as deep as his. He shook her hand. "Hi. Frank Corso."

She held his hand, looking at him the way a mackerel eyes a minnow. "I didn't know David had such gorgeous friends."

The woman's perfume hit his nose like a line of cocaine. He felt a sneeze coming on. His hand remained firmly in her grip while the champagne glass balanced precariously in the other. "Excuse me," he said extricating his hand from Leslie just in time to reach his handkerchief and get it up to his nose a second before the sneeze exploded. "Sorry," he said. "Just a little pneumonia. Nice meeting you, Leslie."

He was into his second glass of champagne when an unmistakable voice from behind him whispered, "Excuse me, but I think I used to be married to you."

He wasn't sure whether to turn around or head for the door. He turned and stood eyeball to eyeball with the woman he hadn't talked with since the day after he'd found her in bed with another man.

"Hello, Frank," she offered her hand.

He stared helplessly at her, ignoring her hand. Déjà vu. He knew what she would say next, repeating the scene when they first met.

"You do shake hands, don't you?" the same husky, friendly tone.

The ice was broken and they both laughed. He took her hand. "I'd say that was a familiar scene."

"I'd say," she said. "How are you?"

"How am I? I don't know. I guess I was O.K. until a minute ago. Now, I'm not so sure."

Her eyes inspected him. He wished she wouldn't look at him like she did.

"You look elegantly handsome as always," she said.

"Thanks," he said. "No point in expressing the obvious about you. I'm sure you hear it every day."

Her eyes hardened for a moment, but regained their luster when she smiled. "It would be nice to hear it from you. It has been a while."

"Yes, it's been ten months and twenty-six days. You look very beautiful. How's that?"

The smile disappeared. "I forgot how direct you are, Frank."

"What'd you expect, small talk and bonbons?"

"Frank, I was excited to see you. In fact, I can't tell you the shiver I felt when I spotted you. I can understand how you feel. But what's done is done. If you don't want to talk, then I'll leave. No hard feelings."

"No hard feelings. Gee, aren't we magnanimous and forgiving." He didn't like what he was saying, but it just kept coming and he knew he'd pushed her too far.

"Go to hell, Frank," she said and started to walk away.

"Carla."

She stopped and turned. At that moment, she looked more beautiful and desirable than he had ever seen her.

"Sorry. You want some champagne?"

She hesitated and smiled. "Sure."

# Chapter Twenty-one

David Weltman's party was a haphazard affair with people coming and going all evening. The drinks flowed freely without interruption. Most people just nibbled from the buffet, while others took time out to sit and consume a whole meal. There was no set pattern or order to things, just wing it as you went along.

Carla and Frank found a quiet corner, where they sat with plates of shrimp, little medallions of beef, and a bottle of champagne Carla had liberated from the bar.

"David's kind of a wild man and so are his parties. People kill to come, though. He's very popular and you never know who you're going to see here," Carla said between bites of shrimp.

"Yeah. I met Barbra Streisand earlier," Frank said. She looked surprised and started to speak, but he continued. "So...no more Henry Manning, you're getting close to the big time in your career...very close from what I see and read in the papers and magazines. And there's no Mr. Perfect in your life right now?"

"There is no Mr. Perfect period," she said.

Frank held his hands out. "C'est moi."

"Close, but no cigar," she said. "You already have a mistress remember? She's called NYPD."

"Thanks. Just what I needed to hear from you."

"And speaking of your mistress, I gather she's keeping you busier than ever. I see your name in the papers, too, you know. They say you may have a serial killer on your hands now?"

"Oh, Jesus. You, too? Why can't I just eat shrimp and drink champagne and talk about sex and residuals like everybody else here?"

"Because this is more interesting. Are you making any progress? The media's giving you a bad time. Says you're not. That doesn't sound like you, Frank."

"The media's a crock. You of all people must know that by now. Anyway, look at those two over there. I don't think they're talking about serial killers. And they're definitely having more fun."

Carla looked over at a man and woman standing on the terrace, wrapped around each other, kissing and dry humping. "They may be having more fun, but I'll tell you what they don't have and that's class. Kind of a stupid display, if you ask me."

"Ooh. Prissy. Prissy."

"No, I'm not prissy Frank. I just get disgusted with vulgarity when I see it, that's all."

"Me, too. That why I hang out with cops."

"Very funny. Are you seeing anyone these days?"

"I see a lot of people."

"You know what I mean. Anyone special in your life?"

"No." Funny how Denise flashed into mind at that question. Maybe no wasn't quite the right answer. But at the moment, it was hard to imagine anything better than sitting in a quiet corner drinking champagne with the beautiful woman who had once been his wife. He hadn't expected this and was troubled at how quickly and easily he slid into it.

"Hard to believe," she said moving in close.

She smelled delicious and the urge to grab her and kiss her everywhere was making him dizzy. She sat looking at him, as if waiting for him to do just that.

The moment passed and she took a drink of champagne and glanced around the room. A young man stood near the bar, smiling, and nodding at her. Her eyes lit up and she jerked forward. She turned quickly to Frank. "Frank, I'm sorry. There's someone over there I must see. Excuse me." She pecked him on the cheek and made a bee line for the theatrical looking young man with the simpering smile.

"Nice going, stupid," Frank growled to himself and left.

\*　　\*　　\*

The week dragged on without much progress on the case. Frank was tired and wondered if he shouldn't have gone to medical school after all. Maybe it wasn't too late. No, he didn't want to be a doctor. Maybe he'd chuck it all and write full time. Sure. Make just enough to live in a Bronx rooming house with a hot plate.

He was still angry with himself for letting Carla make such a fool out of him. When he walked into the precinct, Harry spotted him and came over.

"Frank, they found a guy murdered in an alley off Forty-first Street near Seventh Avenue."

"Big deal. Guys are found murdered in alleys in this city every day."

"Yeah, but there's something about this one."

"What do you mean?"

"The guy was clobbered with a blunt instrument, but that's not what killed him."

"What did?"

"His head was bashed up and down on the pavement, maybe fifteen, twenty times."

"Oh, oh. Wine bottle?"

"No, no wine bottle, but I don't like the looks of this."

"Neither do I."

"Nolan's got Sullivan and Levine on this one but he wants you and me to liaison with them."

"O.K. You work with them, Harry. You got an aspirin?"

*      *      *

Paul Gale knew his days at Breda's restaurant were numbered. "Gale, you're not only stupid, but you sloppy, too. You can't even wash dishes right, you are so stupid. Look at the floor. You spilled more food on the floor, than you scraped into the slop buckets. You so stupid Gale, you should be back in jail. That's where you belong."

Gale's eyes flared.

"Yes, I know about you, jailbird. I don't think I like jailbirds working in my kitchen, Now, pick-up that food off the floor, you slob."

Gale snapped. "You son of a bitch," he roared. "Get off my back. I'm doin' my job. What do you want from me?"

Peter poked his finger at Gale's chest taunting him. "Vot's da matter, Gale? Can't take it? Maybe I fire you and then you don't take no more shit, huh? Maybe you quit, huh, jailbird?"

Vince entered the kitchen just as Gale lunged. He stepped between Gale and Peter, and pushed Gale hard against the wall. He held the other hand out toward Peter.

"Stay right there Gale. Don't move."

Gale leaned against the kitchen wall, breathing in long labored heaves. Sweat poured off his face, as he glared malevolently at Peter. His lips were parted, the gold tooth glistened with spit.

"One move. Make one move, Gale and you're gone" Vince said. "We'll have your ass out of here so fast, you won't know what hit you. Now stay there and calm down and relax. Peter, you come over here with me." He led Peter around the corner of the kitchen, and into the little cubbyhole of an office.

"Peter, I don't know what brought all this on, but you've been riding him something awful lately. Let up a little. The guy works hard, and he's lasted longer than most dishwashers we've had. He's not as bad as some of the idiots we've had here. Now ease up."

"I fire the son of a bitch. I don't like him," Peter hissed.

"Peter, you can't fire him right now. We need him. You got nobody around to do his work. Give it a couple of weeks or so and see how it goes. If you insist on firing him, then so be it, but give us some time to get somebody else lined up, O.K.?" He gently tapped Peter on the jaw with his closed fist.

Peter nodded and inhaled deeply. "O.K., Vince. I follow your advice for a while. But I don't like him. I don't vant him here."

Gale was still leaning against the wall. He had overheard most of the conversation and knew he would soon be gone. He couldn't afford to wait any longer.

At seven o'clock that night Gale left his room and hailed a cab. The cab dropped him three blocks from his daughter's apartment. He stepped into the darkened doorway of a jewelry store to collect his thoughts. His fingers rested on the knife in his pocket. A man wearing a torn woolen shirt, filthy summer weight pants and sneakers approached him.

"Hey buddy. I'm homeless and hungry. Can you spare some change so I can get a bite to eat?" He moved to within a foot or two of Gale.

"Get the hell outta here," Gale snarled, pushing the man in the chest.

The bum moved back toward him. "Hey mister. You don't have to get so tough. I'm only askin' for a little help. What's a matter with you."

Gale flashed his knife. "I said bug off or I'll cut your guts out."

The man's eyes widened. He turned and fled.

Gale watched him and wished he'd stuck the knife into him. He spat on the sidewalk.

He reached the apartment building, opened the door, and entered the small vestibule. Twelve mailboxes lined one side of the wall. Opposite them were the names and apartment numbers of the tenants.

He stood alone in the dim hallway, the sound of his own breathing deafening in the small silent space. So close now. He could barely focus on the tenants' names. Then, there it was. He smiled and rang the bell.

No answer. "Be home, you bitch," he whispered. Again, he rang and again no answer. Finally, on the third ring, a response. The voice sounded impatient. "Yes, what is it?"

"UPS, ma'am. I got a package for you. Need your signature."

No response for a moment and then the voice, again impatient. "Oh, for God's sake. I was in the bathtub. What's the package? Who's it from?"

"Don't know, ma'am. It's just a small package." Gale shifted from one foot to the other and glanced nervously over his shoulder.

"Well…I can't come down. I'm all wet, and I don't feel well. Please come back tomorrow and ring the Super's bell. I'll authorize him to sign for it."

Sweat trickled off his forehead and dripped onto the small package he held. He looked at the bank of names and saw "Superintendent, 1A." No way!

"Hello?" the voice called.

"Uh, ma'am, I can't leave it for someone else to sign. I'm afraid you have to sign personally."

The voice hesitated. Gale's heart pounded. He held his breath, waiting, his hand clutching the doorknob. Finally, the exasperated reply came. "Oh, dammit. All right. I'm on the fifth floor, but wait a minute."

He couldn't believe his ears. He slowly exhaled and smiled, picturing her nude body, stepping into her panties, slipping on clothes, getting ready to receive him. It's gonna happen.

The buzzer sounded. Gale turned the doorknob and entered. He stood inside the hallway, fondling first himself and then the reassuring steel of the knife. The building was quiet as he slowly began walking up the stairs. Not a good idea to take the elevator. When he reached the third level, he stopped. The climb and the excitement building within him were almost too much. The sound of his breathing echoed through the empty stairwell. So close now. He hoped his dark wind breaker would look like a UPS jacket. Once she opened the door, it would be too late for her. His mind raced as he slowly resumed his way up the stairs.

What if she didn't open the door beyond the chain? What if she asked him to slip the receipt through the door with the chain lock still on? Those chain locks weren't worth a shit. He was sure he could rip the chain connector off the wall with one strong push. No problem.

He stood in front of 5B. Eighteen years of waiting and now all that stood between him was a door and a flimsy chain lock. He had suffered and waited for so long and now it was going to happen just as he had dreamed all those nights lying in the cell she had put him in. Trickles of sweat rolled down his chest, stopping at the elastic of his underwear. He rearranged the bulge in his crotch and wiped his forehead. Footsteps sounded from the other side of the door, and after a deep breath and another swipe at his forehead, he rang the bell.

"Yes?" The voice came from near the door.

"UPS Ma'am."

Locks began clicking and a bolt slid. The door slowly opened about four or five inches, as far as the chain lock would allow. A partial face appeared but enough to reassure Gale that it was the face he was looking for. He stood at an angle from her line of vision, his body poised and ready to hurl against the door, his breathing louder than ever in the silence of the hallway. He tightened his grip around the knife in his pocket. Before either could speak, the phone rang from inside.

"Oh, excuse me", the voice said and the door closed. Locks and bolts clicked and slid, and the footsteps moved away from the door.

"Son of a bitch," Gale murmured and leaned his back against the wall next to the door. He closed his eyes and waited.

"Hi. How are you?"

"I'm fine but I've got a UPS man at the door, and I have to sign for a package. I can't talk to you right now. Let me call you back."

"I was just wondering if you'd like to meet for a drink"

"No, not tonight. But I do have to run and sign for the UPS package."

"O.K. but you don't have to sign for UPS. Just tell him to leave it."

"Yes, I do have to sign. He said so. Now, let me call you back.

"You don't have to sign for UPS packages. I get them all the time. It seems late for a UPS man, anyway. I wouldn't open the door if it were me."

The woman never took her eyes off the door. Her stomach tightened. "I've got to go." She hung up and walked slowly toward the door.

"Are you still out there?" she asked, raising her voice to a shout.

"Yes, ma'am, but I'm runnin' real late. Can you sign this so I can get going?"

She backed away from the door. "Excuse me, but either leave the package and go, or I'm calling the police."

"What's this shit?" Gale mumbled. He started to speak to her but she interrupted him.

"As a matter of fact, I'm calling them right now." She picked up the phone, but held the button down with one finger, and walked toward the door. "Hello, police. There's a man outside my door, who won't go away." In a loud voice, she gave her address and apartment number and told them to hurry.

There was no question the man had heard her. She stood just inches from the door, listening. Her stomach churned and she suddenly had to go to the bathroom but was afraid to leave the door. She could hear the slow, steady breathing outside her door, then mumbling, shuffling, and finally, footsteps moving quickly down the stairs. She went to the window and looked down on the street. After a moment, a short stocky man, wearing a dark jacket and a baseball cap appeared, crossed the street, and moved quickly out of sight. She shuddered and double checked her locks. She had heard of similar things happening to other women in New York, but decided to try and put the incident out of her mind and go to bed.

Paul Gale was in a desperate rage. So close. He squeezed the knife in his pocket, and started walking across town. As he neared Lexington Avenue, a raspy voice sounded from the doorway of an antique shop.

"Hey, pal. Can you spare some change for a homeless person?"

Gale turned and recognized the bum from earlier. He moved toward the figure standing in the shadows and edged into the doorway with him. He looked up and down the street. A couple holding hands walked along the opposite side of the street. Another couple strolled about fifty yards ahead on his side, no one else. He reached into his pocket "How much do you need?" he asked.

"Oh man. A couple of bucks would get me some hot soup, and I'd thank you, thank you so much." The man moved out of the shadows toward Gale. They were nearly touching. "Oh Jesus Christ. It's you," the man gasped. Gale spread his legs, blocking the doorway.

"Yeah, it's me, but here, I got somethin' for ya. I'm not really such a bad guy."

The man smiled and held his hand out. "Thank God," he said, as Gale plunged the knife deep into his stomach and pushed him back into the doorway. Blood belched from the man's stomach, when Gale withdrew the knife. The bum's eyes bulged and his mouth fell open.

Gale held him by the shoulder with his left hand, while his right hand moved in a quick left to right motion across the man's throat. Blood and gore spilled onto the store window and the sidewalk. A watery gurgle escaped from the dying man's throat, and he slumped to the ground.

"Now you don't need no soup, asshole," Gale hissed.

# Chapter Twenty-two

Only six a.m. and she'd been lying in bed wide awake for fifteen minutes. Her head felt like she'd been hit with a hammer and the dull heavy abdominal ache that had awakened her now expanded into biting cramps. The headaches always came when she was agitated and upset.

The UPS man. She shivered and pulled the blanket up under her chin. "I'm runnin' real late. Can you sign so I can get goin'?" The rasp in his voice. How could she have been so stupid. She wasn't thinking. That's why.

Of course it was he. He knew where she lived, probably knew a whole lot more. She would have to be careful. He's watching, tracking. And then she smiled. When I'm ready, he will find me.

The smile disappeared She clutched her stomach in pain and rolled into a fetal position. Tears welled and trickled down her face. She unwound and pulled herself slowly out of bed. The movement accelerated the pain in her head, but three Percodan would help. She also took a Darvon for the cramps and made her way back into bed. There was no way she could go anywhere today. Her only obligation would be to herself, to stay in bed and hope the pain in her head, her stomach, and her mind would let up.

\*     \*     \*

Paul Gale finished his work day at the restaurant. Last night he had come so close and he would have had her except for that fucking phone call. He pulled the collar of his jacket up, tightened his baseball cap, and bent into the wind.

Today at work was the worst yet. "Clean the slop bucket, jailbird and after that you go scrub the toilets. That's good work for you, jailbird. You just a piece of shit, too. You feel right at home."

The whole day had been like that and Gale knew he couldn't take it much longer. But he would have to. He had her pattern down pretty good now, and his chance would come soon.

*    *    *

At seven o'clock the woman got out of bed. She'd been sleeping off and on for most of the day, getting up only for more pills. The cramps were nearly gone but she took another Darvon just in case.

She was famished. The apartment was hot and stuffy and she felt fidgety, irritable, out of sorts. She needed fresh air. Without bothering to shower, she splashed on some Jean Naté and quickly dressed in black slacks and sweater. The Jean Naté smelled fresh and clean, just as it did when her mother used it. Memories of her mother came back whenever she put it on.

The night was bitter cold, but no matter. She needed to walk, walk off the anger that was building again.

She walked several blocks, picking up speed as she went along. The more she focused on last night, the more foul her mood, and the faster she walked.

He had actually come to her home, right to her doorstep. She clenched her fists and cursed.

A man of about fifty approached her from the other direction and smiled at her. "Slow down honey. The night's young."

She blew by him, then slowed, and stopped. She turned and so did he. She stood for a moment, looking at him, the stupid smile still on his face. He was short and stocky. The overcoat he wore, fashionably long looked ridiculous on his little short body. It was also too tight around his middle.

She was about to turn and continue on when he spoke again. "You keep walking that fast, you're going to run somebody over." He took a couple of steps toward her.

She watched him approach. And waited.

He took another few steps and stood next to her. "Cold night for a pretty lady like you be out walking alone."

She wanted to wipe the silly smile off his face. But she said nothing, just stared at him.

The smile broadened. His hand went out. "Hi. I'm Phil Chesbro."

Her hand went up slowly. He took it and squeezed it and put his other over hers, like they were old friends. That was probably what did it.

She was back into the world of her own creation, a world dominated by her fantasy of violence where there is no obedience to rules. "Hi," she said.

"What's your name?" he asked.

"My friends call me Lucky."

"You always walk that fast?" He was still holding her hand.

"Yes."

He moved closer. "Well, it's pretty cold tonight. That's a good way to stay warm. I got a better idea though on how to beat it." He nodded his head toward the cafe next to where they stood. "How about if we go in here for a drink?"

She looked down at his hands, still covering hers. He was rubbing it now, probably getting worked up about the progress he was making.

She studied the man holding her hands. His fat face rippled around the obnoxious smile. Come to me, she willed. Come to me.

# Chapter Twenty-three

Jerry Blodgett headed across the precinct bullpen toward Frank Corso's desk. Frank saw him coming and braced himself.

"Get Harry and come into my office," Jerry growled. He continued toward his office, head down, his massive body rolling from side to side. "I just left Nolan's office. Took another sack of shit from him. Last night's murder confirmed his worst nightmare. He's got a serial killer on his hands he tells me."

Frank and Harry looked at each other. "Smart cop," Frank said. "No wonder he's a captain."

"Cut it out, Frank," Jerry snapped.

Harry had been about to add a crack of his own but thought better of it. "What'd he say, Jerry?" he asked.

"What do you think he said? He wants results. Now! He's taking this personally. That wife of his doesn't want to be married to a shitbird captain for too much longer. This is a man feeling pressure from a lot of directions. He's gotta let some out of the bottle and guess who's getting it? Anyway, what've you guys got?"

"I was just writing up the report on this morning's investigations when you hauled us in here," Frank said.

"You finished?"

"Pretty much."

"Go get it."

Jerry paced back and forth. Harry sat quietly, watching Jerry's shirt-tail flap up and down.

Frank returned, thumbing through his report. "Guy was found by his cleaning lady about eight this morning. She knocked several times, then let herself in. Found him on the floor of the living room next to the sofa. Head bashed in with a wine bottle. Hit at least three times. This time the bottle broke. Then his head was smashed up and down on the floor again. Hardwood floor. Full of blood. His head was cracked, maybe a dozen times on the floor."

"What've you got on him?" Jerry asked.

Frank referred to a small notebook. "Phillip Chesbro, forty-seven years old. Divorced six years. No kids. Ex-wife in St. Louis. He lived on West Thirty-fourth Street, not far from Joey Brewer He was an insurance salesman. Worked for Metropolitan."

"No forced entry?"

"None. Whoever did it just strolled politely through the door, sat on the couch with the late Mr. Chesbro, they had some wine together and he got whacked," Frank said. "Maybe the killer was a wine lover, offended by the wine Chesbro served. Real panther piss."

"You say the wine bottle broke?" Jerry asked.

"Yeah, but there was another in reserve." Jerry started to speak and Frank nodded before he could get it out. "Yep. Same as Beatty and Brewer."

Jerry nodded. "These are random picks. But why?"

"Jerry, I'm more convinced it's a woman doing this," Frank said.

"Why?"

"We've got a faint smell of perfume on the body. There's also a touch on the back of the sofa where the killer probably sat. I don't think there's enough for us to do anything with."

"Could be men's cologne?"

"No. It's more like a perfume. Anyway, we checked the victim's cologne. He had several bottles. Totally different from this."

"Could be his visitor's?"

"Could be. But I don't think it's a men's cologne." Frank looked at the picture of Jerry's wife Betty on his desk. Even at fifty-six she was a beautiful woman. Under the picture was a date written and circled. It was Jerry's retirement date, now less than a year away. Nolan wasn't the only one getting nervous about this case.

"We've got some prints out of Chesbro's apartment. They don't match the ones we got from Beatty's place, but the ridges on the prints in both cases suggest that they're female prints. I know we can't be conclusive about that, but our killer could be a woman."

"Guy was single," Jerry said. "Must've had women up there from time to time. What else have we got?"

"We've got hair fibers again. Not sure, but they appear to be from a wig. We'll find out from the lab. We've also got his address book with a whole lot of names and phone numbers in it. Mostly people here in Manhattan, Queens, Brooklyn, and a few, out on the Island. He was an insurance agent. Most of them are probably clients or leads. We'll have them all checked out."

"Best lead we have so far is the woman with Joey Brewer," Jerry said. "Gotta be a hooker. Why else would a good looking woman like that be with Brewer? Bartender said she seemed spaced out. A hooker on drugs. That's how she winds up with a loser like Brewer."

"Yeah, and so far none of the hookers know from nothin'," Harry broke in. "The ones that fit the description all have alibis."

"Yeah. They were probably all with you," Jerry said.

"Cut it out Jerry. That's not funny."

"Wasn't supposed to be. Hell, you're our hooker specialist. You oughta' be able to find out who's bullshitting us."

"We're still checking them out Jerry," Harry whined.

"The guys who roughed up Joey in Barney's don't really have an alibi for that night," Frank said. "Claim they went to the Alcazar after Barney's then to a pizza joint and home. Alcazar and the pizza joint check out. After that they can't substantiate their whereabouts. I think they're hiding something but I don't think they did Joey. Couldn't shake anything out of them when we brought them in, but we're not ruling them out."

"No indication that Chesbro was a client?" Jerry said.

"No. Not yet, but we're working on it. And there's no indication anywhere that they knew Beatty. Beatty had a bank account with fifty-two hundred dollars in it. No withdrawals for almost a year. Nothing but deposits. We didn't turn up any financial problems. I'm satisfied there's no connection there."

"I'll check with the lab on the hairs." Harry said. He was still smarting from Jerry's crack about the hookers.

"O.K.," Jerry said. "I gotta go. Nolan wants me downtown for a meeting at the Commissioner's office. Guess what it's about." He drummed a pencil up and down on his desk.

Harry turned and left, Frank stayed, watching the pain in his friend's face.

"Two weeks between the Beatty and Brewer murders," Jerry said. "Ten days between Brewer and Chesbro. My gut feeling tells me we're gonna have another one soon." He looked up. Frank thought how tired he looked. "How often am I wrong on my hunches, Frank?"

"Not often," Frank said.

\*　　\*　　\*

"Wine Bottle Killer Strikes Again."

"Number Three For Wine Bottle Killer."

"Who's Next?"

"Serial Killer Claims Another Victim."

It was so weird. She had started out killing quite by accident. But now, she felt energized and renewed with each adventure. She hoped he was reading about her. She wished he knew it was her. Hopes and wishes.

She read each article over and over again. Even the *New York Times* had it on the second page. But she didn't like the small headline. "Serial Killer Claims Another Victim."

The *Daily News* and the *Post* were front page. She was the wine bottle killer, a serial killer. And she was a celebrity.

\*       \*       \*

Frank's life was getting complicated. The message on his machine from Denise was warm and friendly. No, more than friendly. "Frank, I miss you. Please give me a call." Short and sweet but for Denise, practically a proposition. He smiled as her voice rattled around in his head. Nice voice.

And Carla was back in his life. The brief time he spent with her at Weltman's party accentuated the scary fact that he still wasn't over her. Even though she had dumped on him again leaving him almost in mid-sentence, she had left her mark and he knew she knew it! And something told him she would be calling.

Running through it all and dominating most of his time and thoughts was the goddamn wine bottle killer. Vultures in the media even had him referring to it as the wine bottle killings. Jerry was right. Somebody is very angry out there. And the way the fury was directed could only be sexual. An angry woman or a violent homosexual. He was betting on the woman.

\*       \*       \*

Denise returned to her office after a meeting with Mike. She had just settled into her chair when she looked up and saw Frank Corso standing in the doorway.

"Hi," he said. When he smiled her hand hit the pencil holder and sent pencils clattering along the floor.

"Frank," she mumbled. A funny feeling hit her stomach.

"Sorry if I startled you." He gathered up her pencils. "Can I sit down?"

"Sure. Sure. My God. What a surprise!"

He moved toward her and kissed her lightly on the lips. His presence filled up the small office. He looked like one of the editors in his tweed jacket, khaki colored slacks, dark blue shirt, and dark tie. She also thought he looked very sexy. She wanted to touch his hair curling around his ears and collar. They both sat awkwardly looking at one another for a moment.

"I was just driving by with my partner and decided to stop in and say hello."

"Hello," she said, surprised at the huskiness in her voice. "How'd you find my office in this maze?"

He grinned. "Well, the receptionist was very helpful."

"Why am I not surprised?"

"Harry's double parked and probably given himself a ticket by now, so I have to run."

She felt the disappointment and actually made a face.

"What I wanted to ask you though is if you're not doing anything on Sunday, you might like to sort of make a day of it. You know like maybe take a walk in the park if it's not too cold, have some lunch and or dinner, a drink, shopping, movie, a trip to Havana?"

"Havana?"

"Just wanted to see if you're listening. What do you say?"

"Sounds great," she said.

"I'll call you in a day or so about the time and all."

"Hey, Dennie, can you help me with…?" Gina careened into the small office nearly bumping into Frank. "Oh, excuse me." She eyed Frank with the same predatory look Denise had seen with the waiter at the Wave. "Sorry," she said, never taking her eyes off Frank. "Didn't know you had company."

Denise introduced them and Frank eased his way out before Gina could get into her routine. "Nice meeting you Gina. I'll call you Denise."

"WHO was that?" Gina demanded.

"A friend of mine."

"A friend of mine," Gina mocked. "There's not a woman alive who'd just be a friend of a guy who looks like that. Where've you been hiding him? What's his name?"

"Down, Fang. His name's Frank and I met him at the health club and sorry to disappoint you, but we are just friends."

"Jesus," Gina rumbled. "He's a doll. What's he do?"

"He's a cop."

"A what?"

"A cop. Actually, he's a homicide detective."

"You're kidding."

Denise shook her head.

"What's he want with you?"

"What do you mean, what's he want with me? You think he was here to arrest me?"

"No, no, I just,…I mean…"

"Gina, you're mumbling."

"Sorry, guess I'm just jealous that you found him first."

\*       \*       \*

Frank walked into his apartment and slumped into a chair. It had been a long miserable day, tracking down leads that led nowhere. In and out of bars, trying to talk with evasive, uncooperative hookers and another session with the two ,Tony and Ron, the friendly loan sharks.

"It ain't gonna be easy, Frankie." His father's advice came back to him.

Dropping in to see Denise gave him a big lift. Best part of his day. He hadn't stopped thinking about her since leaving her office. Now he felt like a kid looking forward to Sunday. The next few days would feel like a month. The phone rang. "Hello."

"Hello, Frank. It's Carla."

The deep voice purred the way a cat would probably sound if it could talk. Something kicked his stomach.

"Hi."

"Oh. The enthusiasm of one hand clapping."

"Well, let's see. The last I saw of you, you trampled six people lunging toward some guy with an earring and too much hair. His parents bring him to the party?"

"Very funny. I know it was rude, the way I left so abruptly. I called to apologize."

He was about to zing her again but thought better of it. "It's O.K.," he said.

"Frank. I did enjoy seeing you. A lot. I meant it when I said I've missed you. I just thought maybe you'd like to get together just the two of us, you know when we both have some time with these crazy schedules."

Oh Jesus, he thought. Don't do this. "When did you have in mind?"

"Well, I'm sure with this serial killer case you must be straight out day and night."

He waited for her to continue but she stopped. After waiting another beat, he replied. "Yeah. I'd say I've been busy."

"Any progress?"

"Not much. How about you?" he asked, wanting to change the subject. "From what you were telling me the other night, you don't have much free time either."

"I'm free this Sunday. All day. All yours," the purring again.

Why do you do this to me? he wanted to say. It was just like her. Vintage Carla with the sixth sense, the instinct for the jugular. Sunday!

"Frank?"

"I'm thinking. I'm thinking. I had something doing Sunday and…"

"We could go out for lunch, go to the new exhibit at the Museum of Modern Art and back here later where I'll make you dinner." Her voice sounded like her lips were resting on the phone speaker. He could almost smell her.

"Ah, well…" He wanted to ask her what she was wearing at that moment. He wanted to ask her if they could make love on Sunday. He wanted to ask her if she would be his girl again. Instead he thought of Denise and asked her if he could take a rain check for another time.

"Oh?" The lips were no longer resting on the speaker. "You mean you can't change your plans or you won't?"

"I guess it means both."

"Well, I guess I understand, thank you. Maybe another time."

"Yeah. I'll call you."

"Sure. Bye bye."

"Bye."

Her phone clicked and he sat holding his, staring at nothing, listening to the silence. Finally, he hung it up. Hard.

"Frankie, I'm proud of you," he said aloud.

# Chapter Twenty-four

Sunday turned out to be the kind of day Frank had been hoping for all week, sunny and warm. By the time he met Denise at Tavern on the Green in Central Park it was an unseasonable sixty degrees.

"Denise, only tourists go to Tavern on the Green," he protested over the phone.

"I don't care. I've always wanted to go there and I never have. Come on, Frank. It's a famous place."

She also insisted on meeting there rather than him picking her up. "It'll be so much easier than you coming all the way over here and we just turn around and leave again."

There was no arguing with her logic. He got there early, claimed their table, and had just ordered a beer when he saw her come in the door. He got a kick out of watching her speak to the maitre d', then look over his shoulder, scanning the room. He waved but she didn't see him. The maitre d' led her toward his table and she broke out in a big grin and waved when she spotted him. He knew it was going to be a great day.

"You look fabulous," he said as she settled in. He took his time, looking her over, admiring her. She was wearing a soft white sweater, hoop earrings, and dark blue pants. Her eyes and hair sparkled and her face looked like she had just washed it in milk. "You also look happy," he said. You must have had a good week."

"It was O.K. Maybe I look happy because I'm about to have lunch with you in Tavern on the Green."

"Sounds good to me."

Lunch was one of those languorous, unhurried affairs. With nowhere to go, no schedules, no appointments, they drifted through it, sharing a bottle of wine and each other.

Frank loved watching her. He liked the way she sipped her wine, never taking more than a half dram at a time. She'd catch him watching her and nervously look away, then dart her eyes back to him.

Every once in a while he would catch her little half smile, her way of telling him she was enjoying herself. It was like she wanted him to know that but wasn't sure how to express it.

"Dennie, tell me about yourself. Where are you from? How long have you been in New York? Any family? What...?"

"Whoa. Slow down, officer," she interrupted. "You've got to leave a woman with a little mystery."

"Hey, right now you're all mystery. I know you work for a publisher and you like decorating and working out in your health club. And you like famous restaurants. That's it."

She laughed. "Maybe that's enough for now. Actually, you've just about covered it all. I'm really pretty boring I guess." She took one of her quick little sips of the wine. "My mother and father are both dead. I've been in New York for about five years. I guess you'd say I'm kind of a loner. Keep pretty much to myself." She laughed again. "And yes, I do have a passion for decorating."

"O.K." He waited but she was finished. It didn't seem like anything more was coming. "That ought to hold me for a while. You forgot one thing. You're even more beautiful when you laugh. You should do it more often."

After lunch they walked through Central Park. It was one of those rare fall days, more like early October than mid-November. The temperature had soared to sixty-five degrees and bright sunshine baked the brown leaves on the ground so they crunched like popcorn underfoot.

"Come on, let's catch a few rays." He led her up a small hill, where they sprawled in the grass under the warm sun.

"What about you, Frank?"

He sat up. "What do you mean?"

"Well, I don't know much about you either. For all I know you could be married. Are you?"

"No."

"Were you ever?"

"Yes."

"I feel like I'm playing twenty questions. Is that how your suspects answer you when you're grilling them?"

"We don't grill people. We interrogate them. Good word, though." He put his arm around her and was surprised at how quickly and easily she snuggled into him. "I was married for a while. It didn't work out."

"I'm sorry. Where is she now?"

"Here in New York."

She turned her face to look at him. "Do you ever see her?"

"Funny you should ask. I hadn't seen her for a year, not since we split up. The other night I went to a party and she was there. We talked for a while before she spotted some young stud she knew and sprinted away."

"Too bad," she said, some distance in her voice.

"No, it wasn't."

"Were you glad to see her?"

"No," he lied.

"Think you'll see her again?"

"Hey, this is twenty questions. First of all, I barely have time these days to see myself in the mirror to shave. Secondly, if and when I do get some free time, I'd much rather see you." He paused. "Than her or anybody else."

She moved in closer and when she did, he kissed her. She responded, at first tentatively, then he felt a shiver pass along her body. They kissed hungrily, the way lonely people do. Some kids walked by, giggling. Neither heard them.

She moved her lips away and whispered into his ear. "Oh, Frank."

He maneuvered to kiss her again but she spotted the four giggling kids standing watching them. She slid away. "My God! Here we are necking in broad daylight in Central Park."

"Yeah. Great, huh?"

"Yes, and no," she said, getting up. "Yes, it's great and no, not here. Come on. Let's go." She pulled him to his feet.

They left the park and walked along Fifth Avenue holding hands.

"That was nice back there," he said.

"Yes, it was."

They walked in comfortable silence for a while. He watched a police car cruise by. The two uniforms inside looked bored. A siren wailed in the distance. Today he was just a citizen for a change. He liked that.

In the park joggers came and went, stylish in the colorful warm-ups they didn't need in the warm sunshine. Was the weather really beautiful whenever he was with her or did it just seem that way?

"So…what else do you do besides be a cop?" she asked.

"I do some writing, teach a little, go to an occasional football or basketball game. And I like to cook when I have the time, which isn't very often."

"What kind of writing do you do?"

"Mostly about police work, investigative techniques, things of that kind. Nothing very creative."

"That's interesting, Frank. Where does your stuff appear?"

"Oh, some really exciting places like *The Encyclopedia of American Crime, The Journal of Forensic Science, Criminal Justice Quarterly*. You know, the kind of stuff everybody has on their coffee table.

"Sounds impressive to me. How's the Wine Bottle Killer case coming?"

"It's not."

"Any progress?"

"No more than what you read in the papers. Hey, let's grab a cab."

"To where?"

"The best Italian dinner in New York. My place."

*     *     *

"I don't believe you, Frank," Denise said, trying to get used to the taste of the brandy she was sipping. "This dinner was a work of art. Let's see. Fettucini with Gorgonzola sauce, Caesar salad, charcoal broiled chicken marinated in pepper, oil, and lemon. Did I get it all?"

"Don't forget the vanilla ice cream with the little macaroons."

"Where did you learn to cook like that?"

"From my parents. Actually, my dad's the real cook. I learned more from him. It's been sort of one of our things together"

"Well, the whole meal was delicious. I'm stuffed."

They sat on the couch in the small living room, sipping brandy and listening to Pavarotti on CD.

"It's been a wonderful day, Frank. Just lovely."

"It's not over." He reached over and gently pulled her toward him. She slid easily into the space between his shoulder and neck. Her hair brushing against his face tickled him. As he adjusted his face downward toward her, she looked up and they kissed. This one began like the one in the park and accelerated as quickly. Their mouths went open, groping exploring, nibbling on one another. He felt a hollow aching beginning in his throat and move through his body as he held her in his arms. He barely managed to whisper her name. "Denise."

"Oh, God!" She arched her back and rolled over on top of him. They kissed and explored one another, groping, moaning, their breathing coming in strangled bursts.

Frank caressed her breasts, then moved his hand down to the two buttons of her slacks. He opened her slacks, slid his hand down, and gently touched her.

She scrambled to her feet. "No, Frank." Her voice was husky and heavy. "Not so soon. Not tonight. I've got to go. It's late."

Frank lay back, still catching his breath, the moment gone. "You're going to go and leave me for dead?"

She stood, her back to him, straightening her clothes. After a few moments, she turned and managed a laugh. "Sorry, Frank. I know it's cruel and unusual punishment. For me, too." She leaned over and kissed him lightly and caressed his face. "You're a wonderful man, Frank Corso. I'm glad we met."

He still hadn't pulled himself together. His head lolled crazily against the couch pillow. "O.K., if you have to go, you have to go. I understand...I think." He got up and stood next to her.

"I do, Frank. And thanks again for a fabulous day. Call me.... Soon?"

He was breathing normally again. "You bet I will." They kissed goodnight and she was halfway out the door when he called.

"Dennie?"

She turned.

He wanted to say something but he wasn't sure what. "Goodnight."

It had been a great day but he hadn't figured on the abrupt ending. Maybe he'd been out of practice too long. Losing his touch. No. He should have known. Denise Johnson is a class act not a woman who hops in the sack on the first date.

He shivered out of the shower, quickly dried himself, and poured a scotch on the rocks.. He sat on the couch and closed his eyes. Her smell was still there. Beautiful, sensitive, vulnerable, sensuous...complicated lady. Nice. Very nice.

# Chapter Twenty-five

Denise took a long hot bubble bath when she arrived home from Frank's. It had been a wonderful day, her best ever in New York. She felt comfortable and safe with Frank. He wasn't one of those wise guys, overly impressed with himself. No, he treated her with respect, like a lady should be treated. Frank Corso was a gentleman Most men swaggered through life, demanding, insensitive. Frank was different.

She could see the women in the restaurant looking at him. She watched their eyes follow him as they walked along Fifth Avenue. She saw them look her up and down as if wondering what it is she has to be holding hands with a man like that. She wasn't sure herself. Maybe he was just playing her along, out for one thing. It didn't take him long to get his hands in her pants.

The water had turned cold and her body felt dank and chilled. She shivered as she toweled her body and quickly put on her pajamas. Eleven o'clock but she wasn't tired. Thumbing through one of her *Architectural Digests,* she saw a small living room not unlike hers and liked the arrangement. It took her only fifteen minutes to rearrange her room. First the couch went over to the other side under the three windows. The table lamp that had been next to her wing chair and the pharmacy lamp near the slipper chair were placed on either end of the sofa. And she knew just the lamp she would buy at Bloomingdales to place on the table she now had between her chairs. She completed all the other little touches, moving so quickly, she was perspiring. She loved her apartment. It was the nicest one she'd had yet in New York.

Now, she did feel tired, more a physical exhaustion and fell into bed. The restlessness returned and she picked up the phone.

"Hello." He sounded sleepy. She pictured him lying in bed in the dark, probably in his underwear.

"Did I wake you up?"

No answer. Was he trying to decide who it was before committing himself? She wished she hadn't called.

"No."

"This is Dennie," she blurted, still not sure he knew.

"No kidding. You think I don't recognize that beautiful voice? I thought you'd be sound asleep by now."

"No. I just felt like calling you and thanking you again for a wonderful day. I loved it."

"So did I," he said. "You know what?"

"What?"

"I was just going to call you."

"Well, I'm glad I beat you to it. But you can call me, soon, I hope."

"Tomorrow soon enough?"

"Perfect. Good night."

*         *         *

At eleven o'clock Monday morning, Frank called. "Dennie, I only have a minute but I just wanted to call and say hello."

She rocked back in her chair. "Hi! You've brightened up my day."

"Mine, too. Listen, we're straight out here and it doesn't look like it's going to get any better. I want to see you soon, but can we just play it by ear this week 'til I can see some daylight? I don't want to make a date and then have to cancel. Let's talk during the week and maybe shoot for something toward the end like Friday." He waited for a reply, but when none came, he continued. "Dennie, I hate being so vague and I don't want to screw up your plans. If something comes up for you, I'll understand. But I really am dying to see you soon."

She wished she didn't feel so disappointed. But she did. Now, she had to sound casual, like everything was O.K. "Sure, I understand, Frank. Call me this week and we'll try for Friday night. What's going on? Anything you can talk about?"

"It's this wine bottle killer. We're just under a lot of pressure. I gotta go. Call you soon." And he was gone.

At three o'clock Gina popped her head over Denise's cubicle. "Hey, Dennie. Let's go downstairs and get a coke or some tea. Come on, you need a break."

Gina was right. She did need a break. It had not been a good day.

The coffee shop was crowded but they found a small table. "Does anybody ever work in this building?" Denise asked. "No matter what time of day you come in here, it's crowded."

Gina looked around. "Yeah, that waitress over there with the cute little body probably makes more than the two of us together. Hey, I called you a few times yesterday to see if you wanted to go to the movies, but no answer. You must've been gone all day on a hot date."

Denise smiled. "I was."

"Oh? Anybody I know?"

"Frank. Remember the guy I introduced you to the other day in my office?"

"Oh Jesus. I just saw him today. I was having lunch with a friend over by one of the police stations on Forty-fifth Street, and I saw him walking down the street." She leaned over and spoke in a half whisper. "Hate to tell you this, Dennie, but a beautiful woman was hanging on to his arm. I thought for a minute it was you. She looked a little like you."

Denise's stomach tightened and she put down her cup. "How nice of you to tell me."

Gina touched her hand. "I'm sorry, Dennie. I shouldn't have just blabbed that out. But you know me. I never was known for my tact. I guess I didn't know you were really interested in this guy...are you?"

"We're friends. I have to get back to work."

"Relax. You haven't finished your tea. Anyway, how about that movie? You want to go tomorrow night?"

Denise finished her tea, pushed the cup aside, and got up. Gina watched her but said nothing.

"Yeah, sure," Denise said. I haven't been to a movie in a while. Sounds good."

She hoped Frank might call Monday night. He didn't. All day Tuesday she hoped and half expected he might call. He didn't. How could she have been so stupid to think that he was really interested in her? It was all BS. She turned off her computer.

"Hey, Dennie." Gina filled her office all perfumed and eye shadowed, looking ready to roll. "Come on. Let's go over to the Park Sheraton and have a Happy Hour Drink. They're cheap for the next couple hours and the hors d'oeuvres are fabulous. The movie starts at seven, so we've got plenty of time."

She had completely forgotten about the movie. And now she was tired and just wanted to work out for a little while and go home and go to bed. "Oh, Gina. I really am beat and I'm feeling rotten. Could I possibly take a rain check?"

Gina's shoulders slumped. She recovered. "Come on Dennie, a drink a bite to eat and a good movie and you'll feel a lot better. Come on, it'll be fun."

Denise felt guilty when she saw how disappointed Gina seemed. But she shook her head. "No. I just don't feel up to it tonight."

"You want to go tomorrow or Thursday?"

"Let's just play it by ear, O.K.?"

Gina nodded. The expression on her face hardened. "Yeah, sure. See ya." She turned and left.

*        *        *

Crystal Wilcox felt out of sorts. It had been nearly three weeks since she'd heard from the one man she had come to enjoy. She was surprised that she was actually missing him and the evenings in his apartment, sharing his wine and the stimulation she got from their conversation and even, if not especially, the kinky sex they enjoyed together. Twice she had called him and left messages.

She was tired, tired of New York, tired of what she did and tired of who she was. She needed to get away. She would, soon.

# Chapter Twenty-six

Edward Nemerow left his office at six-thirty p.m. His Jaguar XK-8 convertible stood waiting for him as he emerged from the building. Joshua Nemerow, Edward's grandfather, was one of New York's most prominent patrons of the arts. Plaques in his honor hung in Carnegie Hall, The Metropolitan Museum of Art, and other bastions of culture throughout New York.

Joshua's son Benjamin continued in his father's philanthropic footsteps, endowing a chair for the humanities at New York University as well as donating one of the family homes to Hunter College to be used as a Center for the Arts.

Although lacking the humanistic orientation of his father and grandfather, Edward did inherit their talent for finance. He was acknowledged as one of the most brilliant arbitrageurs and merger specialists in the country.

He lived in Greenwich, Connecticut with his second wife, Pamela and also maintained an apartment on Fifth Avenue, not far from the Metropolitan Museum of Art. On the rare occasions when Pamela would come into the city, the apartment was a comfortable haven. It also served Edward's other needs.

\*     \*     \*

The refrigerator was empty, some bottled water, leftover limp salad, and a withered, mushy apple. She was tired and the thought of climbing into bed with a book sounded good. But she knew the hunger would only keep gnawing at her.

She leaned against the sink and read the headlines in the *Daily News* again. "No Progress In Wine Bottle Killings." Although she'd read the article three times, she began reading it again. "In spite of working around the clock in an effort to catch the serial killer responsible for the wine bottle murders, police yesterday admitted they have no suspects. But Captain Joseph Nolan continues to be optimistic. 'We have our best people heading the investigation. I have every confidence in Sergeant Jerry Blodgett and Detective Frank Corso. Every homicide detective in the city is assigned to this case, and I can assure you we will not rest until the killer is apprehended.'"

She smiled at the policespeak. "We will not rest until the killer is apprehended." But it was undoubtedly true and she would have to be careful. The hunger wouldn't go away and she thought of the French restaurant on Fifty-second Street that she'd been wanting to try. It wasn't far and if it was as good as she'd heard, it might be just the thing to buck up her spirits, which were low again.

*     *     *

Paul Gale was cold, tired, and hungry. His luck had to change soon. He could see the lights on up in her apartment. But he missed her going in and now it looked like she was settling in for the night. "Goddamn!" He flicked his cigarette high into the air and started to leave. The door to her building opened and she appeared. She stood for a moment and started walking South. Again the door opened and two couples came out and started walking in the same direction. Gale fell in behind them.

No more dry runs. This time he'd stay on her like a bad smell. She moved quickly along the busy street. She wouldn't get away from him tonight. Not the way he'd planned it, but he was running out of time.

Finally, in a little stretch, between Second and Third Avenues she was alone. He was no more than fifty feet from her, staying close to the buildings, being smart and quiet. She didn't know he was behind her. He moved forward silently on his crepe soled shoes. The street was dark, still not a soul in sight.

Now, you bitch. He was closing on her fast, twenty feet, ten feet away from her now. He slipped the knife out and flicked the blade open. It was going to be easy. So close now, he could almost touch her. A couple more steps. He lifted his hand with the knife, and she took a sharp left and disappeared into a restaurant.

He stood outside watching a guy in a tuxedo smiling at her, leading her into the restaurant. Now he couldn't see her anymore. "Well, I ain't letting her out of my sight this time. No way." He unzipped his jacket and entered the building.

"Can I help you with something, sir?"

The man in the tuxedo stood in front of him. His eyes arched and he looked as if he'd just seen a cockroach crawl across his shoes.

"Uh, yeah. I thought I might get somethin' to eat."

The tuxedo man stared at him in disbelief. "Do you have a reservation, sir?"

"No, I ain't got a reservation. Why?"

"I'm sorry. We're booked solid all evening."

"O.K. I'll just get me a beer in the bar." He started toward the bar.

The tuxedo man was around in front of him. "I'm sorry, sir, but the bar is already crowded over our capacity. Why don't you try us another night?" He smiled thinly and gestured toward the door.

Gale stared at him, looked into the bar and back into the face of the tuxedo. Prick was still giving him that phony smile and nodding toward the door.

He headed toward the exit, the tuxedo man right behind him. At the door Gale turned and drove his knee hard into the man's groin. "See ya,

asshole," he said and was out the door. It was the only satisfaction he'd
had in weeks of frustration. That and the bum on the street.

*       *       *

She was glad the restaurant wasn't crowded. The chilled white wine
she sipped and the rich food smells of the place brightened her mood.
The restaurant really was quite elegant. She settled back and tried to
relax. But the room was warm and her mind refused to stop racing. She
felt the twinge of a headache coming on. She also felt an aching loneliness crowding in on her

It saddened her knowing there was a side of her that could have a
good life, a life like other women. She tried, God knows she tried, but
she knew how hopeless it was now.

So many times in the past few weeks, she had sensed his presence.
Was he watching her? He knew where she lived. No question of that.
What else did he know? He was here in the city. Crawling around. He
would find her. Or she would find him.

*       *       *

It had been a long day for Edward Nemerow. He checked his face in
the car mirror and winced at the tired-looking bloodshot eyes staring
back at him. But then last night had been such fun. He took pride in his
sexual prowess. At times it seemed he was indefatigable. And last night
was one of those times. He smiled. "She was a lusty one."

Tonight, though he was grateful for a rare evening without commit-
ments of any kind. He looked forward to a quiet dinner and a good
night's sleep. It was Michelle, his secretary who had told him of Les
Bois, the new French restaurant on Fifty-second Street.

"It's small, quiet and not frequented by any of the investment crowd.
And the food is terrific."

That was good enough for Edward. He called himself and made the
reservation under the name Charles Barton. He didn't want them

recognizing his name and fawning all over him. Nemerow entered the restaurant, glanced around, and nodded his approval. The maitre d' led him to his table. On the way they passed a young woman sitting alone, sipping a drink.

One glance and Nemerow's practiced eye gave him a quick snapshot. The lustrous hair rippled softly over her shoulders onto a wine colored cashmere sweater. A touch of eye shadow gave her eyes the sensuous sultry look that he liked. He also liked the high, firm breasts.

By the time he reached her table he was no longer tired. "Hello. How are you this evening?" He said flicking a smile at her.

She looked up quickly. "I'm sorry. Were you speaking to me?"

"Yes, but forgive me if I startled you. Enjoy your dinner." He continued along with the maitre d' to his table. The maitre d' seemed to have a limp she hadn't noticed before.

She had observed the well dressed, self assured man heading toward her table. He was short, not more than five-eight, but he carried himself erect, with style. She even admired the expensively tailored suit, draped with a loose elegance over his slender frame. He smacked of grooming and money but there was something about him that irritated her. Maybe it was the swagger, the condescending arrogance in his voice.

She heard the maitre d' ask him if the table was satisfactory. Out of the corner of her eye she watched him dismiss the maitre d' with a lowering of his eyes and a curt nod. He preened for a moment and sat down.

"Well, isn't he just too, too much," she snickered to herself. She finished her drink and after a few moments glanced his way. He was looking directly at her, smiling intrusively. She turned her head and was relieved when the waiter brought her meal.

The coq au vin was superb. She ate slowly, trying to enjoy it but something about the man's presence unnerved her. She knew he was still looking at her, waiting for her to look up, so he could favor her with his insolent smile. She decided to skip coffee and get outside into the fresh air.

"Since you've finished your dinner, why don't you have some coffee and brandy at my table?"

She spun around. He was standing with his hands resting on the back of her chair, ready to slide it out and assist her up. She turned her head back to her table, away from him. "I don't drink brandy."

He slid around the chair and stood in front of her. "I'm told that the coffee here is wonderful. You do drink coffee, don't you?"

She looked up at him. The perfect teeth were bared, together in a Jack Nicholson smile. His eyes moved up and down her body. Did he think he was being cute with his sing-songy, "you do drink coffee, don't you?" She thought about leaving but the familiar sensations took over. Time slowed down and she saw herself as a player in a slow motion movie. The sounds, colors, and odors of the restaurant were more vivid, more intense.

"Yes, I drink coffee," she said.

"Well, then you must have one cup of their wonderful coffee with me." Again, his hands went to the back of her chair.

Oh, must I? She continued to watch him.

He beckoned toward his table. "Come. You would so brighten up my evening. Join me." It wasn't a question, more like a command.

Her eyes were still fixed on him, distaste for the man intensifying by the second. A small smile crossed her lips. "All right. I'll join you."

*          *          *

Nemerow's apartment was about what she expected, all gilt, mirrors and expensive art everywhere. She stood in the living room staring at the exquisite figurines and sculptures, Nemerow watching her with his phony smile.

"I can see you like beautiful things, my dear," he said moving around behind her and sliding her coat off. "The two figurines are by Nike de Saint Phale, the ceramics are Picasso and the horse sculpture is a Deborah Butterfield." He laid her coat over one of the chairs. "But come. Do sit down and let me bring you something. I believe you said you like wine?"

She stood rigid as he sidled up to her, put his hand around her waist and placed the other under her buttocks. He tried to pull her into him but she resisted. He was unable to budge her.

"Yes, I would like some white wine," she said. "Why don't you bring the bottle in?"

He removed his hand from her backside and slid it across her breasts. "I have a delicious Chardonnay just for you. Sit down and relax. I'll be right back."

She watched him mince his way toward the kitchen and shuddered. The headache had settled in and her head throbbed. She took a Percodan from her purse, swallowed it dry, and sat heavily on the sofa. Beads of perspiration trickled down her body. The woolen slacks clung to her and pressed against her pelvic area. She opened and closed her legs.

"Here we are, my dear." Edward Nemerow stood in front of her, a dark blue silk robe covering his slender frame, matching slippers on his feet. He held a silver tray containing two half filled wine glasses. He handed her wine to her and sat on the sofa. "I thought I'd get into something a bit more comfortable than all that wretched, heavy clothing. May I offer you the same opportunity?" he asked, caressing her face.

She ignored the question. "I thought you were going to bring the bottle?"

He arched his eyes again in that annoying way and she knew his disgusting smile would come next. It did.

"Oh, you do like your wine, don't you. Don't worry, there's plenty more in the kitchen. I don't like to clutter up things in here." He moved in closer to her and placed his mouth next to her ear. His breath was hot and unpleasant and she choked back the impulse to gag. The Percodan made her dizzy but did nothing yet for her headache. She did not like the direction things were taking.

"You are a beautiful woman, my dear and I'm having very strong feelings for you. There is something about you that arouses me beyond belief. I suspect that you feel very much the same."

She pulled away and stared at the repulsive little man, who seemed to be heading out of control. How could he possibly believe she could feel anything but revulsion for him?

Suddenly he was kissing her hungrily, his tongue licking and exploring. She tried to move away, but his strength surprised her. Then it was he who broke away and put his lips to her ears again. "I want you to do something for me, Lucky." His voice was a harsh whisper. I want you to come into the bedroom and handcuff me to the bed. And then I want you to do unspeakable things to me. Will you do that?"

She pushed him away and gazed at him with eyes that passed through him as if he were a window. "Yes," she said. "I would like to do that."

Inside the bedroom she stood at the foot of Nemerow's bed, watching him take off his clothes. He peeled off his shirt revealing a hairless pink chest the color of a rare steak. The rest of his shapeless little body was soft and doughy, unremarkable except for the ugly erection, grotesquely out of proportion with his puny frame.

She hated looking at it and closed her eyes for a moment. When she opened them, he lay spread-eagled on the bed holding a pair of handcuffs. "Please, Lucky, take your clothes off and come to me." He held the handcuffs out to her.

She wanted to leave this repulsive little man and go home. But the dark entity that raged within her took over. Her eyes fixed him with a distant stare before she moved toward him, slipping out of her slacks along the way.

Nemerow groaned and writhed on the bed. "Oh God, Lucky. Take your sweater off. Now," he commanded.

She slid off the sweater and stood over him.

"Now, Lucky, I want you to put these handcuffs around my wrists and snap them around the bedposts." He barely rasped the words out.

She did as she was told and leaned close to him. "You're mine now, aren't you?" she whispered.

He tried to speak, but he was breathing so hard the words squeezed out in little gasps. "And-now-Lucky,-I-want-you-to-take-off-your-panties-and-sit-on-my-face."

"Yes, of course," she said. She moved onto the bed and straddled him somewhere up around his neck.

"Nemerow's moans grew louder. " Oh! God! Sit on me. Sit on me, baby."

She slowly lowered herself over his head and settled the full weight of her body onto his face. "Now, there. Do you like that, Charles?"

She barely heard his muffled voice. "You still have your pants on. Take them off." He was still commanding her, still thinking he was in charge. She would enjoy this.

She moved her thighs in closer along the sides of his face. "No, I like it better like this. You like it too, don't you? Don't you, Charles?" Her voice was soft, cooing.

She controlled the muscles of her thighs, flexing them into a tightening vice around his face and head. He thrashed like a wounded duck. His legs flailed helplessly. He mumbled and made noises, muffled screams, bits and pieces of unintelligible sound came from under her thighs. She grabbed at a bedpost and pushed up with her arms, forcing her body harder into him.

After a while the squirming slowed, then stopped. There were no more sounds. Edward Nemerow lay motionless.

She slumped forward and lay her head against the wall. Her work was done. She felt satiated, at peace. She wanted to close her eyes and sleep. But not yet.

# Chapter Twenty-seven

Jerry and Frank were in Jerry's car, heading for an appointment, when they received the call directly from Captain Nolan. A prominent citizen had been murdered, and they were to get over to ten-sixty Fifth Avenue immediately. Thirty minutes later, they were let into the apartment by a uniformed police officer, who led them over to a man and woman sitting on the couch.

The woman got up and shook Frank's hand. "I'm Michelle Vivier, Mr. Nemerow's secretary." She nodded her head toward the man with her. "This is Mr. Byrd, the manager of the building."

Frank was impressed by the lady's composure. Byrd was agitated and fidgeted on the couch. Probably worried about the scandal in his nice building.

"Mr. Nemerow failed to show up for an extremely important meeting," Vivier reported. "It just wasn't like him. No one, including his wife, had heard from him. I became worried and came over here. Mr. Byrd let me in and we found him."

Fifteen minutes later, Captain Nolan and Commissioner John Keohane himself arrived, followed shortly by the Medical Examiner, a police photographer, sketcher, two uniformed officers, a finger print specialist, Harry Leonard, and two reporters from the New York Post, who were outside in the hall.

The Commissioner spoke quietly with Michelle for a few moments. He then adjourned to the hall with Jerry and Captain Nolan.

"Gentlemen, as you know, the man lying dead in the bedroom is Edward Nemerow. And you know who Edward Nemerow is or was. I can tell you that before this day is out, the shit is going to hit the fan in this city unlike anything you have ever seen. Those two reporters over there are the beginning of big trouble. I don't know how they got up here but I want them out. I expect no more leaks to the press. I also expect a visit from the Nemerows very shortly, and the pressure they're going to put on me will be passed on to you. Take my word for it. Now, get those reporters the hell out of here, and get busy. I want a full report on your progress, before I leave my office. I'll be there at least until seven tonight."

He grabbed Nolan by the arm. "Come on Joe, I've got to get back. You and I need to talk some more. We can do it in my car."

Nolan glared for a moment at Jerry, then left with the Commissioner.

Jerry went back into the apartment and found Harry. "Harry, get out in the hall and get those reporters out of here. Go down the elevator with them, and make sure they leave the building. There should be an officer down there to see that they don't get back in. Also, find out which doorman was on duty last night and talk to him."

Jerry was now in charge. He tucked in his shirt and walked over to Frank, who was talking with the Medical Examiner. "Frank, check the other occupants of the floor and see if they saw or heard anything. I think we're finished with Mr. Byrd and Miss Vivier for now. They can go."

Frank grabbed Jerry by the arm. "Jerry, have you gotten real close to the body yet?"

"Depends on what you mean by real close. Why?"

"He's got a strong smell of perfume on him. I mean it doesn't smell like men's cologne. It sure as hell isn't the cologne he's got in the bathroom. It smells like a woman's perfume or lotion. Check it out. Check his clothes. I'll see you in a while."

Jerry walked back to the bedroom, where Edward Nemerow lay, as Byrd and Vivier had first discovered him. The photographer was still taking pictures, full body views, general views of the body and the crime scene, close up shots of wounds, photos of contiguous areas, as well as the entire apartment. The crime scene sketcher was also still at work, as were the fingerprint man and the Medical Examiner.

Frank walked along the long, wide hallway of the building. He had learned from Francis Byrd, that there was only one other apartment on the tenth floor. It was located around the corner of the building and faced South.

Frank rang the doorbell, and a woman's voice replied from within. "Yes, who is it, and how did you get up here?"

"Police officers, Ma'am." He held his credentials in front of the viewer in the door, and made certain that the uniformed police officer he had brought with him was visible to her.

The door opened as far as the thick chain on it would allow. The woman's voice was apprehensive. "Please let me see your credentials."

Frank handed them to her. She studied them carefully, and handed them back to him. Her eyes darted from Frank to the patrolman. "May I ask what this is all about?"

"I'm afraid there has been a crime committed in your neighbor's apartment. I wonder if I might ask you a few questions, Ma'am?"

"A crime? What kind of a crime?" She sounded frightened.

Frank spoke softly. "Mr. Nemerow has been murdered. May we come in and talk with you. You may be able to help us."

She gasped and closed the door. Frank heard the chain being unlatched, and the door opened.

A tall blond woman, who appeared to be in her early forties stood in the doorway. Her short blond hair framed deep blue eyes, with just a trace of indigo eye shadow over them. She wore no other make-up, and the news Frank had just delivered to her had turned her porcelain features to chalk white. The blue and white designer warm-up suit she wore fit as if tailored for her, which he figured it probably was. Her white sneakers were spotless. He admired her, in spite of the circumstances.

"Oh, my God," she stammered. "I can't believe I heard what you just said. Please, please come in and sit down."

They sat down in the living room. The apartment was as elegant as the woman. The ceilings in the entry hall and living room had to be at least fourteen feet high. He was sure the crystal chandelier hanging over them was bigger than his whole living room. The artwork alone, if it was original, and he was sure it was, might have been worth as much again as the apartment. He resisted the temptation to press his fingers into the carpet under their feet. The pile was soft as beaten egg whites and easily an inch or more, deep. He wondered for a moment what it must be like to have this kind of money and then got down to business.

Her name was Patricia Greiff. She was a free lance casting director and her husband, Daniel, was a surgeon. They had no children and had been living in the building for nine years. They knew Nemerow, but they would not consider themselves friends of his.

"Let's just say, we didn't approve of his lifestyle," she said.

"What do you mean?," Frank asked.

"Well, it was no secret here in the building that Mr. Nemerow was fond of entertaining women in his apartment. They came in various colors, some black, some white, and they came and went with some regularity."

"Wasn't Mr. Nemerow married?" Frank asked.

"Yes. That's what I mean about not approving of his lifestyle," she replied. "He made no effort to be discreet. My husband and/or I often shared the elevator with him and one of his women. I felt so sorry for his wife."

"Did you ever see him with a man?"

"No, never."

"Did you see him with the same woman more often than with others?"

She thought for a moment. "No, not really. They were pretty much a mixed bag." She looked up at Frank and smiled. "If you'll pardon the expression. Some were tall, some short."

"Any similar characteristics about them?" Frank asked.

She looked away and ran her tongue along her upper lip, then back to Frank. "They were all very attractive women." A hint of pique crept into her voice. "Now, please. Can you tell me what happened?"

Frank nodded. This was not a woman accustomed to being questioned. She was instinctively courteous. Good breeding. But she had an imperious quality about her that warned him she wasn't going to suffer through this very long. "We believe he was killed last night, sometime between ten p.m. and one or two in the morning. Did you see or hear anything at all?"

Mrs. Greiff stared at Frank, her eyes widening. "Oh, my God. Of course we did."

"What did you see?"

"Well, as we were coming down the corridor heading toward the elevator, I could see it was open and I yelled for whoever was in it to hold it. But just as we got there it was closing and I caught a glimpse of someone inside."

"One person?"

"Yes."

"Do you recall what time it was?"

"Yes, as a matter of fact, I remember exactly. My mother was due to arrive at JFK at eleven-forty on a flight from Seattle. Dan and I were leaving to pick her up. I wanted to be certain to be there in plenty of time before her arrival, and I was concerned that we were running late. It was about ten-fifteen."

"Please describe for me if you will, the person you saw on the elevator, Mrs. Greiff."

Mrs. Greiff ran her fingers through her hair again, and shook her head. "Well, that's going to be difficult. We really didn't see much of him, I'm afraid."

"Can you describe what you did see?"

"Well, as I told you, we got to the elevator, just as the door was closing. There was one person on it, and we were a little exasperated, because he could have pressed the button and reopened the door for us. There was still time. But he didn't." She paused and frowned, as if remembering her annoyance.

Something about the way she frowned told him this was a lady with a short fuse. "Mrs. Greiff, how much of this person did you see?"

"Not very much. He was standing with his back to us, which I thought at the time was a little unusual. You know most people get on an elevator and turn and face the front. Don't you?"

"Yes, I do. What was the person wearing?"

"Ah, I noticed that too. A long dark coat, black or dark blue. Dark slacks and a dark scarf covering his head."

"Shoes?"

"I'm sorry I didn't notice the shoes. Could I get you gentlemen a cup of coffee or a soft drink?"

"No thank you," Frank replied.

"No thanks," the uniformed officer spoke for the first time.

Frank continued. "Mrs. Greiff, you keep referring to the person on the elevator as he and him. Are you certain it was a man?"

She was about to speak, but stopped, and paused. "Well..., no as a matter of fact, I guess I can't be totally certain. I mean I didn't really see his—I mean the face. But the person was tall and—actually, yes, I suppose it could have been a woman."

"How tall would you say the person was?" Frank asked.

"Gee. I don't know." She thought again, took a deep breath, and let it out. "No, I just didn't get that good a look."

"Would you say the build was slender or heavy set. I mean could you tell if it was a mannish kind of a build or..."

"Mr. Corso," she interrupted. "Please remember that we caught only the most fleeting glimpse of him or her or whatever." A touch of impatience crept into her voice. She got up and walked over to a table, and withdrew a cigarette from a silver case. She lit it with a small silver lighter.

Frank sensed that she was getting tired and knew he'd have to wrap it up soon. "I'm sorry, Mrs. Greiff. I know this isn't easy, and I apologize for having to take so much of your time. Maybe just a few more minutes?" He smiled at her like they were old friends.

The smile bought him the time he needed. She smiled back and touched his arm. "Forgive me for snapping. I know that your questions are important and necessary. I'll do my best. Please continue." She took another deep drag on the cigarette and inhaled in a quick gasp.

The woman had presence. Even through the warm up suit he couldn't help but notice she had a great body. The kind of woman who took very good care of herself. "I was asking you about the person's build," he said.

"Well, as I said 'the person' was wearing a rather heavy coat, but I'd say 'the person' was tall with fairly broad shoulders. But that could have been the coat. I mean a coat like that can make someone look a lot broader than he or she really is."

"Is there any chance this person could be one of the women you had seen Mr. Nemerow with on the elevator? You did say that some of them were tall."

"Well, I guess it's possible. But as I said, I did not get a good look, and I really paid very little attention to him or her. I didn't expect to be having this conversation you know." She gave him a little smile.

He grinned back and nodded. "I understand. Tell me about the scarf."

"Well, as I think I told you, 'the person' had a dark scarf." She held up her hand and shook her head. "No, I can't tell you what color. It was just dark, like dark blue or black. Anyway, the scarf was wrapped around his…or her head and I think part of it was tucked into the coat collar."

"So, you couldn't really see any hair?"

"No. None at all."

"Mrs. Greiff, it strikes me that wearing a scarf over the head isn't something a man normally does. Doesn't that seem more like a woman's thing to you?"

"Well, now that you mention it, I guess I'd say yes, you're right. Of course, it was cold out last night, and whoever it was might have just been bundling up before going out." She held out her hands and shrugged. "I don't know."

"By the way, was the person wearing gloves?"

She thought for a moment. "I don't recall. I think he…or she had his hands in the pockets of the coat."

"So, I guess you didn't really see enough to know if the person was white or black or what color skin they had?"

"No. I didn't see any skin."

Frank got up and held out his hand. "I think that's about it, Mrs. Greiff. Thank you for your time and for being so cooperative and helpful. Oh, by the way. Did you smell any perfume or any kind of scent coming from the elevator?"

"Hmm…no. I can't say that I did."

"Did the women on the elevator wear perfume?"

"Yes."

"Could you identify any of it?"

"No."

"Just one last question, Mrs. Greiff. You would have to assume, wouldn't you that since Mr. Nemerow's and yours are the only apartments on this floor, the person would have been coming from Nemerow's apartment. I mean, could there be any other explanation for him or her being up here?

She shook her head vigorously. "No. We have very tight security here."

"O.K., thanks, again. I may be calling you."

"I hope so," she said, touching his arm again as she showed them out.

Back inside Nemerow's apartment Frank reported the results of his discussion with Patricia Greiff to Jerry. "I don't think there's any question that the person she and her husband saw is our killer, Jerry," Frank said matter-of-factly. That would put the time of the murder to maybe somewhere between nine-thirty and a little after ten."

Jerry led Frank over to a quiet corner of the large living room, where they settled into matching Louis XIV chairs. The sight of Jerry's massive frame bulging over the delicate chair brought a smile to Frank's face.

"What's so funny?" Jerry growled.

"Don't get up quick. You'll be wearing the chair."

Jerry snorted and leaned forward. "Your thing about the perfume is right on. There's perfume on his suit coat, his shirt, the bathrobe and you can smell it on his chest. At least it smells more like perfume than men's cologne. And you're right. It's definitely not the stuff he's got in the bathroom. We're sending the clothing over to the lab for some gas chromatography."

Frank nodded and sat quietly for a moment. "That's good, Jerry, but you know what I'm going to do? I'm going to take a piece of his clothing down to Macy's, to one of those women at the perfume counters. Those ladies are like bloodhounds. I'll bet any one of them can take a whiff of this stuff and tell us what it is. Then we'll buy some and see if it matches."

Jerry chuckled. "You're right, Frank. Those broads are like bloodhounds. They'll tell you what it is.

Frank nodded. "They pick up any prints?"

Jerry looked toward the bedroom. "Yeah. We got some in the bathroom and a couple off the bedroom door. Nothing on the wine bottle or the glasses. Probably been wiped off."

"Anything else?"

Jerry pointed to a man bent over the sofa with a flashlight and tweezers. "They're looking for hair right now, here and in the bedroom.

"Well, we know that whoever zapped him didn't exactly break the door down to get in." Frank said. "There's no sign of any forced entry, unless he shinnied up the side of the building."

Jerry nodded. "Had to be one of his guests. Hey, Harry!" Jerry bellowed.

Harry Leonard appeared from the bedroom. "Yeah?"

"Harry, come over here. I want you to listen to Frank's interview with the neighbor. What'd you find out about the doorman?"

"He's on his way in now. I talked to him a little on the phone. I don't think he's going to be much help. Said Nemerow always went in through the garage and took the elevator up from there. He didn't see him at all. Didn't see any strangers leave during the time frame we're talking about. The killer probably went down and out through the garage" Harry sat down and Frank filled him in on his discussion with Patricia Greiff.

Jerry turned to Harry. "Go down and talk to Byrd. See if he can corroborate or add anything to what Frank has."

Jerry lowered his voice. "We got something else too, Frank."

"What's that?" Frank asked.

"We got an address book out of his bureau drawer. It's full of nothin' but women's names and phone numbers. Interesting annotations next to most of 'em."

"Like what?"

"'Best blow job in New York'. 'Very kinky'. 'Likes to dominate'. 'Won't screw, but will do anything else'. 'Likes to play rough'. You know, little gems like that."

Harry stopped at the front door and started back toward them.

"Get outta here, Harry," Jerry shouted.

Harry scurried out.

"Any men in there?" asked Frank.

"None. All women."

"We'll check the names and numbers against the ones we found in Chesbro's book," Frank said. "Jerry, I'm ready to bet it's a woman doing this foreign object insertion. Typically happens when men brutalize women. I've checked the computer back through 1985 for similar MO's all over the state. We've got your experience going back thirty years. I've talked with my father and retired detectives going back beyond him. Only a very few cases of foreign object insertion perpetrated on men—

all homosexually related. It's not something a heterosexual man does to another. It's a fag or female thing. I don't think any of these guys were involved with homosexuals."

"I dunno, Frank. Nemerow could've had a fag up here, a transvestite. Who knows what kinda creeps this guy played with."

"Jerry, every time we turn around, we're bumping into signs of a woman. Does it have to jump up and bite you in the ass?"

Jerry started to speak, but gave up on whatever he was going to say.

Frank continued. "We've got Jack Beatty, Joey Brewer, Phillip Chesbro, and now Nemerow all killed with just about the same M.O. Nemerow's wallet and some jewelry were taken from him. The other guys weren't robbed. Two things could account for the difference. One: the other guys didn't have anything worth taking, and or two: the killer wanted to throw us off and make this one look like robbery was the motive. My guess is that it's probably a combination of both. No big deal as far as any change in the M.O. All four appear to be the work of the same person."

"No question," said Jerry.

The Medical Examiner appeared in the room. He spoke with the clipped precision of people in his profession. "Jerry, we're finished with the body, and we're ready to have him removed, unless you have anything else."

Jerry shook his head. He turned to the forensic specialist. "What have you've got."

"We've got some pieces of human hair that were on the victim and on the bed. We'll check that out and see if we have any follicles with it. We've picked up some pieces of fabric off the victim's robe and his shirt. And his shirt and robe are in two separate paper bags for you over there on the table. Frank, I believe you said you wanted them."

Frank nodded. "Thanks, George."

"It looks like the cause of death was suffocation, but he was also hit in the head and face a number of times. Can't yet say for sure how many, but a lot. He was hit with a heavy instrument which I'm sure was the wine bottle on the floor. Besides the bottle, his head was hit several times on the floor-very hard. There's blood and pieces of scalp on the floor."

"Jerry, I showed you the marks on his wrists. They're the marks handcuffs make. They were on very tight, causing pronounced lacerations."

"Handcuffs?" Frank asked.

"Yes, I don't think there's any question that's what's caused the marks, but you boys can confirm or deny that when you've examined him more."

Frank turned to Jerry. "That's a new twist. Any sign of the cuffs?"

"No, but the killer had another wine bottle in reserve. Yep, same deal, Frankie," Jerry said.

"Was he handcuffed to something, the bed?" Frank asked.

"Yep. You can see the marks on the bed posts," Jerry said. "But whoever killed him took off the cuffs and dragged him onto the floor so they could pound his head on it."

"I'm leaving now with the paramedics," the M.E. said.

"What do you think, Frank," Jerry asked, settling back into his Louis XIVth chair.

"No question it's a woman, Jerry. This guy liked getting kinky with his ladies. I'm sure the cuffs bit was part of his repertoire of little games. He just picked the wrong lady this time. She probably couldn't believe her good luck. He made it easy for her."

"Yeah, I'd say this guy was strictly a ladies man from the looks of his journal," Jerry said. "No men in it."

Frank went over to the table and picked up the bag containing Nemerow's clothing. "I'm going to take this clothing down to Macy's and have some of the perfume experts there take a whiff. We'll also have the lab run some tests, but I think we'll get our answer from the perfume women."

Jerry got up and walked slowly over to Frank, his shirt tail hanging from under his sports jacket. "O.K., Frank. I'll be here for a while. See you back at the precinct in a couple hours." He went over to the window and looked out, still thinking of the look Nolan gave him as he walked out with the Commissioner.

# Chapter Twenty-eight

Macy's was crowded, already beginning to show the effects of the upcoming holiday season. Frank made his way to the perfume counter, approached one of the few women not busy with a customer, and identified himself. The woman, in her late thirties, wore a blue smock over a black silk blouse, In spite of the smock, she still managed to look overdressed. Her jet black hair (too dark to be real, Frank thought) was pulled tightly back at the temples and hung in a pony tail, held together by a large sequined donut. False lashes protruded over half an inch from her eyes, and when she blinked, his first instinct was to jump out of the way.

"Well, this is a surprise. What can I do for our police department today?"

Frank set his bag on the counter. "I wonder if you could smell the garments inside this bag, and tell me if you know what the scent is?"

She gave him a quizzical look.

"Please, Ma'am. It's important, and I would much appreciate it, if you don't ask me any questions. I hope you understand."

She smiled at him again and pointed to her name tag. "Officer, please call me Jennifer. Somehow 'Ma'am' makes me feel old."

Frank handed over the bag. "O.K., Jennifer."

Jennifer sat on the stool behind the counter, put her nose into the bag. She quickly withdrew it.

"Oh, that's too easy. Why don't you give me a tough one? It's Jean Naté."

"Can you be absolutely certain?"

"Of course I can. Most perfume scents are easy to identify. Jean Naté is one of the easiest. Listen, I've been at this stuff for nearly twenty years. Take it to the bank. This is Jean Naté."

Another perfume lady approached, this one in a green smock. Jennifer called her over.

"Francine, can you do me a favor?" Jennifer handed her the bag. "Smell these clothes, and tell this gentleman what the scent is."

Francine looked from Jennifer to Frank and took the bag. She put her head slightly into it, sniffed, and handed back the bag.

"It's Jean Naté," she said matter-of-factly.

"Thanks, Francine. Talk to you later."

Francine shrugged and continued on her way.

"Officer, I could hand this bag to every clerk on these counters, and every one will tell us the same thing, believe me. Do you want to try another?"

"No, you've made a believer out of me."

"Good. Glad to help. What else can I do for you?" Big smile.

"What type of women buy Jean Naté, Jennifer?"

"Actually, we don't sell it here anymore. You find it mostly in drug-stores, Walgreens, places like that. It's an old after bath fragrance. Been around a long time. Very common."

"Not upscale?"

"Not upscale."

"One last question and I'll let you go."

"No rush."

"Is it something men ever wear?"

"No. It's a women's fragrance."

Frank left the store satisfied that Edward Nemerow had been in close contact with someone, most likely a woman, wearing Jean Naté cologne on the night he was murdered.

*       *       *

Jerry Blodgett sat at his desk, working on the Nemerow report, when he heard his name roar across the bullpen and through his open door. He jumped, looked up, and saw Joseph Nolan standing in the bullpen area.

"Blodgett," Nolan yelled again.

Jerry got up from his desk, and grabbed his coat from the rack. He plodded across the bullpen, one arm grappling with his coat sleeve, the other vainly trying to stuff his shirttail inside his pants.

"Jerry, come into my office," Nolan growled.

"Look at this newspaper article." He threw the *New York Post* at Jerry, who instinctively caught part of it, while other parts drifted across the room.

Jerry retrieved the paper and put it together. The front page headline jumped at him. 'Wine Bottle Killer Strikes Prominent Financier.'

"Ah,shit!" Jerry muttered.

"Go ahead. Sit down and read it," Nolan said.

Jerry looked at him and slumped into a chair next to him. Nolan remained standing.

"Edward Nemerow, nationally known and respected financier and member of one of New York's most prominent families was brutally murdered last night. Nemerow's body was found this morning by his secretary and the manager of the posh Fifth Avenue building where he lived."

"He appeared to be the victim of the serial killer, who over the past two months has killed at least three other men, the killer's signature being a wine bottle left in the victim's rectum. All four, including Nemerow, were found in their apartments, brutally beaten, with a wine bottle the primary instrument."

"The *Post* learned today from confidential sources, that the previous three victims were killed with the same modus operandi as Mr. Nemerow."

"'There's no question, there's a serial killer working out there,' stated the *Post's* sources."

Jerry threw the paper down. "Ah, shit, Joe. I've read enough."

"Oh, there's more, Jerry."

Nolan picked up the paper. "Listen to this."

"'Joshua Nemerow, patriarch of the Nemerow family and grandfather of the victim, expressed outrage that the police have said nothing about the activities of a vicious serial killer on the loose.'"

"'The public has a right to know about these things, Mr. Nemerow said.'"

"'My family and I expect prompt and decisive action in bringing this killer to justice. We demand to know all the facts in this case, and the other three, and we want a complete accounting on what's been done to date toward apprehending this maniac.'"

Nolan threw the paper back at Jerry. "Nice, huh?"

Jerry frowned and started to speak.

Nolan interrupted. "I got the chief and the commissioner all over my ass. The Nemerows won't let up, and I'm taking nothing but shit from all directions. I don't like that Jerry. I don't care if you guys work twenty-five hours a day. I want results." He turned his back and that was it.

Frank was back at his desk. Jerry called him into his office.

Jerry was pleased with the Jean Naté results. "That's the first good news I've had today," he said.

"We can put some pressure on the lab to get these other tests done right away," Frank said. "I'll have them run the gas chromotography with the scent too, but I don't think it's going to change what we already know."

"We'll check the names out and compare for duplicates. We've got the hair, the prints, the fabric, the perfume. We should be able to nail this down soon, as to whether it's a man or woman we're looking for. Once we do, that little tidbit has got to be kept from the press."

"Absolutely!" Jerry replied. "Fuck the Nemerows. We're going to do this our way."

Frank went back to his desk and picked up the bag of clothing to run it over to the lab. As he closed the bag to tie and tag it, the lingering scent of the perfume hit him and stayed for a moment.

He pictured Edward Nemerow, lying handcuffed to his four poster bed, all worked up over the sight and smell of the beautiful woman hovering over him, about to satisfy whatever his perverted needs. Instead she satisfied hers. What the hell were they dealing with here?

# Chapter Twenty-nine

She was addicted to the newspaper accounts of her activities. A serial killer was loose in the city. The public wanted action. It seemed to her that she was reading about someone else. Her activities had been so isolated, so personal, it seemed odd to be reading about them in the newspapers, that everyone in the city was reading about them, about her. The lead story on both the six and eleven o'clock television news was about Nemerow.

In today's paper she read quotes from the mayor and the police commissioner. Even the governor had responded to a question about the killings in a press conference. He had referred to her as a monster. She wished she hadn't read that. She was not a monster. If only he knew, he would never call her that.

She put the *Times* down and picked up the *Daily News*. "Police continue to follow up on a number of leads and express confidence in apprehending the killer soon." It was the first such positive statement coming from the police. Were they bluffing? Fending off pressure from the Nemerow family?

Nemerow. She'd had a feeling that Charles Barton was a fake name. Like she was some cheap tramp he'd picked up, not worthy of knowing his real name.

No question he was an important man. Not like the others. Now she had opened a Pandora's box. "A number of leads." Had she been careless, made a mistake? Those people at the elevator. How much of her did they see? Of course the police must have talked with them by now. Why no mention of it? She was glad she had the presence of mind to take the handcuffs, but it was stupid to take his wallet and jewelry. How could she think that would fool anyone? What other stupid things did she do?

*       *       *

Three days after Nemerow's murder, at five-thirty in the afternoon, Clark Hamilton called. "Frank, we've got some lab results for you if you want to come over. I think you'll find them rather interesting. I'll be here until about seven-thirty," Clark said.

"Be right over," Frank said. "That's got to be a world's record for those guys, Jerry. Funny what a little heat'll do, huh?"

"A lotta heat," Jerry said."

Frank went over to Harry's desk. He wasn't there. A hurried look around the room and Frank spotted him in the far corner of the precinct talking with another cop. Even in the drab blue uniform, her breasts protruded majestically. Harry's face was inches from hers.

"Hey, Harry," Frank yelled across the precinct. "You think you could pull yourself away and come over here?"

All eyes turned on Harry and the busty cop. She turned and bolted in the other direction, while Harry sauntered toward Frank, trying to look casual. When he reached Frank, he was no longer casual. "Goddamn it, Frank. What do you want to embarrass me like that for?"

Frank shook his head. "Harry, I'm not trying to embarrass you. I just don't think the precinct is the place to be playing grab ass when we've got a serial killer to deal with. Anyway," he grinned, "She's too much woman for you."

Harry started to speak, but Frank interrupted. "Come on. Clark Hamilton just called. They've got some lab results."

The police lab was housed in a typical New York brownstone on East Twentieth Street amid rows of other turn of the century brownstones.

Frank and Harry went straight to Clark Hamilton's office and found him sitting at his desk, typing.

"Well, it didn't take you fellows long to get here. Nice to see you, Frank. Harry." He offered Frank and Harry a seat and walked over to his coffee pot. "May I offer you gentlemen some coffee?"

Harry started to sit but Frank's nudge made him stand his ground. Frank knew Clark well enough to indulge him his geniality and hospitality before they could get down to business. But he also knew that once Clark had you seated you were his, until he was ready to release you.

Clark could be ponderous but Frank liked his courtly manner and elegant bearing, definitely out of place in the conduct of police business. He never swore nor even raised his voice. A refreshing misfit.

Clark handed them their coffee and again beckoned them to sit down. They sat, knowing he wouldn't begin until they did.

"Gentlemen, I have some interesting results for you. I know how busy you are, so let me get right to it." Clark was up and pacing around his office, carrying his notebook to which he occasionally referred. He was all business, in his lecture mode.

"We have done the gas chromatography on the perfume scent and have confirmed that it is indeed Jean Naté perfume." Clark paused to look at his small notebook and Frank seized the opportunity.

"Clark, the scent doesn't last for very long does it? I mean what's the longest period of time ago that the perfume scent would have come off onto Nemerow's garments?"

Clark's eyes widened as he stared at Frank. "Why, it had to have come in contact with him no longer ago than the evening before you found it on him," he said with the cocksure positiveness that sometimes irritated Frank.

"O.K., thanks. Please continue."

Clark resumed pacing.

"Now, unfortunately there were no follicles in the hair we examined, so we can't say for certain whether it's from a man or woman. However,

I can tell you from the pieces we found that this is long, natural dark brown or black hair. There are no traces of any substance to indicate this hair has been chemically treated. These pieces came from a head of long hair. Unfortunately that doesn't necessarily tell us that it was a woman or a man. But I can tell you that the person whose hair we examined had long natural dark hair. Oh, and definitely Caucasian."

"The hair wasn't dyed?"

"Not dyed."

"Not a wig?"

"Not a wig. Now, we've compared this hair with the natural hair found with Mr. Beatty, the first victim. As you know, they cannot be identified as being absolutely identical but they can be classified as similar."

"And the two are similar?"

"Yes." Clark resumed pacing and lecturing, hands behind his back. "The pieces of fabric found on Mr. Nemerow and the sofa are a deep red or wine colored cashmere. From its length and texture, I would say it's more likely from a sweater than from say a sport coat or topcoat. Mind you now, we can't be certain, but the consistency of the weave would tell me sweater.

"As you know, the prints we have from Beatty and Joey Brewer match. We do have several sets of prints from Chesbro's scene, but no matches with the other scenes. The glasses and the wine bottles were wiped clean. The hair fibers found at the Chesbro scene were from a wig of dark brown hair.

"There were prints all over Nemerow's place, but we couldn't get a match with any of the other scenes. Again, the glasses and wine bottle were wiped clean."

With this last pronouncement, Clark fell silent, peering down at Frank and Harry over his tiny spectacles. His soliloquy was over, but his expression told them he would now take questions.

"That it, Clark?" Frank asked.

Clark nodded. "That's it." Clark walked over to his desk, and set his pad of notes on it. "I hope we've been of some help, and please do give me a call if you need anything else." He reached toward a phalanx of pipes propped in a holder on his desk and withdrew one.

Frank backed away. Clark's pipes were known throughout the New York Police Department for the vile and foul smelling tobacco they harbored. Clark reached into a canister and began slowly, methodically stuffing pieces of tobacco into the pipe in that familiar manner common to all pipe smokers.

"Uh, Harry, I guess we're ready to go, aren't we?"

Harry was already at the door. "Yeah. I'm ready. Thanks, Clark. Talk to you later." They were gone, before Clark could light up.

"I'd say we got a pretty good profile of Mr. Nemerow's visitor the night he got killed," Frank said as they drove away. A tall, thirtyish or younger woman with long natural dark brown or black hair, wearing Jean Naté perfume and a dark red or wine colored cashmere sweater. She may very likely also have been wearing a long dark blue or black coat and a dark scarf. And she must be one tough lady."

# Chapter Thirty

Time was running out on Paul Gale. "I have a new dishwasher, Tony," Gale overheard Peter tell Tony. "He can start in one veek. Den I get rid of the jailbird."

One week. Today was Monday. The guy was most likely going to start next Monday. Saturday would probably be Gale's last day.

Eighteen years of waiting and planning and it was all coming down to one week. It wasn't like he hadn't been trying. But everything just seemed to go wrong. If it hadn't been for the goddamn phone call, he'd have had her right in her own apartment. That was exactly how he had planned it. Just the way he saw it happening.

So many misses. Some, so close. He picked up his knife from the table, the knife he had taken from the dead hooker. A smile crossed his face as he thought of how he had outsmarted the tough, street smart broad. The knife was razor sharp, but he ran it over and over against his knife sharpener. When he was satisfied, he pulled a hair from his temple and dangled it between his thumb and forefinger. One easy stroke, and the knife sliced the microscopic hair in two.

He had her patterns down pretty good now. But even with that, he kept striking out. He'd waited so long in the cold outside her apartment building and his patience finally paid off. This time he'd stayed with her and he almost had her…again. And she pops into that fucking restaurant with the fag in the tuxedo. Then another hour in the cold only to have her come out and jump in a Jag with some prick.

These incidents were discouraging. No question. But he was seeing another side of her, too. She liked to pick up men. That gave him some ideas. But one way or the other he would get her this week.

He retrieved the gun from his bureau drawer. It already gleamed, but he cleaned and oiled it, loaded the chamber, and carefully placed the gun next to his knife on the table. He liked seeing them together, silent reminders of his goals. He picked up the gun again and pointed it at the floor. "This one's for you, Peter, you son of a bitch," he whispered.

He replaced the gun and picked up the knife, letting it lie in the palm of his hand while he opened and closed his hand on the handle. He closed his eyes and saw the knife slide into and across his daughter's throat.

*    *    *

Frank stared wearily at his computer. The vodka martini tasted good. On the rocks. Ice cold. Vodka martinis were an acquired taste, but worth the effort.

It was late and he'd been home for only fifteen minutes. Another long week. But they were making progress. Nemerow's black book was shaping up as a gold mine. Somewhere, among those pages of names, he felt certain they were going to find the woman they were looking for.

Somehow he found the mental energy to finish the article for the *Journal of Police and Criminal Psychology*. At eleven o'clock he put the finishing touches on the thirty-five page piece, he'd begun a week ago. Progress was slow these days on the writing. As it was, mailing it tomorrow, he'd be still a few days late on his deadline. Jerry would say who gives a shit. But he wasn't built that way. Sometimes he wished he were.

Was it too late to call Denise? Eleven o'clock. She'd be long since conked out. Call her in the morning.

He turned off the computer and trudged into the bedroom. It was an effort to get out of his clothes. He let them fall on the floor, switched off the light and fell into bed, physically and mentally exhausted but unable to sleep.

It was a confusing time. The Wine Bottle killer had everybody jittery. Jerry's acting weird. Going through the motions, like he's ready to pin the killings on anybody, just not make waves or let this thing screw up his retirement. Running scared.

He was still fumbling with his personal life. He'd promised to call Denise during the week and shoot for something toward the end, like Friday. Then the shit hit the fan with Nemerow.

And Carla was playing games with him again. He wished he'd never gone to Weltman's party. He closed his eyes and saw her standing in the doorway of the detective's bullpen.

"Uh, Frank," Steve Monahan leaned over his desk and whispered. "You've got company."

He looked up and saw her standing there, hair wrapped in a scarf, no make-up, wearing jeans and a wind breaker, a bag big enough to carry Jerry hanging over her shoulder. Somehow she managed to look stunning. For a moment, typewriters stopped, the din and chatter went silent and he thought he was going to lose it.

She moved across the room in that way that she had and stood over him. "Hi. I was in the neighborhood and thought I'd stop in and say hello." She seemed oblivious to the impact she was having on the room, but he knew she wasn't.

He was on his feet. "Nobody is just "in" this neighborhood. What brings you here?"

"You. Actually I was in the neighborhood five blocks away and figured it was close enough to drop by. How about taking me to lunch?"

He wished she didn't look and smell so good. "I was just heading out. I've got an appointment a few blocks from here."

"Are you walking?"

"Yeah."

"May I walk along with you? This is a rough neighborhood and I'd feel so much safer with you." She slid her arm through his.

The room was still silent. He felt like they were talking through a microphone. All he wanted to do was get the hell out of there. "Sure, let's go."

She continued holding his arm as they walked along Thirty-fifth Street. It seemed so natural. Just like normal people.

"Frank, can we duck inside somewhere? I need to talk with you."

Oh, Jesus. Yes, he thought. Walking along the street with her holding him, with her so close, so desirable, a whole year's longing took hold of him.

They went into a coffee shop and sat in a booth. The booth was small and their knees touched. She placed her hands over his and gently squeezed. The physical contact was enough for him to lower his guard. His hand went up to her face. "Nice to see you," he whispered.

"You, too." Her eyes moved up and down him.

He thought she seemed nervous.

"You mind if I smoke?" she asked him.

He shook his head.

She lit it and took those quick deep puffs, blowing the smoke out the side of her mouth, the way she always did when she was stressed. "Frank, I've been thinking about you a lot since we saw each other at David's party. And then I couldn't believe how disappointed I was when I called you and you turned me down."

She was leading up to something that was going to complicate his life. Don't do this Carla he wanted to say. But he also wanted to hear her say the thing he'd been fantasizing over for a year. How would he handle it?

She took the scarf off and started playing with her hair. "Frank, please don't think me crazy and hear me out. When I saw you on the street that day, my stomach did funny things. I didn't know what to make of it. Then, even though I was the one who cut things off at David's, I couldn't get you out of my mind. Still can't."

He eyed her cigarettes. It'd been six years.

She picked up the cigarettes and put them in her pocket. "No you don't."

He grinned. She still had that knack of reading his mind.

"Frank. I know this is going to sound crazy and your logical mind may not be able to process it, but please listen to me."

He wished he'd grabbed the cigarette before she pocketed them.

"I've been offered a movie role in Italy. I turned it down at first, because I just couldn't leave the city at the time, that was a few weeks ago, and still can't. But they've postponed shooting on it until February or March and by that time I should be able to leave the city. So I've agreed to do it."

"Congratulations."

"Please don't take that tone of voice, Frank. I hate it when you do. Anyway, if they like what I do the producer says he's going to want me for another he's planning when this is finished. The bottom line is I'll probably be over there for about a year maybe more."

"Good. Sounds like a dream come true for you. Why are you telling me all this?"

"Because I know you and I know me. I'm going to want to see you and spend time with you before I go. I don't think I'm wrong in saying you might like that too. But it wouldn't be right or fair to either of us. I'm going to be gone for at least a year and a lot can happen in that time. It could even be longer."

He beckoned to the waitress for the check.

"Frank, I know I'd be calling you in the next few days if I didn't hear from you and it would be very easy for me to resume things with you."

"Things?"

"Goddamn it, you know what I mean. So, what I'm saying is I've got to head this off at the pass for my own good and yours. Now, having told you all this if I should call, it shouldn't be hard for you to say no and hang up."

The waitress brought the check and Frank paid her. He turned back to Carla and just looked at her for a moment. "You know, you're right. I never could figure your logic. Hell, even married to you for a year, I never really figured you out. So, what's changed? I gotta go." He got up and left, resisting the urge to turn and look at her.

It was close to two in the morning before he finally fell off to sleep. It had been a crazy week.

# Chapter Thirty-one

On Saturday morning, the first thought on Frank's mind was Denise. A good sign, but he couldn't get the bizarre conversation with Carla out of his mind. There was just something weird about the whole thing. She seemed jumpy, disjointed. What she was trying to say wasn't easy, and it wasn't exactly a fun conversation. But it was more than that. He'd never really seen her like that before.

Eight o'clock. Denise should be awake.

"Hello."

"Did I wake you up?"

"No, I...Frank?" Her voice went up an octave.

"It's your friendly wake-up call."

"How are you?" It went back down two.

"Dennie, I'm sorry to take so long to call. No excuse. I've just been working constantly."

"The wine bottle killer?"

"Yeah. Uh, I know this is not cool, I mean such short notice, but any chance I could see you tonight?"

She thought of his promise to call earlier in the week, his half promise to see her on Friday. She thought of Gina's comment about seeing him with another woman. Her first reaction was to tell him she's busy. "Sure."

"Great. Want to go out to dinner?"

"Tell you what. How about if I have you over here for dinner?"

"Sounds good to me."

"I'll probably suffer by comparison with you, so I'm not going to get too creative. But I do good things with fish. You like swordfish?"

"Love it. I'll bring the wine. What time?"

"Seven?"

"See you then."

*       *       *

Harry was waiting for him when he got to the precinct. "Frank, we got a run-down on most of the women on Nemerow's list. Quite a cross section. Most of 'em are high ticket call girls. Also got a few married ladies, couple actresses, a few models, woman who's a big shot in the garment business. He's even got a college student. Our friend Mr. Nemerow had an active sex life."

Frank nodded. A touch of envy in Harry's voice?

"Most of them have an alibi for that night. The married ones are scared shitless but the ones we've talked with so far can account for their whereabouts that night. Some of the hookers don't remember where they were. You recognize any of the names?"

Frank shook his head. "No, do you?"

"Er, yeah, I, uh, recognize a couple of the hookers."

"Any of them fit the description of the person the Greiffs saw on the elevator?"

"Yeah, a few of the hookers do. I mean roughly, you know? Tall, big women. Haven't been able to reach all of the women yet."

"Any of them wear Jean Naté?"

"Not so far."

"How about Chesbro's list?"

"Nothing but legitimate clients so far. We'll get to them all."

"O.K.," Frank said. "But I think Nemerow's list is our key. One way or the other, it's going to lead us to our killer."

When Frank arrived home late in the afternoon, there was a message on his machine to call his father.

"Frankie, you sign that book contract yet?"

"Yes, as a matter of fact, I did. Is that what you called about?"

"How much you get?"

He pictured his father, sitting on the edge of his chair, leaning forward, nodding his head. "Just what I told you. Five thousand advance and twelve percent royalties on the sales."

"You shoulda held out for more, Frankie. You're gonna write a hell of a book. Can I tell your mother?"

"Course you can. But I haven't written it yet. Just wrote my name on a contract."

They talked about the wine bottle case. Silvio wanted a complete update. But it was obvious to Frank that his sources had him pretty well filled in.

"Frankie, be careful you don't get sucked in too much on the hooker theory."

"Oh? Why not?"

"First of all, cashmere sweater doesn't sound like what your typical hooker wears. Even if she's making a lot of money. Just too soft and wholesome a garment for a prostitute."

"And second of all?" Frank asked, still amazed at how much his father knew about important cases, even though retired.

"Secondly, Jean Naté is not a hooker kind of perfume or cologne. Again, too light. Not sexy enough."

Frank nodded. "Unless she figures she's already sexy enough. Maybe even wants to play it down. Anything else?"

"Yeah. The description of the girl with Joey Brewer doesn't strike me as a prostitute."

Frank went into the shower to start getting ready for his dinner date. His mind whirled.

*        *        *

Crystal Wilcox stood looking out the wide windows of the hotel suite. The vista across Central Park let her imagine for the moment that she was out of the filthy city. Hopefully, she would be soon.

"You like it Crystal?"

She turned back to her host. "It's very nice. The whole suite is spectacular."

"It's all yours, honey. Or I should say ours." He gestured toward the liquor cabinet. The cupboard is full of all the things you like. Nice wines, champagne, Glenfiddich, and of course, some Remy Martin."

Crystal nodded. "You've done well. Of course you always do. And you do know that woman does not live by alcohol alone." She gave him her dirty smile. "Or should I say function?"

"I think if you'll look in the top drawer of the cabinet, you'll find what you have in mind." She opened the drawer and removed a small plastic bag filled with white powder.

"Would you like some now?" he asked.

She shook her head and went over to the couch and sat next to him. "Not right now. Why don't we work up to it slowly? I'm here for as long as you like. There's no rush." Her lips rested on his face as she spoke. He reached for her and she slid away. "Let's first get our business out of the way, honey, so we can relax and have some champagne."

He went into the bedroom and returned with a thick wad of hundred dollar bills, which he handed her.

She counted the bills and rolled her body into his. "Hmm. Feeling generous this trip aren't we?"

"Like you said Crystal. There's no rush. I've got no place to go and neither do you sweetheart. So let's settle in and enjoy."

# Chapter Thirty-two

Frank stood outside Denise's door. He felt awkward standing there holding a bouquet of roses in one hand and a bottle of wine in the other. The flowers were a last minute impulse.

"Hi! Come in."

He stood in the little entry way and her eyes landed on the flowers.

"Oh my God, Frank! Roses! They're beautiful." She took them from him and set them on the table. "Frank, you are so sweet." She leaned forward and kissed him. Before he could react she was whirling around the apartment, setting out wine glasses filling a vase with water, arranging the roses.

"Hey, slow down. Give me a minute to look at you?"

She finished with the roses and turned toward him. The white pearls against her black sweater were one of the little simple touches he loved in her. Each time he saw her now she seemed to look more beautiful than the last time. She walked over to him her hips rolling against the dark slacks.

He slid his arms around her neck and they stood looking at each other. "I got a kiss for the roses. How about the wine?" He pulled her into him gently and they kissed, not with passion, but it was a kiss that promised more.

They made drinks and sat down in the living room. He looked around the room at the array of books and magazines on decorating and picked one up. "Your passion, right?"

"Yes, she said softly. I love sewing and making things and just decorating, I guess. I suppose my dream has always been to have my own home and spend all my time decorating it."

He waved his hand around the apartment. "Beautiful."

"Thanks," she said, took a sip of her drink, and flicked her hand across her hair. He liked the way she did that, too.

"How's your investigation coming with the wine bottle killer?"

"Slowly." He held up his glass. "Where'd you learn to make such a good martini?"

"Frank, why is it you always change the subject when I ask you about your work? Don't you like to talk about it?"

"It's not that. I like my work. But it's with me twenty-four hours a day. When I'm with you, I like to forget it and focus on you."

"I know you like your work a lot. That's why I ask you about it. The papers say you've got some good leads and that you expect, let's see, how did they put it? Expect to apprehend the killer soon."

He laughed. "Yeah. I wish. That's P.R., to take a little pressure off. We're making some progress, but we're a long way from an arrest."

"Are you getting a lot of pressure?"

"Sure we are. Four murders within six weeks. And if you're reading the papers you know that the last one came from a prominent family. That just adds to it. Anyway, I'd rather talk about you. What have you been doing all week?"

"Waiting to hear from you."

"Walked into that one."

She smiled. "Yes, you did."

"I should have warned you. You're dating an idiot who's married to his job. Causes a lot of problems. It's especially bad right now. I did mean to call you all week. It just slipped away from me."

"You sure you didn't have other distractions?"

He looked up, studying her expression, trying to figure out the funny look on her face. And then he got it. "Care to tell me what you mean by that?"

"It's no big deal, Frank. I shouldn't have even mentioned it. Do you want another drink?"

He shook his head. "This may or may not be what you mean, but the only distraction I had other than this case was my ex-wife coming by the precinct. The distraction was short lived, believe me."

"How'd you know that's what I meant?"

"I'm a cop. Let me ask you. How'd you know?"

She told him about Gina and he explained the reason for Carla coming by.

Denise sat for a moment, saying nothing. Frank got up and refilled their drinks, letting the silence hold.

It was Denise who broke it. "She must be very beautiful. I mean a model and a movie actress."

He laughed. "Actually, she looks a lot like you. Tall, long dark hair and if she's beautiful it's because she does look like you." He paused and touched her face. "I can tell you one thing, Dennie. She doesn't have anywhere near the inner beauty that I see in you."

Her eyes clouded over. "Thank you, Frank," she said and turned away.

"Hey, that's not something to cry over." He turned her face back to him and wiped away the tear.

"Sorry," she said. "It was just such a lovely thing to say. Let me get dinner going."

They ate by candlelight and adjourned to the living room with coffee and brandy.

"You like the brandy? I remember you said it was your favorite."

"Courvoisier. What a sweetheart you are."

She studied him. "Frank, I'm curious about what happened to your marriage? How come you got divorced after only a year?"

Another thing about her he liked. They were adding up. The blunt, straight out of the box way she had. Nothing subtle. "I told you earlier. I've been married to the job. That's what broke up our marriage. I was never around. She just got tired of playing second fiddle."

She ran her hand along his face. "Did you love her a lot?"

"Yeah. I did. But I got over it," he lied. "Actually, she did me a favor, a couple of favors. The break-up helped me to understand there's more to life than being a good cop. Too late in her case but, hopefully, not the next time."

"What's the other favor?"

"I met you."

She made a little noise of contentment and snuggled into him.

He felt good holding her and it was funny, but he liked talking about Carla with her. He'd never been able to talk about her. Even with Jerry, he'd cut off the discussion. With Denise, it seemed easy, like a catharsis.

"You know," he continued, " I did love her and I was pretty broken up when we split. But looking back, we didn't really share an awful lot. We had great sex for a while, a lot of laughs and fun for a while, and there was a lot of passion…for a while. But as I look back, I never really knew all that much about her, I mean for being married for a year."

"What do you mean?"

"Well, her parents were both dead and she never talked about them. When I met her she had only been in New York for a short time. Moved here from Chicago, but she'd lived in other places before that."

"Where?"

"New England, Washington, Philadelphia. You know, it's crazy, but looking back, there's just not very much that we ever talked about concerning her. She was very good at drawing me out and then after a while, I don't know, we just never talked much about our backgrounds. Too focused on the present I guess."

"Are you happy, Frank?"

He thought for a minute. Who is ever happy? Jerry? Sweating out his last year of being a cop so he can have a few left to live like a normal human being? Harry? Married three times and still chasing any pig who'll drop her drawers for him. Carla? You gotta be kidding. Susan Barsky? Too busy trying to help dysfunctional people to pull her own life together. "The simple answer to that question a month ago was no. Right now?" He moved her head from against his shoulder and held her face in his hands. "The answer is yes." And he meant it.

Her arms went around his neck and they kissed again, this time hungrily, mouths open, searching, biting. Her tongue played in and out of his mouth and slid across his face.

"Denise," he whispered. "I want to make love to you."

"Oh, God, Frank. I want you so much."

He slid off the couch, took her by the hand, and led her into the bedroom.

# Chapter Thirty-three

Carla Sanders poked listlessly at the filet mignon on her plate. She drained her wine glass and poured more from the bottle.

"For Christ Sake, Carla," her agent Randy Stern whined. "What's eating you? Here I am taking you to dinner at the most expensive restaurant in New York, where we're supposed to be celebrating your good fortune and my genius in your getting a very important part in a very important movie and..."

"Randy, stop giving speeches."

"Carla, I will never figure you out as long as I live. Any other woman I know would be on top of the world and you sit around pouting. Why? Just tell me why. That's all."

She finished off the wine and poured more. She thought of Frank and that stupid conversation. The one time she tried to do the decent thing and be up front with him and what does it get her? Misery. How could she have known that seeing him again would affect her like this? But she had made decisions and there was no turning back now.

"Randy, did you ever stop to think that maybe the reason you look like such a genius in landing these opportunities for me is because I am what I am? Unpredictable, moody, a little off-center, a bit of a pain in the ass, but intriguing, sweetie, right? Now, how about ordering us another bottle of that wine?"

"All right, all right," Randy sighed. "Only just don't change your mind again about the movie, O.K.?"

\*　　　\*　　　\*

On Sunday morning Frank and Denise made love again. And again. The ice was now broken completely for Frank. He'd been wary and cautious for a year, his guard always up. But this was a no-brainer. There was nothing about this woman he didn't like. What you see is what you get. And he loved what he saw.

Denise lay next to him stroking his face. "Frank, you are a wonderful man do you know that?"

He thought about her question last night. "Frank, are you happy?" Right now he was feeling happier than he could remember being for a long time.

"What are you thinking?" she asked.

"I was just wondering if we should get up or...you know, fool around some more?"

"Let's do both. First I'll make you one of my super duper breakfasts, and after that, we can fool around some more...all day if you're up to it. Go take a shower, while I get it started."

The breakfast—a western omelet, home fries, orange juice, toast, and coffee—was the first real breakfast he'd had in maybe a year. He wasn't counting the stuff he threw together at three o'clock in the morning. "You're almost as good a cook as I am," he said.

"Hmm. High praise."

"You know, last night you got me talking about a lot of things, even my ex-wife. We never got around to you. Remember? You seduced me before we had a chance."

"Good."

"It was better than good."

"That's not what I meant."

"So, you've been in New York five years. You're not a New Yorker, where are you from?"

"No, I'm not a New Yorker. I'm from Middlebury, Vermont."

"Vermont. Why does that not surprise me. And I bet you lived on a farm."

"Sort of."

"And you milked cows and drank a lot of it." She smiled the shy smile when she thought he was complimenting her.

"You told me your mother and father are both dead. Do you have any other family?"

"Nope, I was it."

"Have there been any special beaus in your life?" He didn't ever remember using the word beau before, but it seemed to fit her.

She dropped her eyes and turned her head away. He sensed a change in her mood.

"I'm sorry if the question was too personal. Didn't mean it to be."

She turned back to him and smiled. "You're not being too personal, Frank."

He smiled back and waited.

"There was one. We were together for two and a half years. I thought we were going to be married. And then one day out of the blue, he told me he'd met someone else." She shrugged. "And that was it."

The sadness in her eyes told him the shrug was a feeble cover up for pain that hadn't fully left her. "How long ago was that?"

"I met him a few months after I came to New York. So it's been about two years now. He got married four months after he dumped me. I later learned he'd been seeing her while he was talking marriage with me."

"Nice guy."

She looked up at him, the sadness in her eyes joined by a neediness he'd noticed before. He was sorry he'd brought the whole thing up. Sorry to see the pain there.

She nodded. "It's made it hard for me to let a man get close. Guess it turned me into kind of a recluse. I've spent more time alone than with people. That's the way I've wanted it." She reached across the table and put her hand on his cheek. "Until now."

He went to her, took her in his arms, and held her. She slid her arms around his neck and hugged him as if she would never let go.

His beeper went off. "Oh. Oh." He checked the number. "That's the precinct. Can I use your phone?"

"Sure." She beckoned to the one on the kitchen wall.

"I'll use the one in the bedroom."

A few minutes later he reappeared. "It's one of my partners. I've got to go down to the station."

"What's up?"

"Don't know. But I have to go."

"Well, it must be pretty important to drag you out on Sunday. Is it about the Wine Bottle Killer?"

He took her in his arms and kissed her. "Hey, stop grilling me." She smiled at his play on her word.

"Call me?"

"I'll call you. And thank you for sharing with me, Dennie." He kissed her again and was gone.

Harry was waiting for him at the precinct. Frank was not surprised that Jerry wasn't there. He couldn't remember the last time he'd seen Jerry out on a case on a weekend, either Saturday or Sunday.

"Frank, I think we're getting somewhere. Turns out that one Virginia Nichols in Chesbro's book happens to be Sandy Nichols, one of our friendly neighborhood hookers."

"You know her?"

"No. Don't know her. I understand she's fairly new. Hasn't been around long. Also a loner. Doesn't seem to know many of the other girls."

"She say if any of the other girls knew Chesbro?"

"Yeah. Just one that she knows of. Vickie Torrez."

"Ah, old Vickie," Frank said.

"You know Torrez?"

"Yeah. Known her for a long time. She works the streets and bars in mid-town. Tough cookie."

"Yeah, I know her, too. Anyway I went to her apartment. The doorman says she hasn't been around for a couple days. Seems she does that."

"Does what?"

"Disappears from time to time for a few days or so. We'll find her. She can be real helpful, Frank. She knows everybody. If anybody's gonna recognize any other hookers' names, Vickie will."

"What about the other one, Sandy?"

"Says she's seen Chesbro a couple or three times at her place. Strictly business. Never heard of Nemerow."

"What's she look like?"

"Not bad at all. Sandy colored hair like her name. She's tall. Five-eight. I showed her picture around the bars in the neighborhood. Some of the bartenders recognize her. No luck in Barney's or the other two joints Joey hung out in. Says she never heard of Joey. She's got no solid alibi for any of the nights in question, including Chesbro."

"Let's get her in for prints."

Harry looked uncomfortable and started to protest.

"Harry, it's O.K.," Frank said. "Remember, I told you. I'll give it to you verbatim again. There may be 'narrowly circumscribed procedures whereby a judicial officer can authorize the brief detention required to obtain physical traits such as fingerprints without offense to the Constitution'. Now that's straight out of the Supreme Court, a direct quote from Justice Brennan. You can do it Harry. Trust me. We'll get prints on all of them who can't account for that night."

Harry nodded.

"Come on," Frank said. "Let's bring her in now."

*    *    *

Monday passed without Denise hearing from Frank. By Tuesday afternoon still no call. She called him at the precinct. Not in. She was not having a good day. After Saturday night and Sunday morning, she was so sure Frank would be calling on Monday. Here it was getting toward the end of Tuesday and nothing. Was she wrong to trust him?

Would he treat her like this and just take her for granted now that he got what he wanted?

"Hey, day dreamer wake-up."

She turned to see Gina standing in the doorway. "Gina. Come on in. Sit down and tell me what you've been up to."

Gina slumped heavily into the chair. "Same old crap. Little of this. Little of that." She gave her dirty laugh. "Not enough of that."

She was relieved that Gina seemed like her old self.

"How about you Dennie? You still seeing that doll of a cop?"

"Yes." She told Gina about their dinner on Saturday and her concern that he hadn't called.

"That's men for you, sweetie. Once you let 'em get in your pants, they change on you."

"Who says he got in my pants?" Denise demanded.

"Hey. You had him up to your place for dinner. Candlelight and wine, soft music. Come on, Dennie. This is old Gina you're talking to."

Denise shook her head. She liked Gina's bluntness, got a kick out of her sometimes outrageous behavior, but this was too much. Her eyes filled up. "I'm not feeling well, Gina. I think you'd better go."

"Oh, come on, Dennie." She went over to Denise and put her arm around her. "I didn't mean anything by that. It was just another one of my stupid remarks. Can we forget it? I'm sorry." She pulled Denise to her bosom and hugged her.

Denise moved away from her. "It's O.K., Gina. It's forgotten. But I really don't feel well, so can I just see you tomorrow? I'm going to go home now."

"Sure. See you tomorrow."

# Chapter Thirty-four

On Tuesday night the woman lay quietly across her bed. She was tired. Looking back it seemed she'd been tired since that night with Jack Beatty, when all the anger, all the memories that lay buried for so many years, tumbled out.

She knew there was rage inside her. The doctors had prepared her, helped her to understand and accept it. She knew she hated him, but she never knew how much until that night with Beatty. Now, she just wanted it all to end, the only way it could.

She had been aware of his presence for weeks; the phone calls, the phony UPS man, the times on the street where she sensed him so strongly, she could almost reach out and touch him. She knew he was stalking her. He was probably outside, watching her building now.

The phone rang. She picked it up halfway through the first ring. "Hello," a harshness in her voice. "Oh, hi! A drink?" She was about to say no. A drink was the last thing she felt like. But something made her say yes. "O.K. See you there in twenty minutes."

Fifteen minutes later she emerged from the building. She stood in the street, looking in both directions, her head swiveling back and forth. The street was empty and quiet.

The man stepped out of the shadows and started across the street. The light changed up the block and a stream of cars appeared, including several cabs. She flagged one down and drove away. Paul Gale hailed another and ordered the driver to follow her.

Her cab pulled up in front of a bar and she went in. Gale waited outside for a while, pondering his next move. He was tired of waiting. He would wait no more. He opened the door and walked in.

The place was big and comfortable looking. Large easy chairs and tables were lined along a row of windows with booths along another wall and more tables and chairs grouped closer to a grand piano. A pianist played softly. The bar stood in a far corner.

Gale spotted her sitting with another woman at one of the tables by the window. "Perfect," he thought and headed for the bar, where he could see her clearly across the room, but she couldn't see him in the dim light of the bar. He ordered a beer and settled back to watch her.

He liked watching her. Old memories stirred in him. Now she was laughing. Little bitch. Put her in prison for eighteen years and see how much she laughs. She won't be laughing much longer. He ordered another beer.

*     *     *

"Come on, Frank." Harry Leonard stopped at Frank's desk. "The doorman at Vickie Torrez' apartment just called. She's home. Just got there."

Frank grabbed his coat and they took the stairs two at a time.

*     *     *

She'd been sitting with the other woman for an hour. They were nearly finished with their second drink. He noticed that she hadn't laughed or even smiled in quite a while. She seemed serious. Watching her for this long was almost more than he could stand. Something had to happen tonight.

"Uh, oh," he said aloud. The waiter brought the two women the check and they were paying him. Gale paid for his beers and headed for the door from the other direction. He stood hidden in a doorway a few doors down, waiting. His heart pounded and he felt the reassuring touch of the knife in his pants pocket.

The women appeared and stood for a moment talking, before heading in opposite directions. He fell in behind her, as she headed uptown for a block, and turned west. The street was crowded with people moving in both directions. She seemed in no hurry, walking slowly, acting kind of funny, he thought. Twice, she nearly bumped into someone coming the other direction. Like she didn't see them. "Keep walkin' baby, and then come to Daddy."

She approached a bar, very different from the one she'd just left. It was more Gale's kind of place. She stopped, looked in the window, and entered.

All right! He pulled his baseball cap tight over his eyes and walked into the bar.

\*      \*      \*

"I don't know what you guys are buggin' me for. You got no right." Vickie Torrez sat in her living room, chain smoking. "Harry, you know me for a long time. I never give nobody trouble. You know that."

Harry wished she wouldn't cross her legs like she did. He could see all the way up her thigh and it wasn't doing his concentration any good.

"I know that, Vickie," he said. "Nobody's suspecting you of anything. You tell us that you and your boy friend were in Puerto Rico the night Chesbro was killed, I believe you. And I'm sure you can prove it. The only reason we want to talk to you is I know you know everybody. I figure you can help us. Who else did Chesbro see besides you? Any of the girls know Mr. Nemerow?"

Vickie squashed her cigarette out and put another in her mouth. Frank beat her to the lighter on the table and flicked it under her cigarette. She peered down the cigarette and smiled at him.

He looked around the small apartment. Cheap pieces of furniture plopped down in no order. Functional and threadbare. Depressing. Vickie didn't seem to be a big success in her work.

Her clothing reflected her profession. Even relaxing at home, she wore the uniform. Tight miniskirt, peek-a-boo blouse, long earrings, a musky availability about her.

"Vickie, what kind of perfume do you wear?" Frank asked.

"Perfume? Why?"

Frank smiled. "You smell nice. That's why. I'm just curious what it is."

She softened and let a flicker of a smile escape. "I wear Opium. Glad you like it." Again a smile. She was warming up to Frank.

"I guess I like all kinds of perfume," Frank said. "If I had a favorite though, I'd have to say Jean Naté. It's what my mother wore. I always remember it as a kid."

Vickie looked quizzically at him. "Your mother?"

"Yes. She's gone now, but I can never think of her without thinking of that wonderful scent."

"Well, nobody wears that shit anymore. Sorry about your mother."

"It's too bad that nobody wears it anymore, though. Hard to believe. Nobody?"

"Shit, no. It's got no sex appeal, you know?"

Frank nodded and looked at Harry.

"We've got no quarrel with you, Vickie," Frank said. "Nobody harasses you, do they?"

Vickie shook her head.

"And you don't want anybody to start now, do you?" Harry asked.

She shook her head again.

"O.K., then. Let's have some names."

Vickie's demeanor changed. She was no longer cool, no longer angry, no longer flirting with Frank. She lit another cigarette, even though she had she'd just lit one and it was sitting on the ashtray. Frank noticed her hand shake when she lit it.

"I ain't talking to you no more. Get out of my apartment."

\*          \*          \*

She liked the bar. It was dark and faceless. The night at Barney's flashed vaguely across her mind…a hundred years ago. She tensed the muscles in her genital area, systematically applying, and releasing pressure. Her eyes closed.

She looked up and saw a stocky man with a goatee standing in the doorway. Even from where she sat at the far end she could see the sweat trickling down his face. When he lit a cigarette his hands trembled. She wondered why he seemed so nervous.

He made his way along the bar, heading in her direction. She looked at the two empty stools next to her, placed her purse on the one nearest her, and lowered her eyes.

"Mind if I join you, Miss?"

She spun around and faced the man. Stringy hair snaked down over his ears from under a New York Mets baseball cap. The salt and pepper goatee framed his small mouth. He stood with a little half smile.

She felt herself drifting, staring with blank eyes at the man.

He turned the bar stool around and squeezed into it. "Chilly out there." Without asking her, he ordered another glass of wine for her and a whiskey for himself. "So, what's your name, honey?" He passed his hand across her eyes. "Honey?"

She blinked. "My name?"

"Yeah, you got a name, don't you, honey?"

She nodded, her eyes still fixed on him. "Honey? Yes, Honey is my name."

He laughed, a scraping sound that forced an ugly cough from him. "Hey, that's O.K. with me, Honey. Mine's Fred. Hmm, you smell good. I like your perfume."

She gave him a hard smile but still said nothing. The man troubled her.

"Honey, you mind if I smoke a cigarette?" he asked, pulling out a pack of unfiltered Camels.

"Yes," she said.

"Hey, that's O.K. Honey. If I gotta choose between smokin' and talkin' to you, then no contest. No smokes."

She stared at his eyes.

"Hey, you all right? How many a those babies you had, anyway?" he asked pointing to her wine.

"It's nothing," she said. "I'm just getting over a little virus." The sound of her voice jolted her.

"Hey, you ain't got AIDS, have ya?" Again the harsh laugh, followed by a spasm of coughing.

She ignored the comment and took another sip of her wine.

His arm was across the back of her bar stool, parallel with his leg which was positioned between her leg and the bar stool. She was, in effect, hemmed in by him. "Come on, Honey. Have another wine. We're just gettin' to know each other." His fingers touched the back of her neck.

She shivered. "Yes. Let's get to know each other."

# Chapter Thirty-five

"I don't get it, Frank," Harry Leonard said, as he finished off the last of his second Cheeseburger. "Vickie's always been cooperative. I've never seen her like this."

"She's afraid of something or somebody." Frank watched Harry as he wiped the ketchup from his face and remembered why he promised himself not to eat with him again. "Harry, you ever eat anything besides cheeseburgers?"

"Sure I do."

"Oh, yeah. I forgot. French fries, cole slaw, apple pie and ice cream, right?"

"Right."

"You don't look like you're putting any weight on."

"I'm not."

"What about your lady?"

Harry gave him a wary glance. "What about her?"

"Well, you told me she wanted you to get some meat on you. All that shit you've been eating, you're still a bag of bones."

"She's not complaining. Still likes my stamina. Must be the cheese-burgers."

"Whatever it takes. Anyway, I think we leaned on Vickie as much as we could at her place. Tomorrow we'll get her down at the station."

"Something's bugging her, Frank. We'll get it out of her tomorrow. I gotta go. You coming?"

"No, you go ahead," Frank said. "I'm going to have another cup of coffee and try to think through some of this stuff."

"O.K.," Harry said. "You can get the tab then. Thanks for the lunch."

The lunch crowd was gone and the small coffee shop was quiet. Frank sipped his coffee in the booth, grateful for the solitude.

Life was never simple. He missed Denise and realized for the first time that it was two days since he'd told her he would call. And Jerry. He was drifting more and more into the background, like he just didn't want any visibility on this one. Running scared. Get it over with. Nail somebody, anybody.

The case was getting to him, too. They really didn't have much to go on. They might get something more out of Vickie tomorrow, but he was beginning to question the whole notion of a hooker being the perp. Silvio's right. Hooker's don't wear Jean Naté and cashmere sweaters. And the untreated hair fibers they'd found. There's not a hooker alive who doesn't mess around with her hair color. What the hell's bothering Vickie? Beatty. Didn't seem the type to pick up with a prostitute. He and his killer were looking at books. Not your activity of choice when you bring a lady of the streets to your pad.

And why would a hooker bother with Joey Brewer? The bartenders said they avoided him like the plague. Never had any money and he was a deadbeat. Owed most of them. Revenge?

Nemerow. A different story. No common street girls. No Vickies. But a high class call girl would be his style. Expensive, exotic perfumes. Sexy, turn-on clothing. A transsexual? Some of those guys could fool their mothers?

He'd worked so long with Jerry, he'd absorbed his intuition. And it was telling him the killer is overdue for the next one.

*      *      *

Paul Gale continued to caress the back of his daughter's neck. He was enjoying this. Things were finally working out the way he had hoped and planned for so long. "Come on, Honey. Have another drink."

"All right," she murmured.

"Hey, that's my kind of woman." He switched to beer and sipped it slowly. He needed to stay sober, in control.

The bar was warm. She slipped her coat off her shoulders and let it hang over the bar stool. Gale looked at the woman his daughter had become. He liked the firm breasts protruding from her sweater. The vee formed in her crotch looked tight and inviting. His mind raced back over the years and he fought to control his breathing. He coughed and took a deep slug of beer.

She stared straight ahead. Bothered. Something about this one was even more disgusting than the others.

"Hey, Honey. What're you thinkin' about? You're off in left field again. Talk to me." He put his hands on her shoulders and turned her toward him, leaning his face in close to hers. His hands went up and cupped her face. "You're a pretty lady, Honey."

She recoiled from his breath.

"Hey, you look so serious. How 'bout a little smile for old Fred?"

She studied him. The smile came, but it wasn't for him.

"That's a good girl, sweetheart." He smiled back at her.

Familiar. The ugliness of his smile. She blinked. The room was hazy and she felt dizzy and faint. Slowly, the room came back into focus and he was on his feet holding her.

"Hey, Honey. You almost keeled over. If I hadn't caught you you'd a taken a header right on the floor. Too much wine, baby. Here, lemme getcha over to the booth so you can sit back, pull yourself together." He sat her down in the booth and sat next to her, his arm around her.

She closed her eyes and listened to the words, the voice.

"Wake up sweetheart. Talk to me. Come on now." She opened her eyes. "That's a good girl. Here let me hold you."

The smell of whiskey and beer and stale made her nauseous. She opened her eyes and stared at the man holding her and thought of an ugly, hairy mole. "Oh, my God," she whispered.

"Honey, you all right?"

Her stomach had turned sour. The thought of the awful mole refused to go away. She blinked again...a little girl afraid.

"Hey, that's better, Honey. Your eyes are open. I thought I lost you there. You O.K.?"

She opened and closed her eyes until her head gradually cleared. "Yes," she said softly. "I'm O.K." She was thinking clearly now. Thinking the unthinkable.

Her hand slid up around his neck, behind his ear, caressing him. Her fingers, reaching, exploring, slid across a hairy bump and her body went cold. She moved her fingers back slowly across the growth behind his ear.

Gale moaned, his own eyes closed, mouth open, his breath coming in spasms. "Ooh. I like that, Honey."

She pulled her hand away and was on her feet.

Gale opened his eyes. "Hey, Honey. What's the matter?"

"I have to go to the ladies room."

She closed the ladies room door and leaned back against it, breathing deeply. The dizziness hit her again and she splashed cold water on her face. She staggered and went into a stall, locked the door and sat down. "Wake up, sweetheart. That's a good girl."

"It is. It is. It is him," even in a whisper, her voice echoed in the small stall. And she was afraid.

But there was no need to be afraid. This is what she'd been waiting for. The others were only warm ups. And then she smiled.

"I know who he is and he knows who I am. But I don't think he knows that I know who he is." Her hand shook as she reached for the door.

# Chapter Thirty-six

It was ten o'clock when Frank arrived home. He checked his messages. One from Susan Barsky and one from his father.. He hauled out the notes on his book and turned on the computer. But nothing would come. He picked up the phone and called Denise. He was way overdue. No answer. And no machine. She refused to buy one. He couldn't even leave a message and let her know he'd tried.

He felt frustrated, tired, and suddenly lonely. He eyed the phone again but left it alone, took a shower, had a nightcap and climbed into bed. Wide awake, his mind whirled. He sat up, picked up the phone, and tried Denise again. No answer. He hung up, started to put the light out, but instead dialed Carla's number. Her machine told him to leave his number and she'd call him back. He tried Susan but again no luck. He hung up and put out the light.

*       *       *

Paul Gale sat waiting for his daughter, barely able to contain himself. He had watched her long legs take her to the ladies room. Perfect slender lines up and down her body. Blood pumped and rushed into his forehead. It wasn't the only place it rushed. He squirmed in his seat. He had her. She'd be back any minute. He licked his lips.

She returned and sat next to him in the booth. "Miss me, Fred?" She touched his thigh and threw her head back, moving the hair from her eyes, all the while watching him, listening to his coarse breathing.

She needed to stay in control. Her hand moved along his thigh to within inches of his crotch and back down and up again, tantalizingly closer this time.

"Oh, Jesus, baby, you're drivin' me nuts."

He was beginning to sweat and she didn't know how much longer she could take sitting this close to him, "Where's your apartment, Fred?" she whispered, exhaling her breath into his ear.

His eyes were closed. He tried to talk but was incoherent.

"Fred!" she scolded.

"Oh. Uh, my apartment's being re-done. It's all tore up. It ain't fit to entertain in. How about yours?"

She frowned at this unexpected complication. "I don't bring men to my apartment, Fred."

"No sweat," he said. "I know a nice little hotel close by. We can walk there, relax and have some fun."

Risky. But she wanted him tonight. She had waited too long to let it slip away. "Sure, why not?"

They were an odd looking couple walking along Seventh Avenue. The short stocky man with the graying, unkempt goatee, baseball cap, poplin jacket, chinos and crepe soled shoes, walking along holding the arm of the beautiful young woman towering over him, sleek in long black coat and dark slacks. Her hair was tucked into the coat collar and a dark blue scarf covered her head and part of her face.

Her eyes searched the avenue until she saw what she was looking for. "Fred, would you go in and buy us a few bottles of wine to take up with us?" She smiled. "It may be a long night."

When they entered the small lobby of the hotel, she kept her head turned away from the front desk and waited at the elevator with her back to the clerk as Gale registered.

They got out of the elevator on the fifth floor and she followed slowly behind him as he searched the door numbers for their room. Her heart pounded. She was going on pure adrenaline now. She sensed the danger she was in, but she would prevail. She thought of her mother, of the things he had done to both of them.

The hallway was dark and smelled of mildew. "Here we are, Honey. Five-o-nine." He unlocked the door, snapped on the light and they entered.

# Chapter Thirty-seven

Frank awoke from a troubled sleep and looked at the clock on his nightstand. Twelve-thirty a.m. He was wide awake and something was bothering him. He wasn't sure what at first. There were so many things.

But something rattled around in his head. It was there as he was waking up. What the hell is it?

Vickie. Vickie Torrez. Tough woman. Been on the streets for ten years, around the pike and back again many times. Not the kind who gets frightened by a couple of cops talking to her. She'd been in and out of the station a dozen times over the years, always cocky, tough, a lady with an attitude. She knows she's not a suspect in the Chesbro murder. Not with an airtight alibi. Not really a suspect in any of them, and even if she was, it wouldn't faze her. And it sure as hell wouldn't cause her to act the way she did when we asked her for names. She's afraid of something or somebody. And then he got a brainstorm.

\*     \*     \*

She stood at the door, watching him set the three bottles of wine on the nightstand. It was the only piece of furniture in the room, other than the bed and a small bureau.

She eyed the bathroom. "Open the wine, Fred, while I slip in here for a minute." Inside the bathroom she held her breath until her chest threatened to cave in. Had she ever really believed he would come back into her life. That it would come down to this? She fought off the fear and forced herself to think rationally.

Once they'd left the bar, she was able to size him up. He was heavier than the others. And if he knows who she is, he has an agenda. Of course he knows. But she had an agenda, too.

"Hey, Honey. You didn't fall in, did ya?"

She entered the bedroom and saw her father sitting on the side of the bed in his shorts, holding two half-filled water glasses of wine. He tipped one toward her. "Come on over, Honey."

She looked around the room and saw the three wine bottles sitting on the night stand. The one he'd poured from still had some left in it. The others were unopened. Paul Gale sat beckoning with the wine, leering at her. Neither said anything. An eerie quiet settled over the room. In the silence, at that moment, she was certain that the man on the bed knew he was looking at his daughter.

She put her coat on the chair, never taking her eyes from him, and walked over and took the wine glass he handed her. In the same motion she picked up the bottle and poured the rest of the wine into the glass and moved back to the chair.

"I like a nice full glass of wine, Fred," she said. "It gets me a little crazy, if you know what I mean."

"Oh, baby." The words came out in a low growl. He wanted her so bad. "Come over here, sweetheart. What're you standin' way over there for? Come over here." He held his stubby arms out to her.

She walked slowly over to him, rubbing the wine bottle against her crotch. She thought how vulnerable he looked lying there in his near nakedness.

He lay on his back looking up at her. The bulge in his underwear was obscene and she felt like throwing up on him. The ugly sounds coming from him were those of long ago A faint trace of drool trickled from his partly opened mouth. They stared at each other. Father and daughter.

His hands went up and the coarse smile appeared. "Come to me, sweetheart."

She unbuckled the belt of her slacks and undid the first two buttons. He watched her and squirmed.

"Uh, uh, Fred," she purred. "You turn around. I don't like anyone watching me undress. When I'm ready, I'll tell you when to turn." A soft whisper. "You're going to like what you see."

"Oh, Jesus," he nodded and moved his head to the side.

She acted swiftly. Her arm went up and she brought the bottle down with all her strength.

Something about her movement must have alerted him. He moved his head—just enough as she brought the bottle down. It glanced off the side of his head and onto his shoulder. He yelped in pain and spun around.

Again she brought the bottle down and again, he moved just enough to absorb only a portion of the blow. Blood streamed from his head but he was far from finished. Before she could swing it again, he rolled away from her and onto the floor on the other side of the bed. In an instant, he was back up, crouching, smiling. And then she saw the knife in his hand.

They stood on opposite sides of the bed, facing each other. She held the still unbroken bottle. Her father expertly moved the knife back and forth. A smile spread across his face.

"Tried to hurt your daddy, didn't you?" The razor sharp knife gleamed under the ceiling light. He began slowly moving around the bed, flicking the knife in a semi-circle in front of him.

She watched him as if in a trance. And she was afraid.

"You send your daddy to jail, huh, Tookie? You told them on me, didn't you?"

She didn't want to look at him anymore, but his eyes never left her. Those ugly eyes. "Daddy missed you. He wants you take off your clothes and come to him. You hear me, sweetheart?", his voice, low and soothing.

She took a step back and stopped. He was around the bed, in the middle of the room, not four feet from her.

She continued to stare blankly, the bottle at her side. He smiled and moved slowly toward her.

She backed away until she reached the wall and stopped. Arms hanging loosely at her sides, she stood, her back against the wall, staring straight ahead listening to her father's words.

"That's a good girl. Now put the bottle down."

She stood motionless.

"Tookie." His voice was firm and mean.

The bottle slid out of her hand and thumped onto the rug.

"That's the girl. Now, take off your clothes for daddy," the voice commanded.

Slowly, never taking her eyes from him, she began removing her clothes. When she was down to her bra and panties, she stopped.

"Take off your bra, sweetheart. Do it for daddy."

She unhooked her bra and let it slide to the floor. Her father stared. His tongue flicked across his lips.

He moved forward, the knife now down at his side. "Now daddy wants you to move over to the bed and sit down."

She continued staring and moved sideways to the bed.

"Good girl. Now sit down."

He nodded his head and she heard the mean voice again.

"Sit down."

She did as she was told. Her father moved slowly behind her and sat with the knife at the back of her neck.

"Now, I want you to lean against daddy, and take off your panties."

She felt his hot breath against her neck and tears trickled down her face. She lifted her bottom and slid off the panties.

Her father reached around and put his hand between her thighs. Slowly, carefully he spread her legs apart. "That's it sweetheart. Now, Daddy's gonna take good care of you."

She closed her eyes. The smell of the whiskey and beer and the wine and the stale sweat and she was back in her little room. And he was going to do those things again. She began to sob. She felt her father's harsh breathing against her neck.

And then he penetrated her with his fingers.

A scream of horror and rage erupted from somewhere inside her. Her arm flailed and wrapped around one of the full bottles on the bed stand. Before her father could move, she smashed the full force of the bottle into his face. Again, she swung the bottle backward flush into his mouth.

His mouth fell open, the gold tooth surrounded by blood dangled like a piece of spittle.

She rolled away, turned, and swung the bottle again. The tooth tore from his mouth and arced across the room, trailed by a bloody spray.

With the last blow, the bottle slipped from her hand and rolled over the side of the bed. She stared down at what was left of her father. Blood gushed from the hole formerly occupied by the ugly tooth. Thick clots of blood and bone seeped from where his nose had been. The bulging eyes were no longer visible, covered with blood and pieces of peeling flesh.

Miraculously he still held the knife. Even more miraculously he sat up and moved his arm and the knife clumsily toward her. She lashed out at his hand and the knife fell to the floor. He struggled toward it, groping, and she pushed him off the bed. He fell on his back next to the hissing radiator.

Quick as a cat, she was on him, straddling him, pounding his head against the radiator.

"Tookie," he gurgled. "I'm your father. Don't."

She hesitated for a moment. It was just long enough for him to arch his body and catch her by surprise. She lost her balance and fell backward, and he was on her. The weight of his heavy body held her fast. His knee nudged against the fallen wine bottle and he grabbed it. "Now, you little bitch. Let's see how you like it."

That was when she saw the knife and drove it into his stomach. He gave a little cough, dropped the wine bottle, and fell sideways onto the floor.

She scrambled to her feet and stared down at the thing that had been her father. He was dead. It was over.

# Chapter Thirty-eight

Early Tuesday morning Frank arranged a witness warrant for Vickie Torrez to come down to the precinct and answer more questions. Next he called Denise, hoping to catch her before she left for work.

He let the phone ring five times and was about to hang up when she answered. "Frank." Long pause. "Hi!"

"Hi. I uh, didn't wake you up by any chance, did I?"

"Oh, yeah." Her voice was a foggy whisper.

He waited for her to collect herself, to respond. "You there?"

"Hi! Sorry. I was dead to the world." She was beginning to sound semi-normal.

"I called a couple of times last night. Last one was past your bedtime. Good to hear your voice."

"It's good to hear your voice," she was awake. "I've missed you. Missed your call."

"I know. I know. But I did call you last night. Better late than never?" It was a question, an uncertain one.

"I'm sorry I missed it. I was feeling lousy. Took a sleeping pill, which I hardly ever do and went out like a light. Never heard a thing until just now. God, if you hadn't called I might've slept the day away. What time is it?"

"Quarter after seven. Scandalous hour to be still in bed. On second thought, sounds like a good idea. Stay there. I'll be right over."

"No you don't. I've got to go to work."

"What're you doing tonight?'

"Nothing, I guess."

"How about a little Corso special dinner at my place?"

"I don't know. I…"

"Come on. See you at seven?"

"All right."

*    *    *

Frank picked up Vickie at noon. She was surly and uncommunicative. She was also very nervous. He tried a little small talk in the car but she didn't respond. They rode to the precinct in silence.

Frank and Vickie and Harry Leonard sat at the long table in the conference room. It was also the interrogation room. What they called it depended on who they had in there and why.

They sipped coffee for a few minutes before anyone spoke. It was Vickie. "The fuck you want with me, draggin' me down here like this?"

Frank watched her nibbling on her nails, eyes flashing around the room, already on her third cigarette. He wasn't looking forward to this.

"Vickie, you know and I know you aren't yourself. I've been around you too long. I know you. So does Harry. We've always been fair with you, haven't we, Vickie?"

No response. Only her glare.

"You've always been cooperative and straight with us. That's why we never crowd you."

Harry sipped his coffee and eyed Frank. He liked watching him operate.

"Vickie, I know why you're afraid. I know why you're not yourself. I know what you're hiding." He stopped and stared hard at her.

The room was not warm, but perspiration rolled off Vickie's forehead into her eyes. She dabbed at them, smearing the mascara. The sweat trickling down her face turned light brown.

"Vickie, everybody knows your turf. You don't stray more than a few blocks. Forty-fourth, Forty-fifth, Forty-sixth, Seventh Avenue, Eighth Avenue. That about right, Vickie?"

She stared sullenly, looking more and more like a cornered animal. Harry offered her a clean handkerchief. She refused it.

"Vickie," Frank continued. "Three months ago, a man was found in an alley off Forty-fourth Street. He'd been knifed to death. Last night when you were acting funny and then clamed up on us, it bothered me. It just wasn't like you. So, I got to thinking. And guess what I thought of?"

She took five or six quick, deep draws on her cigarette. Her eyes were all over the room.

"Vickie, there was a man on the street that night at about the time of the murder in the alley. After our little talk last night, I called the man. He was kind enough to drop in this morning and I showed him a picture of you. You know what Vickie? He says he saw you on the street that night. At about that time."

"Fuck you Corso." She was on her feet, shaking violently. "I didn't do that," she screamed. "You're not gonna' pin that on me." She sat down and popped up again. Harry stood up next to her, ready for anything.

Frank remained sitting. "We've been taking a lot of heat on this Vickie, Harry and I. The man was an important businessman. The chief is busting our asses to nail somebody on this." He stood up. "And we're getting goddamned sick of the pressure."

He walked over to the door. "Stick around Vickie, I'm going to get our witness back in here to take a really good look at you." He turned to Harry. "Shouldn't take much to pin this one down, Harry." And he left.

*     *     *

Denise looked at her watch. She'd been doing it all day. Three o'clock. Late enough. Mike's away anyway. Time to go home, take a nice, long hot bath. Wash her hair, do her nails, try on a few outfits before deciding. Maybe even have time for a little nap. Or at least rest.

She turned off her computer and dropped by Gina's to tell her she was leaving in case anyone asked. Dave was rummaging around on Gina's desk looking for something. "She's not here Denise. Didn't come in today. I Haven't heard from her all day."

Probably shacked up somewhere Denise thought, immediately ashamed of her mean spiritedness. She told Dave she wasn't feeling well and she was going home.

Dave had moved to the file cabinet in his search. "Must be an epidemic," he said.

Denise nodded and left.

Less then ten minutes after he left, Frank returned to the conference room. Vickie was crying. Her eyes were red and puffed. Her shoulders sagged and she was no longer glaring. She recoiled when Frank entered and gave him a frightened look.

"Sorry about this Vickie," Frank said softly.

"You get him?" Harry asked.

"Yeah." Frank said. He sat down and said nothing more to Vickie. Waiting.

Vickie began sobbing. "I didn't do it. It wasn't me," she squeezed the words out through the heaving and sniffling.

Frank went over to her and put his arm around her. "You want to tell us about it Vickie?"

She nodded. And she told them about the night with Crystal and Crystal's trip into the alley with the John. And she told them about the yelling and arguing and what she found when she went into the alley.

"He tried to screw Crystal out of the money. I guess she went bananas. When I got there, she was just pullin' the knife out of him. And then she stuck it in again. I tried to run but she grab me and hold the knife at my throat. She tell me I ever say anything she kill me. She say even if the cops have her, she knows people who will get me for her." And then Vickie really let go.

Frank called in a policewoman. "Stay here with Vickie. Get her any-thing she wants. Come on, Harry."

They went into Jerry's office who was still home with the flu. "You know, Harry," Frank said. "There are times when I really hate this fucking job."

"Frank, how did you know Vickie was connected to the murder of that guy?" Harry asked.

"I didn't. I knew something was bugging her bad. And then, I don't know. I just had a hunch. The guy was found in her area. Shit, she prac-tically lives on those two or three streets. You can walk down to Forty-fourth Street and make book that you'll see Vickie cruising along. Why should that night have been any different? So, I just threw it at her. What'd I have to lose?"

"And the guy, the witness you had in here? The guy you went to call. Just bullshit?"

Frank nodded. "I doubted Vickie would have killed the guy. She's not the type. But I was hoping she might know something."

"And you hit the jackpot. That was Tommy Sullivan's case wasn't it?"

"Still is. He talked to Vickie early on but nothing came of it. Sullivan's handling the murder in the alley last Tuesday, too, isn't he? The one you and Levine are working on with him?"

"Yeah."

"When Vickie calms down, we'll see if she knows anything about that one. My instinct says she doesn't. Too far out of her territory. Anyway, let's find Crystal, fast."

Harry called the number Vickie had given them. He got her machine. "Come on, let's get over there," he said.

"I can't," Frank said. He held up his hand to quiet Harry. "I've got somebody coming over and there's just no way I can get out of it." He looked at his watch. "In fact, I've got to fly now. Find Crystal. Use as many people as you need. Get inside her apartment if she's not there.

Get a search warrant. Look for pictures of her, cashmere sweaters, Jean Naté. Take the pictures over to Barney's. Show 'em to Billy.

"We're going to find her and get her in for prints. I've got a feeling we're going to find some matches. I'll be home all evening. Call me if you get anything or if you need me. We're getting close, Harry."

# Chapter Thirty-nine

Gerard Williams, the night clerk at the Haven Hotel, arrived for duty promptly at seven p.m. The hotel wasn't fancy nor was the clientele, but Gerard took his job seriously and took pride in his official title of night manager even though he was the only one there at night and had no one to manage. He felt nothing but contempt for Ned Haskins the day man.

As usual, Haskins was only semi-sober, when Gerald arrived to relieve him. "Hey, Williams, where the hell ya been, pal?" Haskins' speech was slurred, and he stumbled, making way for Gerald behind the counter.

"Ned, you reek of booze again. Don't you ever stay sober?"

"Who wants to stay sober, workin' this flea trap? Guy needs a couple a pops get through the day here. What a day. Maid didn't even show up to clean the rooms."

"What? Did you call a temporary service?"

"Nope."

"You mean none of the rooms have been cleaned?"

"Nope."

Gerard picked up the check in-check out register. How about check-outs?"

"Um, I dunno. Yeah, we had a few check-outs."

Gerald looked again at Haskins and realized he was worse than usual. "Ned, you're drunk. You been drinking all day haven't you?"

"Yep. How 'bout a lil' snifter, Gerard old boy." He reached under the counter and pulled out a nearly empty fifth of Seagrams. Gerard ignored him, so he took a sip himself.

The check-out book was a mess. Gerard would have to personally check every room to see which rooms were occupied and which were vacant. "Ned, take your booze and get out of here."

Haskins grabbed his bottle and stumbled out the door.

Gerard hung up the phone in frustration. He had called three of the temporary agencies he dealt with. None of them could provide him with a maid until tomorrow morning. The Diamond Agency promised to have a maid there by six a.m. He had used them before and they were reliable. If the hotel's own maid showed up, all the better. They'd have the place shaped up in no time.

He checked the register again and confirmed that eleven rooms had apparently been occupied. Five of them held permanent residents. So he was only dealing with six rooms. He still had nine rooms free that he could rent until the others were made up in the morning. Things weren't so bad after all.

*       *       *

Denise arrived at Frank's promptly at seven. She stood in the doorway, a tentative uncertain smile on her face, a tiredness in her eyes that dulled their usual sparkle. "Hi!"

She looked like she wasn't sure she was in the right place. He hugged her and everything else in his life stood still. "It's O.K. You can come in."

She leaned forward and kissed him gently on the lips. He wanted more, pulled her into him, and kissed her hungrily. He hadn't realized how much he'd missed her.

"Well." She caught her breath. "I'll have to drop in more often."

He handed her a glass of wine and stood for a moment admiring her. She wore a pale blue cotton top, camel pants, little or no make-up, hard to tell with her, and a pair of whimsical multi-colored earrings. "You look like a college kid."

She slumped into a chair at the kitchen table. "I don't feel like one. God, I slept like I was drugged. Come to think of it, I was. I can't remember the last time I took a sleeping pill. It's had me punchy all day." She gave him a little conspiratorial look and grinned. "I left work early."

"Denise!"

"I know. But I wanted to have plenty of time to get myself looking pretty for you."

"You did a good job. How come you weren't feeling well last night?"

"Oh. I was O.K. I think it was more disappointment than anything else." She paused for a moment, letting it sink in. "After you left Sunday, I thought about you a lot. When I hadn't heard from you, I was kind of sad and just wanted to sleep." She gave her little laugh. "Guess I felt abandoned."

She just laid it right out. No subtlety. No games. Just blunt honesty. "Sorry, Dennie." He really was sorry. Sorry he'd let two more days go by without seeing her or even talking to her. She was the best part of his life and he was screwing it up. "No excuses. Just the same old reason. My days and nights get away from me. Last night I had an early night. Got home about ten. That's when I called you."

"I know, Frank. Intellectually, I know why you don't call. But I'm a woman. I don't always think intellectually, when it comes to..." She groped for a word but let it drop. "How's the case coming? Any progress?"

"A little."

"Want to talk about it?"

He grinned. "No."

"O.K. Want to pour me some more wine?"

"Yep. And in a little while, I'm going to make you some of the best pasta you've ever had."

"You're so modest when it comes to your cooking."

"Nothing to be modest about. How does pasta with fresh tomatoes, capers, garlic, black olives and a touch of lemon sound?"

"Ah, putanesca."

"Right. Know how it got its name?"

She shook her head.

"The Putas, the Italian Harlots. In between tricks, if they got hungry, they'd whip this little number up because it was quick and easy. Then back to work."

"You're a regular fountain of knowledge."

"Yeah," he said and slid his arm around her waist. She leaned into him and he felt the heat coming from her. It was going to be a late dinner.

\*        \*        \*

At six-o-five a.m. the maid from Diamond arrived. Gerard gave her the list of rooms to be made up. There were two on the second floor, three on the third and one on the fifth. She decided to start on the fifth and work her way down.

\*        \*        \*

It was seven a.m. when Frank's phone exploded in his ear. The obnoxious ring was relentless.

"Frank, the phone." Denise's voice was foggy with sleep. She barely heard him answer it. Her mind floated with memories of last night, the spontaneous passion of their love making, dinner, and the sweet conversation, followed by more gentle, loving sex.

"Dennie. I've got to leave right away. Something's come up." He was up and already moving toward the shower.

She sat up on her elbows, bleary-eyed. "What is it?"

"Can't say right now." He closed the bathroom door, and was out of the shower and dressed in ten minutes. He said nothing, nor did she as she lay in bed watching him.

When he was dressed, he sat on the bed and took her in his arms. "Last night was wonderful. Perfect in every way." He kissed her. "And so are you." He started to pull away, but she held him.

"Frank, I love you," she said very softly.

He looked at her for a long moment. The sadness was gone from her eyes. In a perfect world he would have torn off the clothes he had just put on and snuggled back into bed with her. Instead, he closed his eyes and held her. When he opened them he said even more softly, "I love you, too." He was surprised at how easily it came out and how much he meant it. "Bad time to leave, but I have to. I'll call you tonight."

*       *       *

The scene inside room five-o-nine of the Haven Hotel was not pretty. They never were. Even with all the windows open, the smell was bad. The air was putrid with decay and offal. Blood was splattered every-where, the room in disarray. Frank saw the uncovered body, lying on its side next to the radiator. A wine bottle protruded from the rectum and a knife was still imbedded in the victim's stomach.

His face was undistinguishable, covered with dried blood and large welts. There was not much left of the nose and there were two ugly gashes in his head.

Frank had never seen so many people at a crime scene. The small room overflowed with a battery of specialists. CSI officers with their fancy evidence collection kits crawled around the floor. Fingerprint specialists, a photographer, video taper, criminalist, and the medical examiner with a forensic pathologist at his side all did their thing, somehow managing not to get in each other's way. The department had pulled out all the stops on this one. He thought of Silvio's stories of the old days when he and a partner were pretty much it at a murder scene.

Jerry stood in a corner of the room talking with a man Frank didn't recognize. He was glad to see his friend back on the job. He spotted Frank and came over. Jerry hadn't shaved. He looked jowly and tired.

"How're you feeling, Jerry?"

"I've been better." He looked over at the victim. "Maid found him at six-fifteen this morning. The medical examiner says he's been dead for about thirty, thirty-six hours. Probably killed sometime Tuesday night."

"When'd you get here?"

"Harry and I got here a little before seven. The patrol officer was here at six-thirty."

"What have you got?"

"No prints so far. Everything's been wiped clean as a whistle. Our killer is getting more thorough. The knife's a big break by the way."

"What do you mean?"

"It's got an unusual handle, covered with some kinda woven thick thread. Made by Talex. Never heard of them as knife manufacturers. It's definitely not your basic, run-of-the-mill knife."

Frank looked around the room. "There was a hell of a fight in here."

"Yeah," Jerry said. "The victim was bashed pretty good with one of the full bottles of wine. There are pieces of flesh and dried blood all over it. The other one's pristine." He glanced at the bottle still protruding from Paul Gale's rectum. "You can see dried blood and stuff all over the heavy end of that one, too."

Frank walked over to the pile of bed linens, bent over and smelled them. "You've got a slight odor of the same perfume in here. Come here and take a whiff."

"Yeah, I know. Faint, but it's there. Same smell as Nemerow's."

Frank went into the bathroom and returned. "There's some on the towel in the bathroom, too. Some pieces of hair, also. Any I.D. on him?"

"Nothin'. Not even a house key."

Frank motioned to Harry to come over. Jerry noticed and nodded.

"Yeah, Harry's got something interesting that you're going to want to hear."

Harry came over. "Frank, I went over to Crystal's. The super of the building hasn't seen her since he saw her go out Sunday night."

"What time?"

"About eight-thirty. He let us in her apartment. She's got four cashmere sweaters in her closet."

So much for one theory, thought Frank.

"And are you ready for this? One of them is red."

"You find any Jean Naté?"

"No, but she could be out. Or maybe she carries it with her in her purse. You know, to keep freshening up?"

"What else?"

"Not much. I mean clothes, shoes, purses, toiletries, books. Nothing so far that's going to offer any help.

"You lift prints out of there?"

Harry gave Frank a pained expression. "Course we did, Frank. What am I, a rookie? And guess what? The prints we took out match prints we got at Beatty's and Joey Brewer's. We also got a match at Nemerow's. We can place her at three of the murder scenes."

"All right! Find any pictures?"

"Nothing. We've got a good description of her from Vickie, and the police artist is working up a final sketch with Vickie now. We've got a rough one for now."

Frank looked at the sketch. "Doesn't look like somebody I'd want to go into an alley with. How'd she get the scar?"

"Nobody knows."

"What did Vickie say about the stiff in the alley last week?"

"Says she doesn't know anything about it. I believe her. Course Thirty-ninth Street is only a block away from Crystal's place. Except she's on the East Side. Oh, we picked up some wigs that were in the apartment. Sully brought them over to the lab to compare with the fibers we picked up at Joey's and Chesbro's. No report yet."

"How'd Vickie describe her?"

"Tall, about five ten or eleven. Well built. Very long black hair. She says the long hair's a wig, because she's seen her with her real hair, which is much shorter and she's seen her as a blonde and as a red head."

"So she dyes her hair."

"Right." She's got blue eyes and wears a lot of make-up. and the little scar. Vickie says she's a real looker."

"O.K. When's the sketch going to be finalized?"

"Maybe done now. When it is, we'll take it around to Barney's and the other bars and the victims' apartment buildings."

Jerry broke in. "She knows we're looking for her. No point in being subtle now. We'll plaster that sketch all over this city. Frankie, we're closing in on this broad. We're going to nail her."

Frank had never seen his partner so worked up. "Slow down, Jerry. You'll have a relapse."

"We've got her name in the National Crime Information Center Computer," Harry said. "Nothing yet. We're also got an APB out on her. And, we've got the word out on the street. We'll find her, Frank."

"Bet your ass we will," Jerry growled. He took Frank by the arm. "Commere Frank." He led Frank over to the man he'd been talking with when Frank arrived. "Mr. Williams, this is Detective Corso. Please tell him everything you've told me."

The neatly dressed black man smiled and shook hands with Frank. "How do you do, Mr. Corso. This is a terrible thing, and I'll be glad to cooperate any way that I can."

Jerry beckoned to him to continue.

Gerard Williams glanced at Jerry and turned back to Frank. "Well, Tuesday night around eleven o'clock, I was on duty and two people walked into the lobby. I was doing some paperwork at the desk, and didn't notice them at first. When I did look up, a man was standing at the front desk. I noticed the other person standing over by the elevator, facing away from me. The man said he wanted a room for two with a double bed for just the one night. He registered and paid in advance with cash."

"How did he register?" Frank asked.

"He registered with just his name, sir. I'm afraid we're not very particular about that sort of thing in this hotel."

"What name?"

Gerard had the registration book in his hand. He opened it and handed it to Frank. "There, you see it. John Jackson, room five-o-nine. That's his registration, sir."

Frank looked and handed the book back to him. "Tell me about the other person. Was it a man or woman?'

"That's just it. I couldn't tell. The person's back was to me. He or she wore a long dark coat and dark pants. They had a dark scarf over their head. The person was tall I'd say maybe six feet. Quite a bit taller than the man who registered."

Frank pointed toward the body. "Is the victim the man who registered?"

Gerard closed his eyes and nodded his head. "Yes, sir."

"Mr. Williams, you couldn't possibly tell if the person with the victim was a man or woman? Could you smell any perfume? Did the person walk like a man or walk like a woman? Do you have male couples checking in here or is it all heterosexual action? Is this a hotel where hookers bring their customers? Let's take the questions one by one, Mr. Williams, starting with the first."

"Could I possibly tell if it was a man or woman? No sir, I couldn't. As for walking, as I told you the person was over next to the elevator. When it opened, they both just stepped in. There really wasn't any walking involved. Perfume? No, I didn't really smell any perfume. And as for clientele, we have all kinds, including some male couples, and, yes, I have to tell you that prostitutes do come in here with their customers. I'm afraid it's one of their most popular hotels. I don't approve of a lot of the goings on in this place sir, but I just work here and try to do the best I can."

Frank was impressed with the man's thoroughness and his sincerity. The guy deserves better than this dump, he thought. He pulled out the sketch of Crystal. "Have you seen this lady come in here?"

Gerard looked at the picture and squinted his face. "It's hard to say with any certainty from this sketch, sir. But I think so. There is a tall woman with a scar like the one in this sketch who has been in here once or twice with a man. Not a pleasant person."

"The person with the victim Tuesday night. Could it have been this woman?"

Gerard put his hand over his mouth and studied the sketch. "Yes, it could very well have been. But there is no way I could say that the person with the victim Tuesday night was this lady. No possible way. I can only say that the size and build of the woman I've seen who resembles the woman in this drawing would be about the same as the person I saw with the victim.

"O.K., Mr. Williams. How about the victim. Had he been here before?"

"No sir. I never saw him before."

Frank pointed to the sketch. "When was the last time she was in?"

"Ooh. That's a tough one. But I'd say maybe five or six weeks ago. I know I saw her sometime in late summer, early fall."

"Do you remember what she was wearing then? Was she wearing a coat?"

Gerard thought for a few moments again before answering. He nodded slowly. "Yes, yes. She did wear a coat, a long dark one with the collar up. It was quite cool that night."

Frank wasn't surprised that Gerard would remember. he would have been surprised if he hadn't. "Was it like the coat worn by the person who came in with the victim?" He waited while Williams went through his thinking, nodding routine again.

"Yes, I'd say so. Dark, longish coat. Yes."

Frank turned to Jerry, who had been standing, listening. "Jerry how far did you and Mr. Williams get?"

"We were right about up to the part when the victim and his companion were checking in. You're doing fine, Frank."

Frank smiled. "Thanks." He turned back to Gerard. "Mr. Williams, did you see the other person leave the hotel?"

"Well, sir, I think so, but just barely. You see, I was watching TV and I heard the door open and close. I turned and looked and caught a glimpse of the person with the black coat and scarf heading out and up the street."

"Did you watch the person walk out?"

"Just a little. By the time I looked out, the person was going out the door, turned left and walked for an instant and disappeared."

"Mr. Williams. If you were a betting man would you bet this was a man or a woman?"

"A woman, sir."

# Chapter Forty

She was puzzled and a little upset that there'd been nothing in the media yet about the events of Tuesday night. Nothing in the papers, the radio, TV, nothing. It wasn't fair. She was tempted to call the papers, TV, or somebody to tell them. Tell them what a good thing she had done. Tell them how she had eradicated an evil person. Tell them what he did to little girls.

Maybe it wasn't very important to the media or anyone else. But it was to her. It was the most significant thing she had ever done in her life. It wasn't fair.

But still, she didn't let it take away from the good feeling she had. The sickness that she carried inside her was gone, left in that ugly hotel room.

\*     \*     \*

Frank spent the rest of the day trying to track down Crystal. He tried her apartment again, talked some more with the super, talked to maybe a dozen prostitutes, some of whom either knew Crystal personally or knew of her. Nobody had seen her for several days.

Although he'd never met Crystal he was beginning to feel like he knew her. He'd studied the sketch, committing it to memory, the long hair hanging well below her shoulders, the blue eyes highlighted with mascara, lips thick with bright red lipstick the lashes too long and thick to be real, and the scar on her left cheek.

Jingi Nelson was the only one who considered herself a friend of Crystal's. "We always keep in touch. She's not so bad when you get to know her. Why you looking for her?"

"No big deal. I just want to talk to her. When did you see her last?"

"I don't know. Four, five nights ago. We had a couple of drinks together."

"What time?"

"Hmm, it was about eight-thirty or so."

"Where did you have your drinks?"

"Place on Forty-eighth Street. Seasons. Nice Place."

"How'd she seem?"

Jingi laughed. "She was pissed off. She usually is about something."

"Why was she pissed off?"

"Well, I guess she was holed up in a fancy hotel suite with one of her rich dudes. Getting high on some coke, champagne, room service. You know, the whole bit. She's going to really milk the guy for a couple of days or more."

"And?"

"The guy gets a call from his wife. Their kid got hit by a car or something and he has to take off right away and go home to Chicago. So he checks out and her little gig is over. I mean, I guess she got some money from him but she had big plans for this guy. Anyway that's the last time I saw her."

"What hotel was it?"

"She didn't say."

"What time did you leave the bar?"

"We weren't there that long. Maybe an hour. Yeah, I'd say we left about nine-thirty."

"Where'd you go?"

"I headed downtown and she went uptown. That was it. That's the last time I saw her."

"O.K. Don't leave town, Jingi," Frank said. "I might want to talk with you some more. Oh, by the way, do you know if Crystal dyes her hair?"

Jingi looked at him for a moment, not quite sure how to take the question. She shrugged and shook her head. "You sure do ask some funny questions, Frank. Anyway, yeah, she dyes her hair. I never knew a hooker who didn't. She's had three different colors since I've known her. How come you want to know all this stuff?"

"I'm nosy. You wear a diaphragm?"

"You want to find out for yourself?"

"Jingi! I'm on duty."

"You're always on duty."

"Tough life, being a cop."

*   *   *

The afternoon papers carried the story of Paul Gale's murder. "Number Five for Wine Bottle Killer." It was on the front page.

"A fifth victim has been claimed by the Wine Bottle Killer. An as yet unidentified man was found early this morning beaten and stabbed to death. A maid found the man in a room at the Haven Hotel in Midtown. The killer left the usual calling card, a wine bottle inserted in the victim's rectum."

"Police are still attempting to determine the identity of the victim. According to an unnamed source, police now believe the murders are being committed by a woman. No further details were available."

She dropped the paper without finishing the article. They know it's a woman. She wasn't worried. That narrows the field to only a few million. Eventually, they had to figure it out. But soon there could be a more serious problem that she might have to deal with. She refused to let it dampen her spirits.

*   *   *

The phone was ringing as Frank entered his apartment. "Hello."

"Hello, Frank," the unmistakable husky voice. Carla.

Oh, God. He wanted to hang up the phone, but at the same time he felt glad to hear her voice. The same contradictory confusion that she always caused him. "Carla, I thought you'd be in Hollywood by now, rehearsing your Academy Award speech."

She ignored the dig. "Frank, I wanted to call you. I need to talk with you. Do you have a few minutes?"

It was a while before he answered. "A few minutes? Let me give you a direct quote. 'Having told you all this, if I should call, it shouldn't be hard for you to say no and hang up.' That sound about right?"

"Frank."

She was struggling. He could tell.

"Frank, please listen to me. This morning I made reservations for Milan for this Sunday."

"Good for you."

"But I've been depressed all day for some reason. And I couldn't figure out why. I was sky high when I accelerated my plans and decided to leave now instead of waiting 'til February or March."

"Carla, why are you telling me all this?"

"You haven't figured it out yet?" She gave a little mirthless laugh. "Why should you? It took me all day. Frank, it just hit me smack in the face. I don't want to leave and lose you again. I could chuck this whole thing for you. Does that tell you something?"

The phone line was dead silent. He could hear her breathing, waiting for his reply. Why does she do these things to me? Why am I holding this phone, shaking? He wanted a slug of scotch.

"Carla, I'm going to get me a large drink. I'll be right back."

"O.K."

He poured some scotch, drained it in two gulps, and poured some more. He waited for it to kick in, then picked up the phone, and took a deep breath.

"Carla, I loved you as much as a man could love a woman. And maybe I still do." He took another deep breath and another hit on the scotch. "But I'm seeing someone else now." He felt like a schoolboy, not sure what to say, or how to say it…or even if he should say it. "Anyway, enough is enough. I'm sorry Carla."

She didn't skip a beat. "It's O.K., Frank. It's been nice knowing you. Good bye." And that was it.

He poured another drink and called Denise. "Hi. It's me. What are you doing right now?"

"Frank, I'm lying here missing you."

"How about if I grab a razor and some clean underwear and come over?"

"I'll give you five minutes to get here."

# Chapter Forty-one

Driving to the precinct on Friday morning, Frank knew beyond a doubt, if there ever was one, that he had made the right decision. Last night was the best yet. He couldn't get enough of her. It was like the early days with Carla, only twice as good. Jesus, it was great to feel something again.

Jerry was in a surprisingly good mood when Frank reached the station. "Good news, Frankie. We got an answer back already from the Bureau. Amazing what the commissioner's signature will do."

"You got an I.D. on the victim?"

Jerry nodded. He didn't have to. The smirk on his face said it. "He's an ex-con named Paul Gale. Paroled from Norfolk State Prison in Massachusetts just three months ago. Served eighteen years for killing his wife in North Adams, Massachusetts."

"Nice guy."

"Yeah. Anyway, that's as much as we know. The information just came in."

Captain Nolan came out of his office and spotted Jerry. "Blodgett, come into my office," he yelled.

"The hell's he want now?" Jerry muttered. He tucked in his shirt and headed for the waiting Nolan.

Frank watched Jerry scurry over to answer Nolan's summons. No matter how many years in the department, how solid your work is, how much respect you deserve, there's always somebody who's going to make you snap to; somebody, depending on his mood who can push his weight around and make you feel like shit. He hated the way Nolan could do that to Jerry. But then, he felt sure it was no different in big corporations. They just make it seem a little more civilized and use bigger words to carve people up.

He went to his desk and called the North Adams police. The officer he talked with didn't remember much about Gale, but said he'd check some and call him back. Fifteen minutes later the man called and told him Gale has a sister-in-law named Janet Kateley still living in North Adams.

"She the sister of Gale's wife, the woman he killed?" Frank asked.

"I believe so," the officer replied.

He hung up and spotted Jerry, head down moving quickly toward his office. He went in and slammed the door.

Frank followed and opened the door. "Can I come in?"

Jerry sat, studying the top of his desk his face in his hands. He nodded.

Frank told him about his phone conversations. "I'm going up to North Adams and poke around a little, see what I can find out about Paul Gale."

Jerry nodded again. Frank wasn't sure he even heard what he said. "I'll call you either from there or when I get back." He stopped at the door and turned. "What'd Nolan want?"

Jerry brought his head up and looked at Frank for the first time. "If we don't come up with the killer by the end of the year, he's going to put somebody else in charge of the case. Take me off it completely. End of the year, that's five weeks from now. The son of a bitch."

Frank started to say something but thought better of it for now. Jerry was hurting too much at the moment, and he knew nothing would penetrate. "We'll talk when I get back," he said and left.

It was a little after five when he arrived in North Adams. He drove down Main Street, a depressing scene of boarded up storefronts and tacky retail stores. The buildings were the old red brick, built in the twenties and thirties. The town had the look and feel of decay. He checked into a small hotel at the end of Main Street and called Denise.

"Dennie, I can't see you tonight. I had to go on a little business trip this afternoon. I'll most likely be back some time tomorrow or Sunday. I'll call you."

"Where are you?"

"I can't really say right now, but it's no big deal. Just some police business. I do have to run now. I'll tell you about it when I get back."

"O.K." She sounded disappointed and maybe even a little peeved. He'd heard the tone before.

"Be back before you know it."

He called the number the cop had given him for the sister-in-law. It was still early.

"Hello."

"Ms. Kateley?"

"Yes."

He thought she sounded fragile, even a little wary already. "Ms. Kateley, my name is Frank Corso. I'm a detective with the New York City Police Department. I'm sorry to bother you Ma'am, but do you have a brother-in-law named Paul Gale."

There was a long pause. He waited. No answer.

"Ms. Kateley?"

"Why do you want to know that?" she asked in a tremulous voice.

"Is Mr. Gale your brother-in-law, ma'am?" He asked again. And again he waited, not sure if she would hang up on him this time or what.

"Yes, he is, but why are you calling me? I've had nothing to do with that man in years."

"Well, I'm sorry to tell you Ms. Kateley, but Paul Gale was murdered in New York on Tuesday night, and I wonder if I might talk with you."

"Oh, my God!"

He waited for it to sink in for a moment. "Ms. Kateley, I'd like to talk with you, if I may. If not tonight, then tomorrow morning. I need to ask you a few questions about Mr. Gale."

"Yes," she said softly. "You might as well come over now and get it over with. I'm not going to relax much anyway after what you've just told me. By the way, it's Miss Kateley, not Ms. I hate that word."

\*     \*     \*

Carla Sanders moped around her apartment. In less than forty-eight hours she was scheduled to leave for Italy for God knows how long. And she hadn't even started packing yet.

There was no question she was leaving. She had to get out of New York. She'd be on her way tonight, tomorrow if she could have gotten a flight.

She was keeping the apartment though. You never know. She glanced again at the newspaper on the kitchen table. Frank's face peered out of it. He seemed to be looking directly at her. She read the article again.

"'But this time the killer made some mistakes,'" Detective Corso said. "'And we're optimistic that we may get a break soon.'"

She threw the paper down and began packing.

\*     \*     \*

Harry Leonard walked into Jerry's office, carrying two Styrofoam cups of coffee. No matter how long they'd worked together, Harry still felt intimidated by Jerry. He looked upon him as his boss, which he was, and he'd just never been able to connect with him the way Frank did. And when Jerry was in a bad mood or pissed about something, he always seemed to take it out on Harry. He was particularly wary this morning.

"Anything on Crystal yet," Jerry asked. He took the coffee from Harry with a little nod.

"Nothing yet, Jerry. Nobody's seen her since Sunday."

Jerry frowned and cursed. "I told you, didn't I that we don't have any record of her prints here or anywhere. Looks like she's kept herself clean."

"Doesn't surprise me," Harry said. "From what I hear, she's a pretty slick customer. When we pick her up and print her you know her prints'll match the ones from her apartment, and the murder scenes. I'm going over to the Greiffs, Nemerow's neighbors. See if they recognize the sketch."

"We're making some progress with the knife," Jerry said. I got the Talex people on the phone yesterday. The knife at the murder scene was a limited anniversary edition. They only made a couple thousand of them. Big break. Only five retail stores in New York carried them. Four in Manhattan, one in Brooklyn."

"That's fabulous," Harry said. He nodded toward Jerry's cup. "You want more coffee, Jerry?"

Jerry shook his head. "A lot of stores will keep records of people who buy knives like this. Or somebody might remember buyers of unusual weapons. Anyway, you keep looking for Crystal. We'll get these stores checked out. Any word from Frank?"

"No, I was going to ask you."

*    *    *

She lay in bed, trying to focus. The last several days seemed almost too much for her. The newspaper articles. Optimistic?

It was over now. She knew it was. But had she gone too far? Been too careless? Of course they're going to find out who he is. She always knew that. But she couldn't let it stop her. She had to do what she had to do. It was always that simple.

*    *    *

Denise's phone rang. Frank. Thank God. He's back.

"Hello. Dennie. This is Gina."

What in the world did Gina want? "Gina. How are you feeling? Dave told me you've been sick."

"Yeah, I have." She sounded subdued, nowhere near the Gina she knew. "I think I'm gonna live, though. Listen, Dennie, I wonder if I could talk with you today."

"What's up?" She was waiting for Frank's call and she didn't feel like a session with Gina anyway.

"I don't want to talk on the phone. Can I meet you somewhere? I really do need to talk with you, Dennie."

An urgency there, Denise thought. "Well…," she stammered. "I'm waiting for a call and…"

"You'll be back in an hour. Please, Dennie, it's important."

"All right. There's a place called Jason's a couple of blocks from here." She gave her the address. "It's sort of a coffee shop. I'll meet you there."

"See you there in twenty minutes," Gina said.

\*     \*     \*

Late that afternoon Jerry hit the jackpot. At about the same time, Harry Leonard got a tip that sent him sky high.

\*     \*     \*

Janet Kateley's directions were easy and Frank was there in ten minutes. The porch lights were on. He rang the doorbell and a small, gray haired woman appeared behind the glass storm door.

"Mr. Corso?"

"Yes, ma'am."

"May I see your identification please?"

He held up his badge and picture and followed the woman into the living room. The absence of any color in the room gave the impression of someone who had bled the emotion from her life.

He watched the nervous little woman straighten the doilies on an overstuffed chair before beckoning him to sit. She and the room looked like they were frozen in time in the fifties.

"What a terrible thing," she said sitting on the edge of the sofa. "But I guess I'm not totally surprised. He was a violent, twisted man and I suppose it's fitting that he should die in a violent manner."

"I gather you didn't much like Mr. Gale."

"No, I didn't. There wasn't much to like. You probably know by now that he killed my sister?"

"Yes," he said and asked her to fill him in. She did, providing him with a vivid description of the events leading up to her sister's death. She spared no details.

The room was hot. She must have had the thermostat turned up to ninety. No matter how hard he tried to slice through her rambling and keep her on track, she was not to be denied her catharsis. He was tired and beginning to wonder what the hell he was getting out of all this. Until she mentioned the wine bottle.

"Tell me some more about the wine bottle business, Miss Kateley. You say he abused her with it?"

"Yes, he…," she stopped.

"I understand," Frank said, satisfied for now.

"He'd done it before. Sarah even told me about it once. And then it all came out in the trial. Oh, God. It was so disgusting."

He was no longer tired. "Miss Kateley, can you tell me more about the daughter?"

Janet Kateley's eyes clouded over. "She was such a sweet little thing. The poor baby, God love her, she tried so hard to be a good girl for her mother. And she was." She stopped and looked out the window into the darkness.

"Yes, go on."

"Well, it seemed like all of a sudden her father started taking an interest in her. At night when he'd come home from work, he would go into her room and lie down and play with her. Even if she was asleep, he'd still snuggle up with her. At first Sarah thought it was nice that Paul was finally showing an interest in the child. But then she started hearing dirty sounds coming from the bedroom."

"What do you mean, dirty sounds?"

"Well, Paul would be groaning and moaning. You know, like sexually? And the poor little thing would start to cry and Sarah…it took her a while to figure out what was going on, and when she did, she refused to believe it."

"Gale was sexually abusing his daughter?'

She nodded and her lips quivered.

"Did Sarah tell you all this?"

"Well, a couple of times I was actually there. I'm the one who first told Sarah what I thought was going on. She had trouble accepting or believing it, but then one night when the baby was about five and a half, she caught him red handed. When she confronted him, he beat her terribly. Beat the baby too, when she started crying."

He thought of the battered mess lying next to the radiator in the dingy hotel room and felt some satisfaction. "How long did all this continue?" he asked.

"Right up until the night he killed Sarah. He would abuse that poor child almost every night. And Sarah was by then so terrified and confused, she just started ignoring what was going on, hoping it would end eventually. My sister was not a strong person, Mr. Corso."

"Why didn't you report it to the police yourself?"

Her eyes flared and for the first time this mousy, gray lady showed some passion. "I did Mr. Corso. I did. The police went over and Paul told them I was a meddling busybody. Of course he denied it. And sadly, so did Sarah."

She looked away from him again and they sat in silence. For the first time, he noticed the smell of dampness in the house and a little mildew, the kind you find in a cellar. He studied her for a moment. The loneliness and sadness in the woman was palpable. She had kept every detail close to the surface all these years. Best to let 'em keep flowing. "Go on, Miss Kateley," he said quietly.

She turned back to him. "Can you possibly imagine, Mr. Corso what a night that must have been for that poor little eight year old? Watching her mother beaten and murdered, and then sexually abused herself? Well, I can tell you, she wasn't ever the same again."

"She came to live with you?"

"Yes. Somehow, she got through the trial, I stood not two feet from Paul when he told her he'd kill her someday for turning him in and testifying. She just fell on the floor of the court and cried her eyes out. We had to carry her out of the room."

"It must have been hard for you, bringing her up."

"Yes, it was. She was not an easy child to get close to. I tried my best but it was so sad and a little frightening to see the resentment and hatred for her father start to build and build as she grew older."

"Jesus." Frank muttered to himself. He was getting more than he bargained for. She suddenly looked very tired. But he had to keep it going tonight.

"Tell me more, Miss Kateley. Where is she now?"

"She's in New York City. Been there for five years." Janet Kateley looked away again, the sadness clouding her eyes. "Yes, I never see her and rarely ever talk to her. She's in her own world and wants nothing to do with me or anyone or any memories of North Adams."

"How long since you've seen her?"

"Over five years. She'd be almost twenty-seven now and I'm sure she's even more beautiful than when I last saw her. So tall and shapely, so lovely."

He watched her fight back the tears, an aging, lonely lady who was still suffering for what happened after all these years. It seemed like she deserved more than the kick in the teeth she got for bringing up her niece. "When did you last talk with her?"

"Well, she called me about two months ago and asked if her father was out of prison yet. I told her I'd heard he was due out any time. She asked me to be sure to call her when I knew. I called her about a week later to tell her he was out of prison. Then, a couple of weeks later, I tried calling her and found that her number had been changed to an unlisted number. I hadn't talked with her for about two years before that."

Frank sighed. He felt for her but she was getting tiresome. There was a constant whine to her voice. He pressed on. "Do you know where she lives and works in New York?"

She looked around the room. He tried to make eye contact but she avoided looking at him. She was a strange, nervous little woman, and he was having trouble figuring her out.

"Mr. Corso, I don't even know that. I did have her address up until a few years ago, but then she moved and never told me the new one." She started to pucker and sniffle again. "She's all I have, and now I have no way to reach her. I tried so hard for that girl and…." She gave up fighting the tears.

"Miss Kateley." He tried not to let the impatience show in his voice, but the mildew smell was getting worse and he had a headache. He doubted she was telling him the complete truth, but he knew he had to handle this brittle lady carefully or she could blow completely. "Do you know where she works?"

She took a crumpled Kleenex from her sleeve and blew her nose. "No, I don't know where she works. I never have."

"Did she go straight to New York after college?"

"I think she worked in Boston for a while, but I don't know where or for how long. Like I said, we just completely lost touch."

"Let me have her old address, please."

She wrote it down and handed it to him. Her eyes told him she was about at the end of her rope. He had to wrap this up and get back to New York. The hell with the hotel room. Miss Kateley, what was her phone number before she had it changed?"

She gave it to him and he noted it was a Manhattan exchange.

"Do you have any pictures of your niece," he asked.

"No, her father took the only ones I had."

"You don't have any of her at all, even when she was a child?"

She looked up sharply at him and appeared wounded that he seemed not to believe her. "No. We weren't much of a picture taking family."

He wasn't surprised. He doubted there had been much joy or fun in this woman's life. "Miss Kateley, I have just one more question."

"Yes?"

"What's your niece's name?"

She stared at him for a moment and the sniffles came again. "Well, she changed her name some years ago because...well, again you see she just wanted to erase everything from North Adams, so...well, it's not Gale anymore."

"Miss Kateley! What's her name?"

# Chapter Forty-two

After Frank left, Janet Kateley sat in her living room, trying to pull herself together. So many things had happened and now this. She wondered how Lucky was handling it and wished she could talk with her.

The phone rang, and she looked at her watch. Eight-forty-five. Who could be calling at this hour?

"Aunt Janet, this is Lucky."

"Oh, Lucky. Have you heard the news about your father? Oh, God, I'm so...."

"Yes, I have. How did you hear?"

"A New York City police detective came to see me. He just left about a half hour ago."

"Yes. I thought the police might be contacting you. What did he want to know?"

"Well, he asked about your father, and I told him about all the things that happened way back and all. And he wanted to know all about you."

"I see. And did you tell him all about me?"

"Yes, I mean I told him everything I could. But..." She started to whimper.

"What is it, Aunt Janet?"

"Well, I was worried about you, and I was afraid to tell them where you live. It was foolish, I know but I just wanted to have a chance to talk with you first. I was hoping you would call me. But now I'm afraid I'm going to get in trouble. I've got to call him back and tell him the truth."

"What did you tell him?"

"I gave him your old address, the one you had about three years ago."

"That wasn't very smart, Aunt Janet."

"I know," she wailed. "I just wasn't thinking. Oh, God, I'm going to call him first thing in the morning."

"No. Please don't do anything until we talk again. I'll call you in the morning."

"All right, Lucky. Oh, sweetheart, I'm so glad you called."

"Yes, I am, too. Aunt Janet?"

"Yes?"

"What was the detective's name?"

"Oh, let's see. I have his card here somewhere. Yes, here it is. It's Corso, a nice young man named Frank Corso."

*     *     *

Frank entered his apartment and slumped into the nearest chair. It had been a long day. The answering machine blinked relentlessly. He pulled himself up long enough to pour a drink and fell back into the chair. The apartment was pretty raunchy. Dirty dishes from his dinner with Denise still sat in the sink. Even now, he could smell the garlic. A roach skittered across it all and disappeared down the side of the sink cabinet.

He took two long pulls on the scotch and closed his eyes. He'd had better days.

The trip back from North Adams was long and ugly. He had managed to catch the last flight out of Albany at eight-thirty, but the weather turned bad and the flight was ragged and bumpy. Then LaGuardia was socked in and they had to circle for nearly an hour before getting clearance to land. Now, at one a.m. he was exhausted. But he was also wired.

The session with Janet Kateley rattled around in his head. Her niece, Gale's daughter, could be the key to the whole goddamn case and could very possibly be the killer.

He closed his eyes and was back in the small, stale living room in North Adams. "What is your niece's name, Miss Kateley?"

"You may find this hard to believe, Mr. Corso, but I don't know."

"You don't know?"

"I told you she changed her name, both first and last, and she would never tell me what she changed it to. Whenever we talked I simply called her Lucky, the nickname her mother and I used when she was little. I never even knew her address. What little communication we had were the few cards she sent and by phone."

He opened his eyes and they landed on the answering machine again. He reached over and turned it on. Three urgent messages from Jerry. "Call me at the house no matter what time you get home." Two from Denise, and two from his father.

He dialed Jerry's number.

"Yeah?" Jerry's voice was a hoarse whisper.

"Frank," Jerry. "I just got back. You said to call you no matter what time."

"Frank!" Jerry's voice came alive. "What time is it?"

"Ten after one."

"Frankie. It's over."

He had a feeling something had happened while he was gone. "What do you mean, it's over?"

"Hold on, let me pick up the phone in my den."

Frank poured some more scotch and paced around the kitchen. He was no longer tired. He'd been away from the city for about thirteen hours. What the hell happened?

"Frank?"

"Jerry. For Christ sake, what happened?"

"O.K. Kid, listen to this." There was a pause and some puffing. Frank knew what Jerry was doing. He was lighting his victory cigar. And then he got going. First he told Frank about their good luck with the knife, about it being a limited edition. "We traced it to Haley's Gun Shop on

West Fortieth right after you left yesterday. The owner, Ben Haley, remembers it. He only had a few of them and they sold fast. He's always kept records of who buys his knives and handguns. I've known the guy for a long time. He's very thorough. You still with me?"

Frank continued pacing around the small kitchen. "Yeah, course I am. Go on."

"O.K., he's absolutely certain who bought this knife. The serial number matches with his records. And he remembers her. You got it, Frankie, the lady who bought the knife at Haley's Gun Shop is none other than our hooker, Crystal Wilcox."

"You pick her up yet?"

"Not yet, but she was seen earlier today. She's still in the city. We should have her within twenty-four hours."

"Getting close. Anything else?"

"Yeah, it gets better. The knife was the same knife that Crystal used to kill the guy in the alley. It checks out with the pictures and slides from the autopsy. We measured the wounds and the knife. Perfect fit."

"Jerry, Vickie told us that Crystal gave the knife to Jenny Clark, the black hooker that was stabbed to death in a room near Times Square, remember?"

"No shit. Vickie said that, huh. Must be true then. Come on, Frankie."

"What else have you got?"

"Oh, nothin', except your buddy, Jingi Nelson, told Harry she saw Crystal on the street near the alley where the guy was bludgeoned last week. Saw her about the time the M.E. estimates the guy was killed."

"What about the hair?"

"What about it?" Jerry's voice took on an edge.

"The hair, Jerry. The hairs we found at some of the crime scenes were natural, untreated hair, remember? And some were wig fibers. Crystal dyes her hair. How do you account for the natural hairs we found all over Nemerow, Beatty and Gale?" He waited for an answer. Silence. "Jerry?"

"We'll check that out when we find her?"

"Yeah, well how about the wig fibers? None of them match the wigs that were found at Crystal's apartment."

"Oh for Christ sake, you think they were the only wigs she had? She probably has others with her. Frank, she's the one. We got her on the first guy in the alley. Vickie's an eye witness and she's going to testify. Crystal Wilcox is a killer."

Frank sat down and polished off his drink, still trying to process all of what he'd just heard. He wanted to share Jerry's excitement but it just wouldn't come. Maybe he was just too tired.

"Frank?"

"Yeah?"

"Nolan wants to see you and me in his office at eleven in the morning. Then at one-thirty the Chief wants to see us. Be nice to get a little praise instead of all the shit they've been throwin' at us, especially me."

"Jerry, I hope you haven't jumped the gun on this. You don't..."

"Frank. It's done. It's over. And now I gotta get some sleep. You go to bed, and I'll see you in my office at ten-forty-five." And he hung up.

Frank looked through the phone at Jerry before hanging it up. It's over. Is it? Did Jerry actually believe it? He doubted it. He knew Jerry too well. Nolan and the commissioner. Did they really care one way or the other? Too many loose ends.

He was too tired now to deal with it. Tomorrow.

# Chapter Forty-three

The first thought that hit him when he awoke was Denise. So much going down but there she was, ahead of everything. Too late to call her last night or this morning or what the hell ever day it was when he got home.

"Hello." Even half asleep she sounded wonderful.

"Hi. It's me."

"Frank?"

Still a little fuzziness in her voice. He pictured her lying in bed, hair splayed out across her face, her breasts rolling out of her nightgown, the way she looked when he last left her. "Your wake up call, ma'am."

"Frank, where have you been? Why haven't I heard from you. I've been so worried. What…"

"Whoa. Enough with the grilling. I'll tell you all about it tonight. I didn't get back 'til one this morning. Too late to call you."

"Just as well, I guess. I wouldn't have been much good. I had kind of a trying session with my friend Gina, advising her whether or not to accept a job offer out of state. She was a nervous wreck and it was exhausting. I went to bed early, started reading and must have conked out before nine. I'm dying to see you."

"How about coming over for dinner? What time can you get here?"

"I have to go to New Haven. I'll call you when I get back."

He lay in bed for a few minutes focusing on her. He knew those minutes lying there, thinking of her would be the best part of his day-until tonight. He'd been so wrapped up in this goddamn case again that he'd put her on hold. Good way to lose her. No way. The phone rang and he bolted up.

"Frankie! Where the hell have you been? I been tryin' to call you. Congratulations." His father's voice crackled with energy.

"Oh, yeah, thanks, I guess."

"What do you mean, you guess You guys have cracked one of the biggest cases this city's had. And you did it in three months. You should be celebrating. You sound like you just came from a funeral."

He didn't want to get into it right now. But he knew that whatever he said Silvio would pick up on. So, he might as well say what he was thinking. "I'm not sure that Crystal did all these guys. I think we've got a rush to judgment here. Maybe that's why I'm not celebrating. It's just not that cut and dried." He told Silvio about some of his doubts. "Maybe she did these guys and maybe she didn't. I'd just hate to be part of railroading somebody because of public pressure. I can't shake the feeling that everybody, Jerry, Nolan, the chief, even the commissioner just want to put this to bed and they don't care about irrelevancies like some holes in the evidence or like maybe somebody else could be doing these guys. I mean, it looks bad for Crystal on the guys in the alleys, but I'm not totally convinced yet of the others."

There was a long silence. Frank knew his father, and he knew that when he was angry and about to blow, he forced himself into silence, collecting himself, gathering his cool.

When he finally spoke, Silvio's voice was low and measured. "Frank, I already heard last night that you're up for a commendation and a promotion. There's an old saying, been around the department since way before me, and I know you've heard it. 'If you want to get along, you go along.' You've got your killer. This is a big day for everybody from the commissioner on down. Let them enjoy. And you enjoy."

Frank started to reply, but nothing would come out. He really needed to collect his own thoughts, gather his own cool before going at it any further with Silvio. "Yeah," he said simply. I gotta go." And he hung up.

He had a lot to do before meeting with Jerry at ten-forty-five. He obtained a subpoena for the phone company and presented it to Donald Ware, Assistant Director of Security.

"Always happy to be of service, Mr. Corso," Ware said. He examined the phone number Frank had given him and settled into one of the computers lining the room. "O.K., so this number was changed to an unlisted number about two and a half months ago you say? And you want to know who this number was assigned to, right?"

Frank nodded. The adrenaline was flowing now and he wanted this officious little shit to shut up and just give him his information.

"Now, you see Mr. Corso I can just dip into what we call our Coles Directory which provides me with a breakdown of phone numbers by number, name and street address. You give me a name and I'll give you the phone number and address. Give me an address and I'll give you a name and number. Give me a number and I give you the name and address of the person who has or had that number."

"Mr. Ware, I know how it works," Frank said. "I've had people do it before."

Ware shrugged and replied curtly, "O.K., let's get to it. We're both busy men." He poked away at the keyboard for what seemed forever to Frank. Finally he pointed to the computer screen and said. "There it is. That number belonged to Crystal Wilcox, 226 East Thirty-eighth Street."

Frank was relieved. It was beginning to look like Jerry and the others were on the right track after all.

Feeling better about things, he handed the address to Ware, the old address of her niece that Janet Kateley had given him. "O.K. How about giving me the name that goes with this."

"Certainly, sir." Ware went into his routine again while Frank sat back, confident of what he would find. It was really now only an exercise.

Ware turned from his computer. "There you are. There's your information."

Frank looked at the screen. "Oh, my God," he yelled and rushed for the phone to call Janet Kateley. There was no answer. He made two more phone calls but again, no luck.

It was time to meet with Jerry, Jerry who had the case wrapped up, on the verge of becoming a hero.

Jerry was already sitting in his office drinking coffee when Frank arrived. The coat to his gray suit hung on the coat rack and he had on a white shirt with a necktie that Frank had never seen. His shirt was tucked neatly into his pants.

As usual when he felt edgy and out of sorts Frank tried to cover with a flipness he didn't really feel. "Jerry, you look pretty spiffy in your new necktie and I see you've got my favorite suit on."

Jerry got up and hugged him. Then he grabbed Frank's face in his massive hands. "We did it, kid. It's all over." He said it softly, his voice full of emotion. He went back to his desk and handed Frank a cup of coffee. "Here, I poured it for you just before you walked in."

Jerry got up again and walked around the office. "Frankie, we shut up a lotta doubting Thomases in this city. We've gone from the outhouse to the penthouse, and I don't know about you, but I like that penthouse."

Frank nodded. He'd hear Jerry out before saying anything. "Fill me in some more on yesterday."

Jerry sat down again and went over the events of yesterday in detail. "I knew we were going to nail that broad, Frankie."

Frank got up and walked over to Jerry's desk. He looked down at the newspaper sitting on it and there were Jerry and Nolan, big smiles, holding court.

Jerry pointed to the paper. "Nice, huh?"

Frank sat next to him. The room felt hot and stuffy all of a sudden. "Jerry, we've got Crystal on the alley stabbing, but you don't believe she's the wine bottle killer, do you?" It came out more abruptly than he had planned, but it was out.

Jerry's expression changed, all the joy and good fellowship replaced with a narrow-eyed stare. "What the hell are you talking about?"

It was the tone he expected. "Jerry, I know you. You're too good a cop to overlook all the holes in the case on Crystal."

Jerry's eyes were now slits, the color drained from his face. Frank had seen the expression before but never aimed at him. He pushed on. "First of all, as I said on the phone last night the hair we found at three of the crime scenes matched and they're all natural hair. Crystal's hair is dyed. "When we showed Crystal's picture to Billy, the bartender at Barney's he couldn't positively I.D. her."

He waited but there was no response from Jerry. "What are we going to do when we print Crystal if her prints don't match the ones at the crime scenes?"

Again, no reply, only the look of rage that Frank had seen many times but never directed at him. "We don't have a positive ID on the sketch from anybody yet and you don't even have Crystal in custody."

Jerry finally spoke. His voice was hard and flat. "You finished?"

"No, goddamn it, I'm not," Frank flared. "You want to hear about my trip to North Adams or don't you give a shit? Well, let me tell…"

"I don't give a fuck about your trip to North Adams," Jerry roared. He was on his feet and around the desk in Frank's face. "You go off on some wild goose chase to Massachusetts and don't even bother to call in. Harry and I are putting this thing to bed while you're screwin' around up there and you have the nerve to come back here and question me, question the chief, question the commissioner? How dare you?" His voice trembled with rage.

Frank walked to the other side of the office, afraid one of them would throw a punch. They stood on opposite ends of the room, looking at one another, Jerry's harsh breathing the only sound.

But Frank refused to let it go. "Jerry, I'm troubled by this. I'm troubled that you're all in a rush to nail somebody. You're reacting to the pressure and you're going to close this thing out no matter what." He spoke calmly now, trying to reach his friend, his partner who had taught him so much. "Jerry, What if she's not the killer and next week or next month we find another guy with a wine bottle jammed up his ass? How are we going to look then? All I'm asking. Jerry is let's just cool the rush to publicity and not jump to conclusions until we check a few more things out. We don't want to be embarrassed, do we?"

After a moment of studying Frank, Jerry looked out the glass panel into the bullpen. A small group stood looking in at them. Jerry glanced at his watch and walked over to Frank. He spoke quietly. "I hear what you're saying, Frank. I know there are some loose ends. But we have a murderess with an eye witness. We have a substantial amount of evidence that seriously implicates Crystal Wilcox in these serial killings. I'm retiring in ten months. I'm going to go out the way I always dreamed I would. Don't spoil that, Frankie. Share it with me." He put his hands on Frank's upper arms and held them there for a moment.

Frank stood motionless, looking into his friend's eyes. He decided to say nothing further for now. All he wanted was to get out of the building as soon as possible.

Jerry looked at his watch again. "It's eleven o'clock. Let's go see Nolan."

# Chapter Forty-four

Frank and Jerry's meeting with Nolan was very different from those of the past several months. Nolan was cordial and complimentary, especially to Jerry.

"Jerry, we've had our differences over the years, but I'm impressed with the way you and your men have pinned this case down. The department has taken a lot of heat over these murders, especially after Nemerow. I've never, in all my twenty-four years as a cop felt such pressure over a case.

"I'm sure I don't have to tell you what a relief it is to me that you've identified the killer. Now, get out there and bring her in fast. I want to be able to sleep again."

"We'll get her, Joe. We've got every detective and half the patrol officers in the city looking for her. It won't be long."

"Good. I'll see you at the Chief's office at one-thirty. I think he's going to have a little incentive for you boys to find her."

Jerry grinned and looked at Frank. Frank looked straight ahead.

Outside Nolan's office Frank and Jerry stood in an awkward silence. Jerry started to speak. "Frank, I…."

"Congratulations, Jerry", Frank interrupted. "You're going out in style." He turned and went over to his desk and absorbed himself in a thick folder of something. Jerry watched him for a moment, grabbed his coat and left.

Frank sat at his desk staring into the open folder. He didn't know what was in it but it didn't matter.

He looked around the precinct. The air was thick and heavy with the stale sweat of overworked cops. He got a whiff of the sweet, sickish smell of the cheap perfume and cologne worn by the hookers and pimps that paraded in and out all day. It was lunch time but he had no appetite.

He tried to think through the last crazy twenty-four hours. His head felt like a chunk of wood. Jerry. Today was probably the happiest day in his pal's life. Everybody's pumped up. But his mind was back in the phone company, staring at the screen. He could focus on nothing else. He chipped away at the block of wood, trying to clear his mind. The information he had could blow everything sky high. He would have to proceed carefully, handle it in his own way. There was too much at stake. Too much. He buried his head on his desk.

It took him forty minutes to obtain a subpoena in order to get the information from the post office regarding the forwarding address for the old address Janet gave him. It was now one-fifteen. No time to get the new address now.

The session with the Chief was much like the meeting with Nolan. The Chief's little incentive was a promotion to Detective Lieutenant for Jerry and Detective Sergeant for Frank when they brought Crystal in and everything fit together, which he was confident it would.

By the time they left, Frank was sick to his stomach, feeling like he would vomit any minute. His apartment was not far. He was in no mood or shape to go to the post office. He would go home, take some Pepto-Bismol, and try to calm down a little, first.

It was three-thirty by the time he arrived home. He tried the phone again and again had no luck. Instead of the Pepto, he poured himself a heavy dose of scotch, straight up, slumped into the kitchen chair, and downed most of it. He knew why his stomach was a mess, and it wasn't medicine that would make it go away.

There had to be a simple answer that would clear things up for him. Everything pointed to Crystal. Maybe what he had was little more than a blip.

He sat gazing at the kitchen wall. His apartment was in semi-darkness. The gloom of a sunless December afternoon had settled in. The empty scotch glass dangled from his hand. He got up to wash his face before heading for the post office when the phone rang.

"Hello."

"Hi, it's me. Can I come over?"

"Can you come over now?"

"Yes, I'll be there in half an hour.

# Chapter Forty-five

Frank hung up the phone and began pacing the apartment. A craving for a cigarette gnawed at him. It made him think of Carla and the day in the coffee shop. He resisted the urge to run out and buy a pack.

Not much time. He wasn't sure how he would handle this, how it would play out.

He gnawed at his thumbnail and wandered into the living room and back to the kitchen. It could be risky, but he had to do it this way. There was no way he was going to bring Jerry or anyone else into this yet. Not until he had more answers. And he hoped they were the right answers. They would be. His gut told him that. He sat at the kitchen table and popped up again, poured some of the morning coffee, sipped it and spit it into the sink.

She was very possibly Gale's daughter. So? What if she is the daughter of an abuser who liked to use a wine bottle. So he gets the wine bottle treatment like the other four. Coincidence? No. Crystal is the daughter and Crystal did these guys.

From everything they'd learned about Crystal, she was sadistic, a man-hater. Abusing a man with a blunt instrument after he was dead would be consistent with her profile.

Still, he had to consider all possibilities and he couldn't shake the worst. A thought that wouldn't go away sent him over to his library where he pulled out a book called *The Murderer* by the psychiatrist Emanuel Tanay. Something Tanay had written sticking in his mind, he had to read again. He went immediately to the passage. "—the murderer appears to carry out the act in an altered state of consciousness. In such an ego-dystonic homicide a person kills against his conscious wishes and thus the murder is carried out during this altered period of consciousness. When this occurs, part of the psychic structure is split off from the rest of the personality." He held the book, pondering the passage for a few moments before picking up another by W.I. Thomas. He quickly found what he was looking for. "In homicides whereby the individual has suffered a cycle of trauma in childhood and is faced with a psychologically unresolvable conflict, one dissociative reaction often is a quest to gain revenge, an act that can be repeated over and over until the need for vengeance is satisfied. When and if this occurs, the individual could be freed from further dissociative actions."

"In other words, the killings would stop," he said aloud.

Vengeance. It had been his theory after the second murder. Payback was the word Silvio used. He read on. "When the vengeance is satisfied the individual could be freed from further dissociative actions." He was tracking now into unsettling territory but he could no more stop than he could erase the name on the screen in Donald Ware's office.

The person could go back to being a normal human being again. No more killing against conscious wishes. No more need to. No more....
The door buzzer jolted him to his feet. He reached for the intercom button but his hand stopped short. The buzz zapped through the apartment again, this time longer, insistent.

He pushed the button.

"It's me."

He waited for her, wondering what he would say, what direction the evening would take. The doorbell rang and he braced himself.

She stood in the doorway, a little smile on her face. He thought she looked as beautiful as ever.

"Hi," she said and stepped inside.

He looked at the large tote bag she carried. "Going somewhere?"

"No, I just came from working out."

"Oh?" There was something about her scent. "You smell good. What is that?"

"It's Jean Naté. I've worn it before."

He studied her face for a moment, nodded and lowered his eyes. When he looked up again, her smile had faded.

"You seem different, Frank. What is it?"

"I went to North Adams and talked with Janet Kateley last night. Does that name mean anything to you?"

Her eyes glazed over.

He waited but there was no response. "Did you know that an old address she had for her niece, Paul Gale's daughter, had a telephone listed under your name?"

Her eyes seemed to clear just before she lowered them. "Yes," she whispered.

"Do you want to talk about it?" He still wanted to believe she could explain everything.

"Yes," she said. "I do." She moved into the living room and he followed. I hope you're going to give me the benefit of talking this through and explaining everything before making a big deal out of it."

"I've said nothing to anyone, not until I've talked with you. I think you would know that."

He watched her, looking for a sign, something, anything that would help him get through this.

She turned her face. "Frank, I'm so nervous about all of this. It's all very confusing and I want you to hear me out." She started fidgeting and gave him a little self-conscious smile. "I've got to go. Can I use your bathroom?"

He nodded and she headed through the bedroom toward the bathroom. He heard both doors close and the phone ring at the same time.

"Frank, this is Jerry."

"Yeah. You find Crystal?"

"Not yet. Frank, when you went up to North Adams, who'd you talk to?"

"I talked to Gale's sister-in-law, Janet Kateley."

There was a pause at the other end. "We just got a call from the North Adams police. Janet Kateley's been murdered."

"Oh, Sweet Jesus! When."

"They say she was killed sometime very early this morning, about three, four a.m...."

Before he could respond, Frank heard the bedroom door open. "Jerry," he whispered. "I'll call you back in a few minutes."

He hung up the phone and turned. Crystal Wilcox stood facing him.

# Chapter Forty-six

He closed his eyes and rubbed them and opened them again, expecting the apparition he had just seen to be gone. She was still there, staring at him, smiling. The police artist had failed to capture the coldness in her blue eyes. He doubted anything could.

She wore the kind of mini-skirt he'd seen in the sketch and stood over six feet tall in her spike heels. Her lips were thick with the heavy lipstick, the scar on her cheek, heavy make-up and hair well below her shoulders gave her a menacing presence.

"I understand you've been looking for me," she said in a voice nearly as deep as his.

Where did she come from? He tried to think clearly, shake off the numbing shock that kept his brain from working.

Before he could speak or move, she produced a gun. She appeared to be holding something with her other hand, but he couldn't make out what it was.

"I'm sorry, Frank."

Her voice had changed. "Oh, Jesus Christ. Oh, Jesus Christ. No."

She nodded.

He closed his eyes and shook his head. "No, no, no," he whispered. He had wanted everything to be explained, all the awful questions to be answered. And now they were, in horrifying clarity. The nagging familiarity of the police artist's sketches; the sterilness of Crystal's apartment. But there were still so many questions.

"Why? Just tell me why? I think you owe me that."

"Why? Why Crystal? Is that what you're asking me, Frank?"

"We can start with that."

"I liked turning myself into a woman men needed, were willing to pay money for. I enjoyed being in control. I was always the dominant one."

"What about going into alleys with drunks and…"

"Oh, yes. I'm sure you have trouble with that. If it makes you feel any better, I didn't like it very much. But I was always a low life. My father saw to that. It seemed fitting that I should play the role of the worst kind of low life for a woman, a street-walking prostitute. I was the dirty little girl doing dirty little things. But you could never understand."

He could understand. Even with her there, holding a gun on him, he could understand and his heart ached with sadness for her. But he knew the danger he was in. He needed to keep her talking.

"What about us?"

Her face softened for a moment. "I thought I loved you when we were together. I tried but Crystal wouldn't let me."

Even now, looking at Crystal, it was difficult to see the real person underneath. In a way it was better that way. He preferred to think of her as Crystal. Keep her talking. "The blue eyes. Contacts."

She nodded.

"And the scar? Make-up."

She nodded again, without expression.

"How long has Crystal…been with you?"

She hesitated and looked away. "A very long time."

"How did the killings begin?"

Beads of perspiration formed on her forehead, trickled along her eyes, picked up mascara and continued down her cheeks, creating black stripes in her make-up.

"Jack Beatty was an act of rage. I didn't plan to kill him. It was sort of an accident, but I liked the feeling.

"It's hard to explain the man in the alley because Crystal killed him. I...." Her upper lip glistened with the perspiration that had made its way down her face, and her eyes narrowed. The deep voice of Crystal returned. "When we got in the alley and he turned nasty, I saw her father, disgusting, foul drunk, and I enjoyed sticking the knife in him."

"What about the knife, Crystal? You never gave it to Jenny Clark like you told Vickie, did you?"

The smile returned. "Yes, I did."

"Then how...?"

"Don't you understand, you fool? That animal killed Jenny and took the knife."

"And you killed him with it in the hotel room."

Her expression softened and the old familiar voice returned.

"Crystal didn't kill my father. I did. I killed Jack Beatty. And I killed the little scum, Joey. And I killed Nemerow." She jutted her head toward him, her voice emphasizing each word.

She's losing it, he thought, watching her face contort each time she hissed the names. "And who killed the others?"

"Crystal killed the man, Chesbro. And Crystal killed the other man in the alley."

Jesus. His stomach turned sour and a wave of nausea swept over him. Dark shadows cut across the room, casting her in eerie silhouette. How long had they been standing there? How much longer could she remain rational? He knew she could blow at any minute. "What about the natural hair and the wigs. Crystal's hair is dyed. Yours is natural. How did you work that?"

"Crystal's hair wasn't dyed. She wore different color, shorter wigs sometimes, and told those stupid women that it was her real hair dyed. They never knew any better."

"And the old phone number and address?"

"When I gave my aunt the phone number, I gave her the number to Crystal's apartment. I wasn't there very much so it was better that way.

Later, I gave her my own address because I knew she would give it to my father. I wanted him to find me. He had pictures of me, not Crystal."

"Why did you kill your aunt?"

"I had to do that," she screamed. "She was going to call you and give you more information. And she would have identified me. And now she can't. No one can, except you."

She started to sob. "I don't want to kill you, Frank."

He spoke softly, gently. "Sweetheart, I can help you. You're very sick. You need help and we'll get it for you." He moved in her direction and put his hand out to her. "I know you don't want to kill me, sweetheart."

The hammer of the gun clicked. "No." The harshness of Crystal's voice returned. "She doesn't need you. She's finished with you. She doesn't need you or your help. She has me and that's all she needs. I will go away for a while but she knows I will always be with her.

"She can't kill you, but I can." She stepped toward him and raised the gun. The phone rang, distracting her long enough for him to grab the gun from her hand. As he did, she raised the other hand and brought the wine bottle down on his head.

He fell to the floor and the room turned to darkness for a moment. When he opened his eyes, he saw her about to bring the bottle down on him again. He raised the gun and fired.

The phone continued to ring. He pulled it to the floor and answered it.

"Frank. I thought you were going to call me back. What...?"

"Jerry, you'd better get over here right away."

"Why? What's...?"

"Jerry, just get over here. Please."

He hung up the phone and cradled the dead woman in his arms.

# Chapter Forty-seven

He opened his eyes. The room was nearly dark. He had no idea how long he'd been sitting on the floor, holding her. Had he blacked out? He thought he'd heard his buzzer, but he couldn't be sure.

He put his hand to his face and pulled it away, covered with blood- her blood from where he had cradled her against him. His head throbbed, and he realized some of the blood was his own.

He closed his eyes again and felt the wetness of the tears still there. The nightmare began coming back in bits and pieces.

A commotion at the door. Someone knocking, pounding. Voices. When he opened his eyes the building superintendent stood in the doorway.

Someone behind the super. He couldn't make out who it was until Jerry pushed his way into the apartment. And stopped.

Frank looked up at his friend and partner. Jerry stood motionless, his mouth open, lips moving, making no sound. He stared at Frank sitting cross legged on the floor, cradling a woman in his arms, both of them covered with blood.

And then the words tumbled out. "Frank, what happened? What's going on here? Who…?" He went to Frank, looked down at the woman, and blinked several times. "Crystal? Crystal Wilcox?"

Frank slid away from the body and started to get up. He staggered and Jerry helped him to his feet.

"You all right, Frank?"

Frank leaned against the wall. "Yeah, I'm all right."

"Frank, talk to me. What happened? What the hell is Crystal Wilcox doing here? Is she dead?"

Frank made his way to the window and raised the blinds. He looked out at the lights of the city below.

"Yes, she's dead," he said softly. Only it isn't Crystal Wilcox, Jerry. It's Carla."

# Chapter Forty-eight

Frank finished his second scotch, pushed the seat back as far as it would go, and looked down at Denise, sleeping on his shoulder. They were somewhere over the Atlantic Ocean, maybe halfway between New York and Barbados.

It was a week to the day since he buried Carla, poor tormented Carla. The toast of New York. And there were three people at the cemetery, Frank, Jerry, and Betty. Even her agent stayed away.

Only a week, but it seemed so long ago that they stood in the cold December drizzle. After a while Jerry and Betty got into the car, while Frank knelt next to the casket. His lips moved silently for a few moments before he got up and eased himself into the car's back seat.

It was over now. High in the air, away from everything, he peeled away the nightmarish images and thought of tequila sunrises and the woman next to him. He leaned over and kissed her. A gentle moan interrupted her soft steady breathing and a hint of a smile crossed her face. He kissed her again and closed his eyes.

The End

# About the Author

*Spin the Bottle* is Wayne Barcomb's first novel. His second, *All Are Naked,* is scheduled for publication in early 2001. His short story, *Good Night Mrs. Chisholm,* appeared in the anthology *Mystery in the Sunshine State,* published in 1999, and his story *Predator* will appear in the anthology, *Horror in the Sunshine State* scheduled for 2001. Barcomb also writes free lance articles for a number of magazines.